lock

me

inside

USA *TODAY* BESTSELLING AUTHOR

C. HALLMAN

Dedication

To all the readers who crave dark romance and all the authors who dare to write it.

Stay kinky my friends.

-C. Hallman

FOREWORD

Dear Reader,

Please be advised that this book is considered dark fiction/dark romance. This is NOT a love story. This book deals with many hard to read subjects which could be triggering to some. If you would like to look at a list of triggers or ask about a specific one, please email us at admin@bleedingheartpress.com

Thank you for reading!

XOXO
    Cassy

CHAPTER 1

I feel him before I see him. His overpowering presence that fills every room creeps up behind me. The sound of my rapid heartbeat almost drowns out his approaching footfalls.

I glance down both sides of the hallway. Empty. Fuck.

My mouth goes dry, goose bumps pebble across my skin, and the small hairs on my neck rise.

"Hey, love bug," his deep raspy voice taunts. A moment later, he appears on my right side, leaning against the locker next to mine. "Still haven't shed your armor, bug?" He taps his index finger against the side of my back brace.

"Leave me alone, Colt." My feeble request is met with a dark chuckle.

"Is that really what you want? According to rumors, you have a little crush on me."

I don't hide the way I roll my eyes. "You know that's not true." It's really not, but of course, everyone would believe it. He is popular, a star player on our football team, tall, muscular, and of course, handsome. What's not to love? For me, it's his nasty personality.

He takes another step closer, eating up all the space until he is so close I can smell him. His spicy aftershave tingles my nose when he leans in, and his hot breath fans over my cheek as he talks.

"I don't know... those texts were pretty convincing."

Before I realize what's happening, he grabs my wrists and twists me around to face him. He turns us both so my back is against the locker, and his body cages me in.

"What are you——" The words get lodged in my throat as Colt grabs the corner of my brace and pulls the velcro off with one hard tug.

"No!" Panic takes over, and I drop everything in my hand to fight Colt off. I look down at my body, just to find myself completely naked.

All my clothes are in a pile at my feet, leaving me completely bare in front of him.

"Oh my god! Look at this freak," someone calls.

My head snaps up, and I find the hallway filled with students and teachers. Everyone is looking at me, laughing and pointing at me.

Humiliated and exposed, I frantically try to cover myself with my arms, looking for a way out, while Colt stands in front of me, laughing the loudest out of the crowd.

"LAST STOP!"

My eyes fly open, and my fingers dig into the sweater draped over my lap as if the soft fabric could protect me from my bad dreams.

A fog of sleep and confusion is still heavy as I look around the now-empty bus.

"Last stop, miss," the bus driver calls down the aisle.

"Oh. Sorry." Scrambling off my seat, I grab my sweater and backpack and make my way out. "Thank you," I tell the driver when I pass him. I only receive a grunt in response, but I don't hold it against him. This was a long-ass bus ride.

It's good to stretch my legs after getting off the bus, the third —or was it the fourth?—since leaving Grandma's. I'm still not sure whether she was sorry to see me go or not. She said she was, but she didn't waste any time getting me on the bus and walking away.

The weeks I spent with her were a nice escape from regular life. Sometimes, when Mom is in one of her really low moods, she looks at me like I ruined her entire life. And I guess I did, in a way. She wouldn't have gone bankrupt paying my medical bills if it wasn't for me getting injured so badly while I was training. She wouldn't have lost her job, either. I needed round-the-clock care in the early days. I know I cost her a lot—much more than I can ever make up for.

At least the last few weeks were a break from the guilt, even if my grandma isn't exactly the loving maternal figure most people picture when they think of a grandmother. Mom's never been that way either, so I guess it runs in the family. But there was no guilt at Grandma's, and she at least tried to make sure I was comfortable and happy while I was with her.

It's over now, and I'm actually looking forward to spending a night in my own bed again. It might be small, and it might be in a trailer, but it's mine.

The walk from the bus station doesn't take long, or maybe it's anticipation making the walk seem quicker than it is. Either way, the sight of the familiar trailers up ahead gets my feet moving faster. I got plenty of sleep during the long bus ride, but that didn't mean I was comfortable. And I could use a shower after all that traveling.

Nothing could have prepared me for what I walk into after unlocking the front door.

Somebody robbed us. Somebody cleaned us out completely because the place is empty. "Mom?" I call out in a shaky voice, almost afraid to move. I can hardly even breathe. "Are you here?" The only answer I get is the echo of my own voice.

I've been gone for two weeks. What could possibly have happened in two weeks? I search my memory for any hint of us getting evicted, but everything was going okay as far as I knew. Was this visit planned as a way to keep me out of here while something awful happened? Could Mom have at least warned me before I got here? Or what if it was something even worse than that? What if she had an accident and is in a hospital somewhere? What if she—

The sudden blaring of a car horn outside the trailer makes me jump before I spin around to look out the still-open door. A car much nicer than any I've ever seen around here is sitting out there, and a moment later, the door opens, and a familiar head pops out. "You're earlier than I expected! I was going to meet you at the bus station, but you were already gone."

"Mom?" I whisper. It's her, but it's not her. I mean, she's driving a Mercedes, for one thing, and she looks great. Like she just had her hair done, and she's dressed in clothes much nicer than the jeans and T-shirts I'm used to seeing her in.

"What happened?" I blurt out as she gets out of the car. "Where is everything?"

She reaches me and gives me a brief hug, which is still better than what I expected. Mom has never been big on displaying affection. "Why don't we get in the car, and I'll tell you about everything along the way?"

"Along the way, where?"

Just like that, her beaming smile slips, and now I'm looking at a woman who reminds me more of my mother. "Honestly, Leni. Why do you have to make everything so difficult? I'm your mother. Do you think I would take you anywhere dangerous?" She laughs like it's actually funny, like she would never do anything like that. And it's not that she's ever hurt me, exactly, but she's also never gone too far out of her way to protect me.

I get in the car like she asks and look once more at the trailer. It looks so sad and empty now. Not that it ever looked that great before. "Is all my stuff gone, too?"

She clicks her tongue, impatient. "Yes, dear, the whole place is emptied out." She quickly returns to her chipper attitude, smiling from ear to ear. "It has been a very big couple of weeks. I would have called you at your grandmother's, but I wanted it to be a surprise."

She succeeded. "So what's the big surprise? What happened? Did you win the lottery?"

"In a way, yes. I hit the jackpot."

"Meaning?"

"Meaning, I fell in love! I met the man of my dreams, and we're getting married next week."

If she crashed the car right now, I wouldn't be more surprised. "You're what?" It's not April Fool's Day, is it?

"Is it so surprising a man could fall in love with me?" she chirps, giggling. "Yes, we're in love. I know it's all happened so fast, but like they say, when you know..." She gives another little giggle. "He is the most incredible man. Kind, generous, funny, intelligent. And all he wants, Leni, is to take care of us. This is the end of all of our struggles and concerns. We're finally going to live the life we both deserve."

I'm still stuck. I can't piece any of this together in my head. "So where are we going?"

"To his house—our house, now."

"We've moved in with him?"

"Well, silly, what did you think? Yes, naturally, we're moving in with him. Actually, I already have. It was only a matter of waiting for you. Now, everything is complete. We'll be a family together."

Maybe I fell asleep on the bus and haven't woken up yet. I actually pinch myself just in case that's true, but no, I'm awake. And more confused than I can remember being in a long time.

"I know it's cliché, falling for your boss," she continues, oblivious to my shock. "But there was no stopping it. The second we set eyes on each other, it's like it was meant to be. Destiny."

"So this is your boss? At the new law firm you started at?" She was only there a few days before I left for my trip.

"Yes. I can't wait for you to see the house! It's a mansion. James is so looking forward to having you there, too. He's been so excited all day. He even wanted to pick you up, but I thought it would be better if I did since this is all such a big surprise. You deserved to hear all about it from me."

"What's his last name again? James what?"

"James Alistair."

Alistair. Fuck no.

I'm going to be sick. As if the rest of this wasn't bad enough.

I no longer see the scenery we pass as Mom drives us to our new home, babbling the whole way. I see the hallway back at school, back before everything fell apart. Back when I was still in training a few years ago. When I had a whole bright, shining future ahead of me.

I could walk through the halls with my head held high as people greeted me, waving and saying hi as I passed. I was popular. I had friends. People wanted to be near me, the local celebrity on her way to the Olympics. I never saw myself that way. I wasn't anybody special. If anything, I used to wonder if all those people who wanted to be my friend would lose a little bit of their excitement if they saw how grim and tough life as an aspiring Olympic gymnast could be. I didn't have much room for fun or parties, or all the other things kids were into. But it was nice, feeling their approval as I walked to my locker and looked forward to chatting with my best friend before class.

Until somebody slammed into me from behind hard enough to knock me against a row of lockers. "Whoops," a male voice said, nasty and cold. I barely had time to shake off my surprise before being jostled again by a second person.

"Stuck-up bitch." Colt Alistair sneered at me while his brother laughed. Nix was already on his way down the hall, snickering over his shoulder. But Colt continued staring at me, almost like he was challenging me to fight back. I was too stunned and confused to offer anything but a puzzled stare.

I couldn't understand why they didn't like me. Everybody liked me. I had never done anything to them, either, not even close. We had hardly ever spoken to each other, and when we did, it was usually because they were saying something nasty to me, and I was asking what I ever did to deserve it.

They hated me, and nothing has changed in three years.

And now, my mother is marrying their father. Dread plants itself in my stomach and starts to spread through my body, sending waves of icy disbelief down to my fingertips and toes.

I wish I had never gotten on that bus to come home.

CHAPTER 2

"*H*ave you been here before?" my mother asks, closing the car door behind her.

"No." I shake my head, a bit confused by the question. "Why would I have been here before?"

"You went to school with Colt and Nix. I thought you three were friends."

I almost laugh at the idea. Us, friends? We couldn't be further from it. Of course, if my mother would have listened to me back then, she would know that. But just like my mother has always been, she only listens to the part she wants to, and her daughter being bullied wasn't something she was interested in.

Tilting my head up, I take in the large three-story family home. Of course, the Alistairs live here. A beautiful, luxurious, and well-taken care of home. A perfectly manicured yard and a garage big enough to hold three cars. Everything is flawless on the outside, but it's what's on the inside that I'm worried about.

I sling my backpack over my shoulder and follow my mom up the small path leading to the front door. My heart beats irrationally fast against my ribs, and my stomach churns at the thought of what awaits me behind this door.

My mother doesn't knock. She simply reaches for the brass handle and pushes it down. The door opens, and we step into the large foyer. The old sneakers on my feet squeak on the polished tiled floor while my mother's high heels click and clack, both sounds echoing off the walls.

An eerie feeling festers in my gut. Something tells me I'm not supposed to be here. I don't belong here, and I still don't believe my mom does either. Nothing about this feels right.

"There you two lovely women are," a deep male voice fills the space. My head snaps to its origin, and I come face-to-face with James Alistair.

I have only seen him once before, at a school event, but I've never actually talked to him. He is leaning against a doorframe, his body language relaxed. His light blue eyes are soft as he smiles at me with genuine fondness. His demeanor takes me by surprise.

James looks very much like an older version of his sons. His short hair is graying, and his masculine face weathered, but he clearly still works out. The white polo shirt he is wearing stretches over his muscular chest and arms. Most people would say he is a handsome guy.

"James, meet Lenora—my beautiful daughter," my mother coos.

"She is beautiful, indeed. Just like her mother." He grins at my mom like a lovesick puppy.

Wow. This is so weird.

"Oh, stop it with your compliments. You're such a charmer."

My mom giggles and swats the air. "Let me finish dinner. Why don't you show Leni to the dining room?"

"Don't you need help?" James seems nice and all, but if his sons are around, I'd rather not see them.

"No, no, it's fine. I prepared everything this morning. Just need to heat it up. You go and relax. I'll bring dinner out in a few minutes."

"Uhm, okay."

"Come on, Leni, let's sit. I'm sure you've had a long day." James motions for me to follow him, and I do so begrudgingly. "How was your flight?"

"Oh, I took the bus, actually."

"All the way from Wisconsin?"

"Yeah, it wasn't too bad, though. I only had to switch buses a few times. Plus, I slept most of the ride."

"I don't like the idea of you being on a bus by yourself, especially sleeping. That's not safe. I would have bought you a plane ticket if I had known." There is a real note of concern in his voice, and I'm so taken aback that I don't even notice how he is walking me straight into a lion's den.

"Don't be fooled by her looks, Dad. Leni can take care of herself. She bites." Nix's voice meets my ear, and my legs stop moving immediately.

My gaze swings past James to the two guys sitting at the dining room table. I haven't seen Nix and Colt in two months, but it feels like yesterday. Being tormented every day is not something you forget easily.

Nix has always kept his hair buzzed while Colt grows his out at the top. Besides that, they look almost identical with their piercing blue eyes, dimples, and athletic bodies. In school, they were regularly mistaken for twins, though they were actually born ten months apart.

"Boys," he warns. "Be nice. Please, Leni, excuse these knuckleheads. Sometimes they forget their manners."

Once again, I'm left shocked by the way James so easily takes my side, almost as if he is protective of me. Maybe he is just being courteous, but with only us four in the room, there is no one to put on a show for.

James takes a seat at the head of the table while I stand in the doorway with my feet cemented to the ground.

"Come on, Leni. Sit with us," Colt invites, but I don't miss the undertone of sarcasm nor the devilish smirk on his lips.

It takes me another few seconds before I'm able to make my legs move and slowly make my way to the chair farthest away from Colt and Nix. Dropping my backpack on the floor next to me, I sit down, looking around the room to avoid looking at them.

"So Leni, how was your summer? Did you have a good time with your grandmother?" James asks curiously.

"Sure. It was nice. I hadn't seen her in a long time." I'm very cautious not to give too much information. In high school, I learned the hard way that bullies will use everything against you. It's better to keep to yourself. Stay quiet, hidden, invisible. That's where I'll be safe.

"Do you have any plans for the rest of your break?"

"Not yet." I need to get a job as fast as possible, so I can get out of here. I have less than a hundred dollars left from helping my grandma's neighbor with yard work and cleaning houses. That's not going to get me far.

"Well, I'm sure you'll find something to fill your time. Or you just relax until school starts. We have a pool, you know? You are free to swim whenever."

Relaxing? Unlikely.

"Yes, maybe we can go for a swim after dinner," Colt chimes in.

"I don't have a bathing suit," I blurt out a little too fast. Lifting my gaze to the brothers, my blood boils when I see their smug faces.

"We won't look." Nix smirks. "We can go naked as well if it'll make you feel more comfortable."

Instead of giving him a snide remark, I grind my teeth together and hold my tongue. Under the table, I fist my hands and dig my nails into my palm. I concentrate on that pain just so I won't feel the emotional agony bubbling up from being in the presence of Colt and Nix.

"I hope you guys are hungry." My mother's cheerful voice breaks the awkward silence.

She walks into the room holding a large serving bowl, and James immediately jumps up to grab it from her. I also moved to get up and help her, but both James and my mother tell me to sit down. Together, they quickly grab everything from the kitchen and set the table so we can eat.

I can't remember the last time I sat at a table with my mom and ate a meal that didn't come out of a microwave. I didn't even know she could cook food that tasted better than a piece of cardboard. When I was training for the Olympics, and she would prepare my meals, it was about nutrition and not taste. Boiled chicken, steamed vegetables, and tasteless protein shakes were my daily life for years.

If it wasn't for Colt and Nix sitting across the table and

ruining my appetite, I would wolf this down like a starved animal. But thanks to their presence, each delicious morsel lands heavy in my empty stomach.

Completely oblivious to the tense mood in the room, my mom goes on about how great of a week she had. "I just love working at the office. Everyone is so nice. It makes the day go by in a breeze."

"Everyone is nice to you because you are so amazing." James smiles, placing his hand over my mother's, who giggles like a little schoolgirl.

They look so happy, and I am glad my mom finally found someone who makes her feel this way. I just wish he didn't have kids, or at least different ones.

CHAPTER 3

"*A*re you sure you don't want me to help you clean up?"

"Yes, I'm sure. You just go and settle into your new room. We moved all your stuff from your old room. Well, everything that survived the move. We had to replace a lot of stuff."

"Oh…" I'm not sure what to say. I wasn't particularly attached to my old furniture, but with all these sudden changes, I was kind of looking forward to my familiar bed. "You didn't have to do that."

"We didn't want your moldy old furniture in our house—"

"Nixon!" James snaps at his son. "Stop being so rude."

"What? It's true." He shrugs, completely unapologetic. "Maybe we can replace some of her clothes too?" He looks down at my shirt in disgust.

"We could go clothes shopping this weekend," my mom interjects. "Girls' day?"

"Sure." I force a smile. Anything to get away from these two assholes.

"Perfect! Do you want me to show you to your room?"

"We're going up anyway," Colt offers. "We'll show you where your room is."

"I'm sure I can find it myself." Grabbing my backpack off the floor, I stand up, looking for a way to escape this place.

"It's upstairs, the last one at the end of the hallway," James explains.

He has barely finished giving me directions when I start speed walking out of the dining room and up the stairs without looking back.

Only when I'm on the second floor, and I don't hear anyone coming after me, do I sigh in relief.

"Last one at the end of the hallway..." But he didn't say which one. The staircase leads into a wall with hallways on either side. I try my luck on the left side.

As I walked down the hall, I count the doors, wondering whose room is behind each one. I pass five before I get to the sixth and last door. If I took the correct turn, this should be my room.

Lifting my hand, I reach for the doorknob. My index finger brushes over the cool brass, the small hairs on the back of my neck lift, and a shiver runs down my spine.

"Wrong room, love bug," Nix whispers behind me.

I spin around so fast that I lose my footing and stumble backward until my back hits the wall. Nix takes one large step toward me, eating up the distance between us.

"Don't call me that." Love bug might seem like a cute pet name but knowing why he calls me that leaves a bitter taste on my tongue for simply hearing it. After my accident, I had to wear a bulky back brace. Someone had the bright idea to call me a stink bug since I had an outer shell, and in the summertime, I would smell like sweat, no matter how much I tried to cover it up with perfume. Nix and Colt turned stink bug into love bug at some point, but they say it with the same kind of disgust still.

"I'll call you whatever I want. After all, you are in my house, and you'd do well to remember that. Don't walk around and stay in your room. I don't want you touching my stuff."

"You think I want to be here? I didn't even know about any of this until a few hours ago." I try to push past him, but he places his hands on either side of me, caging me between him and the wall.

"I don't care what you know or what you want. All I care about is getting rid of you. You and your gold-digging mom need to find some other guy to leech off."

He dips his head low, leaning into my face until his nose brushes against my cheek. "You don't belong here. Go back to your trailer park."

"Trust me, I'd rather live in a run-down trailer than here with you." I shove against his chest as hard as I can, taking him by surprise. Ducking under his arm, I take off down the hall, past the stairs to the other side of the floor.

When I get to the last door, I don't hesitate to open it. I rush inside the room, slamming the door shut behind me. Dropping my backpack on the ground, I reach for the lock, only to find none.

What the hell?

Is this some kind of mistake? Instead of there being a latch on the doorknob I can turn to lock in place, the surface is smooth. I have no way of making sure there's any privacy in this room.

Then my heart lurches, and I rush for the adjoining bathroom. I don't even care what it looks like. I only want to examine the door. Sure enough, there's no lock here, either, not on either side of the doorknob.

An icy chill runs through me, and I shiver, rubbing my arms as goose bumps cover them. This is wrong. This whole thing is wrong. Why would I not be allowed to lock my doors while living in a house with all these men? I would say something to Mom about it, but I'm sure she would laugh it off—if I got lucky. Otherwise, she'll demand to know why I'm making her life so difficult. I don't know what would be worse, being laughed at or blamed for something I'm not trying to do.

Another thing I'm not trying to do is take a shower without being able to lock the door. I feel so dirty after spending hours in those bus seats, sometimes falling asleep while my head rested against a window countless other people touched. The thought of it makes me wrinkle my nose. How am I supposed to clean up when I can't trust Colt and Nix to stay out?

One of my new bedroom furnishings is a desk and a matching chair. It's about the right size, so I pick the chair up and carry it to the bathroom, where I wedge it under the doorknob. At least now I can breathe a little easier, even if the idea of having to do this in what's supposed to be my house disgusts me. Then again, there isn't much about this situation that isn't disgusting. Wrong.

I pull off my clothes and leave them in a pile on the tiled floor before hanging one of the stacked towels on a hook outside the shower door. My own bathroom. I wish I could be more enthusiastic about this because I've always dreamed of having my own bathroom. One of those *Someday, when I'm rich* fantasies. And compared to the tiny little bathroom back at the trailer, this is massive.

I wish I could enjoy it.

Still, the shower is nice, already stocked with all kinds of good-smelling soaps, shampoo, and all kinds of other items I always wanted to buy for myself but never had the money for. I take advantage of all of them, too, using sugar scrub to rid me of the feeling of being soiled and nasty before soaping up. Even the shampoo is better than any I've ever used, and I never thought it really made that much of a difference how much a person paid for it. Now I understand. By the time I'm finished rinsing out the thick suds, I think I could get used to living this way.

If only it wasn't for my fear. Not to mention how strange this all feels and how sudden. Not that my mother is notorious for making the best choices, but this is over the top even for her. Is she this desperate to escape our old life? I guess so, and that's my fault, too. I'm sure if I ever complained, she would throw that in my face. *If it wasn't for you getting hurt and everything that came afterward...* I don't even want to think about it.

Stepping out of the shower, I catch sight of myself in the mirror. My long reddish hair is caked to my neck and shoulder. My green eyes are framed with pale lashes that can barely be seen unless I put mascara on. Just as I reach for a towel, the reflection in the shower stall catches my eye. The way I'm standing lets me get a good look at my back. I rarely look at the ugly scar I'm left with, mostly because I don't need the reminder of it all.

"Come on, Leni, one more time." Coach has been pushing me hard this week. *"I know you can do this. You have to nail that landing."*

"You got this, babe!" my mom yells from the sideline.

Drowning out everything around me, I run toward the high bars. My mind is laser-focused, every muscle in my body taut as I use the small trampoline to jump up and grab the lower bar. Using my momentum, I swing around the low bar. I let go at just the right moment, launching into a full twist before catching the high bar. I continue my routine perfectly. Then go for the dismount. Knowing I have to let go at the perfect time to make a backflip with a one-and-a-half twist work. I spin around one last time, not knowing it would be my indefinite last time.

I let go of the bar half a second too early, maybe even less than that, but it's enough to mess up the trajectory. My body twists in the air, and I know I'm going to hit the mat before I do. What I didn't know was how hard I would hit it.

For a moment, everything goes black. When I come to, I'm in the most excruciating pain of my life. It feels like someone has cut my back open and is digging through it with claws. The pain is so severe I can't breathe. My vision is blurry, and all I can hear is my mom's sobbing voice telling me everything is going to be okay.

She lied. After my accident, nothing was okay.

By the time I'm wrapped in a fluffy robe and returning to the bedroom, I've almost resigned myself to this. At least James seems like a decent guy, even if he's a little much. He wants to impress me and make me feel at home, which is a lot better than how he could treat me. Like a burden, he would rather not deal with.

This bedroom is no joke. I see now that my paltry furniture would look entirely out of place—the room is so large, my bed and cheap Goodwill dresser would have been swallowed up, looking more like furniture from a dollhouse than anything else. Now, I have a bed twice the size, heavy and sturdy looking, and a mattress so soft I want to sink into it and pull the blankets over my head on contact.

Maybe this won't be so bad. So long as I can find a way to secure the door, so I feel safe, I might be able to make it through this ordeal. I'm sure Colt and Nix have their own busy lives. All I have to do is stay out of their way.

But I'd feel a lot better about this if I knew I could lock my door. I need privacy. Everybody does, right? I don't think it's too unusual to ask for a means of keeping the world out.

Maybe if I put it that way, that all I'm looking for is the guarantee of privacy, my mother will be a little more understanding. I want to try, at least. Otherwise, all I have in front of me is an endless string of nights spent worrying whether one, if not both, of my stepbrothers will come barging through the door.

If only she wanted to understand how they treated me back in school. How they're still treating me. Yet those stories would fall on deaf ears, so I'm not going to waste my time.

My own clothes are in the dresser, and they don't take up much space. But they're mine, so I put on clean jeans and a tee, preparing to sweet-talk my mother into finding a way through this. A new bedroom door can't cost that much, can it? I'm sure James could afford it.

I go to the door, prepared to put on my happiest face—but when I try to turn the knob, I get nowhere. It's stuck in place.

Somebody locked it from the other side.

"Are you kidding?" I call out, my heart pounding so hard I'm afraid it will burst out of my chest. "You're going to lock me in here like this?" Which one of them did it? It could be either of them. The odds are equally in both their favor. When no one answers—I don't even hear so much as a snicker from out in the hall—I touch my forehead to the wood and try desperately not to cry. I didn't do anything to deserve this. When is it going to stop?

No. I am not going to let them break me down like this. I'm not going to stand here and cry like a baby because of a locked door. Instead of giving in, I fish my phone out of my backpack. Mom probably won't be happy that I'm bothering her over something I know she's going to think is trivial, but maybe I can make it sound like a big misunderstanding, something we can laugh off together. I have to hope.

As it turns out, I have a text message from a number not stored in my contacts.

Unknown Number: If you know what's good for you, you'll stay in that room and not complain. Otherwise, you're going to regret it.

Are they that determined to avoid the sight of me? Is my presence in this house that much of a problem for them? I can't understand why. I have never done a single thing to either of them, ever. I wasn't even here when our parents supposedly fell in love. I had nothing to do with it.

I guess with people like them, there doesn't need to be a reason. They decided from day one that they hated me, and nothing is going to change their minds. The harder I try, the worse it's going to get. So why bother?

I don't bother responding to the text, instead throwing my phone onto the bed and dropping down beside it. I hate this sense of letting them win, even in this little way. But I have no doubt they meant what they said. They'll find a way to make me regret it if I make a big deal about this.

So instead of marching downstairs, like I'd intended, I

change into pajamas. Then inspiration strikes, and I go to the bathroom to retrieve the chair, which I wedge under the door-knob in here. Just because I'm locked in doesn't mean somebody couldn't decide to unlock the door and do whatever they felt like. I'm not going to make it that easy for them.

Once I'm sure there's no getting in from out in the hall, I go to bed. The events of the day have left me drained, physically and emotionally. I might be able to handle things better if I get a good night's sleep.

CHAPTER 4

*I*t's the first thing on my mind the moment my eyes open on my first morning in the new house. Before I've even shaken off my sleepiness, I get out of bed and go straight to the door to test the knob. Unlike last night, it turns freely. That doesn't mean I'm about to move the chair from in front of the door, but I know now that they don't plan on keeping me locked in here like a hostage night and day.

After washing up and changing out of my pajamas, I have a decision to make. Do I stay up here, or do I risk facing my enemies downstairs?

There's really nothing to think about. I'm not leaving this room until I absolutely have to.

In the meantime, I'm going to do something I thought over last night while I was trying to fall asleep, one eye always on the bedroom door. I wanted to see whether the knob turned like somebody had unlocked it, but I fell asleep before that happened. It's amazing I slept at all, really.

I need to get a job, and fast. I need to make enough money to get out of here and find a place on my own. I can't live the rest of my life this way, that's for sure. Lying in bed, staring at the door, expecting somebody to break in.

I set up the laptop on the desk before taking the chance to remove the chair from under the doorknob. Soon I'm scrolling through job listings, and within an hour, I've applied to six different places—stores, a pizza place, and a coffee shop. It doesn't matter what time of day I have to be there. If anything, the earlier, the better. More of a chance to avoid my bullies. I've never worked anywhere like this before, but if there's one thing I know about myself, I'm strong. I can handle a little hard work.

To my surprise, there's an email waiting for me by the time I finish the sixth application. It's from the pizza shop. *Can you come in today for an interview at 4:00?*

My eyes widen. I didn't expect to hear back from anybody so soon. I type out a quick reply, telling them yes, I'd be happy to. Now, I never exactly dreamed about slinging pizzas all day, but then I've never dreamed about being afraid to fall asleep in case one of my hateful stepbrothers decides to terrorize me in the middle of the night.

I've barely finished sending the email when there's a brief knock on my door, followed by my mother's entrance. "Good, I see you're settling in nicely."

"I'm doing my best, but—"

Before I can so much as hint at what went on last night, she continues, "Breakfast is nearly ready."

How am I supposed to eat with a pit in my stomach? "Are we all eating together?" I ask, mentally crossing my fingers in hopes of her saying no.

No such luck. "Of course." I guess my reaction isn't what she was hoping for since her eyes narrow in a familiar way. She can try all she wants to be the happy, chipper bride-to-be, but those little flashes of the real person behind her smile insist on slipping through. "Now, you listen to me. I don't want any of your complaints. I don't want you dragging your feet or muttering things under your breath. I refuse to allow that. You will not ruin this for me, understood?"

All I did was ask a simple question. Clearly, she's waiting for me to answer, and she'll accept only one answer. "Understood," I whisper, and the words curdle in my mouth.

"Good. Be downstairs in three minutes." She's out of the room a moment later, and I sink back in my chair with a heavy sigh. So much for staying out of everybody's way, hoping they forget about me for a little while.

Sure enough, the men are already sitting around the table when I arrive. Mom is carrying in the last of the platters—already, she's covered the table with pancakes, bacon, and sausage. Now, she's adding a pile of scrambled eggs.

James laughs indulgently at the feast she's put together. "You don't need to go to all this trouble." He takes her hand and lifts it to his lips before planting a kiss that, for some reason, makes my stomach turn.

"This is nothing. I love cooking, and it's been so long since I had a reason to whip up a meal like this." She's smiling brilliantly as she takes a seat, every inch the glowing, happy homemaker. "Besides, this is our first breakfast together as a family. I thought it should be special." From the taste of it, even the orange juice is freshly squeezed. I wonder how early she had to wake up this morning to put this together.

"Yes, I imagine there wasn't much reason to cook up a feast

in the trailer park." Nix glances over at Colt, and the two of them share a snide little chuckle. Either the adults didn't hear it, or they're ignoring them. I decide to pretend I didn't hear it, instead reaching for the eggs. I hate the feel of their eyes on me—like they're waiting for an excuse to pounce.

One thing about me they'll never understand is my ability to block the rest of the world out, a skill I had no choice but to hone when I was in training. The only reason I was able to reach the level I did before my injury was learning the mental game of being an athlete. All the physical conditioning and practice in the world won't make a difference if your mind is weak.

My body might not be in the same condition it was a few years ago, but my brain is still sharp. I'm able to eat without paying them much attention. When it was just Mom and me, there wasn't much of a reason to whip up a celebratory meal. Plus, we didn't have the money for food like this.

"So Leni." Around halfway through the meal, James turns his attention on me. I wish he wouldn't. I'm sure his heart is in the right place, but he's only making things worse. "What's your plan for the day? I wouldn't blame you if you do nothing but sit by the pool."

He seems to have conveniently forgotten the fact that I don't have a bathing suit. "Now that you mention it, I was going to ask a favor." I look toward my mother and hope her fiancé's presence will have the right effect on her. "I have a job interview at four o'clock this afternoon. Could I borrow your car to get there? It's a pizza place in town."

"You don't need to go to the trouble," James assures me with an easy smile. "I would gladly drop you off there and wait for you to finish."

Not what I wanted. I'm sure he's only trying to be friendly and helpful to get on my good side, but he's already pushing a little too hard. If I refuse, on the other hand, Mom will lose her shit. As it is, she's practically vibrating as she stares at me. I'm pretty sure she'll crack a tooth if she doesn't stop smiling so hard.

"You know what?" Colt interjects. "Is it Lorenzo's? Is that the place? I heard they're looking for help down there."

Terrific. I can either lie or tell the truth and see where this is going. I'm sure it's nowhere good. "Yes, as a matter of fact. They must really be in a hurry to hire somebody since I only applied this morning, and somebody already got back to me about coming in."

Nix lifts a shoulder. "We could drop you off on our way to the gym." Just when I thought things couldn't get any more uncomfortable. And it's obvious from the smirks both boys wear that they know I'm stuck. There's no good reason for me to refuse—and considering Mom's intense stare, I have no doubt she expects me to accept. It would look childish if I didn't.

She must get tired of my sputtering because she answers for me. "That is such a generous offer. Leni is so lucky that she'll have brothers like the two of you. I always wished she'd have somebody to protect her the way a brother would." The woman is even tearing up, for god's sake. It's one of her best performances. I wonder if anybody would think it was odd if I started to applaud.

"Sure," I murmur. "That would be great." And now I have no appetite for the rest of the food on my plate, which I move around with my fork while Mom changes the subject to the wedding. I'm fine with that since it means nobody's paying attention to me anymore.

Even if I can't shake the feeling that the guys never stop paying attention to me. I catch Nix grinning at Colt, and a pit forms in my stomach. They're already planning something. I'm tempted to suggest they both get a life.

"Let me help you with that." I almost jump up from my chair when Mom stands and starts gathering the plates.

"See?" James points out to his sons. "This is what it looks like to be helpful around the house. The two of you could take a lesson from your sister." I have to force myself not to look at either of them since I wouldn't be able to wipe off my smirk. No doubt they don't appreciate hearing him talk about me that way. Hell, I don't appreciate it, either. At least he's trying, unlike them.

Before long, we've cleared the table. Once we're alone in the cavernous kitchen with its shining appliances, Mom launches once again into wedding talk. "It's all such a blur!" she says with a laugh. "A whirlwind. But when you've got enough money, you can plan things like this at the last minute. James is so generous. He wants to make sure I have everything I want. I won't have to miss out on a single thing, even if the vendors insist on charging extra in rush fees and all that."

"You're absolutely sure you want to do this?" I whisper. I know it's a risk, but I have to know. She's known this man for, what, less than three weeks?

"Don't tell me you're going to start in on lecturing me about how quickly this is all going."

"Mom, I'm just saying, you hardly know this man." I have to whisper, just in case somebody is standing close enough to the kitchen that my voice echoes. "He seems like a very nice man, but do you really know him?"

"Sweetheart, I've lost count of how many women I know who waited for years before deciding to settle down with the right person. They were afraid of making a mistake and wanted to be sure they knew their partner. And you know what?"

"What?" I ask even though I know what's coming.

"Every single one of those marriages ended in divorce. Every. Single. One."

To be fair, my mother has never had the best taste in friends, either. "Okay, sure. But I mean, we're already living here and everything. And you two seem happy together. Why not give it a little more time? This way, you won't have to pay all these crazy fees or whatever. And you can still have exactly the wedding you want."

"I don't want to wait. I've been waiting for a man like James my entire life. Don't I deserve a little happiness?" Her voice is sharper now, her meaning direct.

"Of course you do," I whisper with a sinking heart.

"Stop being so negative," she implores with a light laugh. "One day, you'll understand."

"Understand what?"

"How it feels when you find the right person. Your soul mate." She's so breathy, and I'd swear I was talking to somebody closer to my own age, not a grown woman who should know better. "When you find them, you can't let anything get in your way. Not the so-called rules, not what society says you should do. Why live by some stranger's arbitrary rules that don't apply to you? And that's what this is. Those rules don't apply to us. The moment I looked into James's eyes, I knew I was looking at the man I would spend the rest of my life with."

"I'm happy for you," I whisper, if only because it seems like the right thing to say.

"Don't worry," she assures me. "One day, it will be your turn. And on that day, when you find your soul mate, you'll come to me and say you finally understand. I look forward to that day. I really do."

She doesn't have me fooled. She wants me to tell her she was right all along. She's never been very interested in my happiness, only in hers.

We're as alone as we're ever going to be in this big house, and she's in a good mood—feeling all warm and maternal and whatnot. Now is as good a time as any. "There was something I wanted to talk with you about."

"What is it?" she asks as she scrapes the last of the leftover food into the garbage disposal. I hate to see so much waste, especially when we spent so long scraping together every last cent for the basics. One more way the two of us are different. She experienced deprivation and wants to make up for it, while all it did was make me want to avoid being wasteful.

"I know I never talked about this before, mostly because I didn't think it made a difference whether or not you knew. But remember yesterday, when we first got here, you mentioned me going to school with the guys?"

"Of course."

"Mom, they were never nice to me. Not once, not ever. In fact, they went out of their way to be mean and nasty."

"I'm sure you misunderstood their intentions."

"They walked around calling me a stuck-up bitch."

"Language," she warns.

"I'm only telling you what they said. They used to push me around, all sorts of things, but I never did a single thing to them. I swear," I insist when she arches an eyebrow.

"You expect me to believe those nice young men, who, by the way, offered to drive you to a job interview, went out of their way to bully you? Besides, even if they did, that was a long time ago. People do change, you know."

I knew she'd go out of her way to misunderstand what I was trying to say, but I had to try. "Mom, I'm just saying they hate me. You don't hear the things they've said already behind your back—"

Suddenly, she slams her hands against the counter, and I jump in surprise. "You listen to me," she whispers, drawing close until she's looming over me while I cower against the refrigerator. "I will not let you destroy this for me, understood? I don't want to hear your complaints. I don't want to hear your sob stories where you make a victim out of yourself."

"I wasn't trying—"

"You've already ruined my life once," she hisses. "I will be damned if I let you do it again."

She thrusts an arm toward the doorway. "Now get out of my sight and stay that way."

This is the woman I know. The woman I was so glad to have two weeks away from. It didn't take long for her to show her true colors, but then James is nowhere around, so I guess she feels like she can get away with it.

I waste no time going to the stairs, then take them two at a time and practically run down the hall to my room. Thankfully, nobody follows me, and I check both the bedroom and bathroom are empty before using the chair again to barricade myself in.

I ruined her life. She was singing a different tune a few years ago. Back then, I was ruining her life if I didn't make it onto the Olympic team. *"Fifteen is already cutting it close."* She never missed an opportunity to remind me of that, and it was her voice that always rang out in my head when I was the last one at the gym. When it was late at night, so late even the cleaning crew left. I used to set the alarm before leaving the building rather than make them wait for me to finish up. Even they used to shake their heads at each other like they felt sorry for me while I worked and worked until my entire body hurt, until my muscles were at the edge of their endurance and closing in on exhaustion. *Fifteen is already cutting it close. This is your last chance.*

Only knowing how she'd never forgive me if I didn't make the team kept me alone at the gym. Pushing through the pain, running my routines "just one more time," though it always turned into two or three more runs. I had to be the best. I had to be a champion, or else I'd ruin my mother's life.

Nobody ever told me I'd end up ruining it either way.

CHAPTER 5

J knew this was a bad idea as soon as the guys offered me a ride. Nervously, I shuffle my feet around at the front door. Looking down at the watch on my wrist, my annoyance grows exponentially. My interview is supposed to start in five minutes, and we haven't left yet.

I'm just about to start walking when I finally hear the guys coming down the stairs. Neither one of them is in a hurry, which shouldn't come as a surprise to me. I guess I thought they wanted to take me to this interview to make sure I do not *leech* off of them.

"You do know that if I don't get a job, I can't get my own place, right?"

"Shut up and get in the truck," Nix snaps.

I suppress an eye roll and follow them outside to a matte black F-150 parked in front of the garage. The sleek truck probably cost more than my entire college tuition would. Nix uses the key fob to unlock his truck before he gets into the driver's seat. Colt walks around to the passenger side, and I get into the back.

The engine roars to life just as I buckle up. It's good that I didn't waste any time because Nix pulls out of the driveway like a madman, and if I wasn't buckled up, I'd be slung through the cab like a rag doll.

"Did you fuck that chick from the party last weekend?" Nix asks his brother like I'm not even in the truck.

"The blonde? Yeah, once, her pussy was weird."

"I know. That's why I fucked her ass," Nix quips, and they both break out in laughter. "Her mouth wasn't bad either, but she was a sloppy mouth fuck, gagging like she was about to puke all over me."

Looking out the tinted window, I try my best to ignore them, which makes Colt only raise his voice.

"Ugh, I did have a chick puke on me once. Maybe I should have stopped fucking her face when she frantically tapped on my leg."

Now I'm gagging myself just thinking about this. "You can just drop me off here. I'll walk the rest." I'm already late anyway.

"What's up, love bug? Does our sex talk make you uncomfortable?"

"You mean your assault talk? Yeah, I could go without hearing it."

"Assault?" Nix chuckles. "Girls like getting their faces fucked. They basically beg us to do it. I know this must be unbelievable for a virgin like you."

"At least my pussy doesn't feel *weird* because I let every guy I meet fuck it."

Colt tsks. "That's no way to talk about your friend. What would Piper think if she heard you say that about her?"

Just mentioning Piper's name feels like a sucker punch to the gut. She used to be my best friend. I trusted her with everything, and she turned her back on me like I was nothing. She's the only one who really hurt me deeply. But the worst part of all is that even now, hearing that the guys hurt her in any way makes me mad. Did she really want it? Or did they take advantage of her? Even after everything she did to me, a part of me still wants to protect her.

"She's not my friend," I murmur, more to myself. I have to remind myself of that for my own sanity.

"Sorry, we forgot. You don't have any friends," Colt says over his shoulder.

"I'd rather have no friends at all than fake friends."

"Whatever you have to tell yourself." Nix chuckles. "Did you bring a change of clothes, or is that really what you're wearing to your interview?"

Scrunching my nose, I look down at my skinny jeans and tank top. It's nothing fancy, but there is also nothing wrong with it. It's clean without holes in it. I could use some new sneakers, but I wasn't gonna spend my last money on shoes.

"I'm interviewing at a pizza parlor, not a law firm."

Finally, we pull up to a strip mall, and the sign above the shop is like a welcoming beacon.

"Good luck," Nix mutters, snickering, and his brother joins him while I scramble out of the truck. The sooner I'm away from them, the better.

I do wish Nix hadn't said anything about my clothes. Now I feel self-conscious about my outfit. I have to remind myself that his entire life revolves around making me uncomfortable and questioning myself. I can't take him seriously. It's with that in mind that I'm able to keep my chin up as I open the glass door, setting off a bell that jingles merrily overhead.

The clock above the cash register tells me I'm five minutes late. Dammit. I knew they'd find some way to mess this up. I could always make an excuse, but no matter what the reason, this looks unprofessional. I'm starting out on the wrong foot.

If I don't get this job, I'm sure there will be other opportunities, but the more time I spend with my soon-to-be stepbrothers, the easier it is to remember why I'm in such a hurry in the first place.

When the girl behind the counter clears her throat, I realize I've been standing here without having said a word. "Hi," I offer. "My name is Leni Peters, and I had a four o'clock appointment to speak with the owner about a job."

She can't be any older than me, so why does it sting so badly when she shoots a pointed look up at the clock? It reminds me of when I was training, and my coach would make a face like that and convey a hundred kinds of disappointment without saying a word. "Yeah, let me tell him you're here," she mutters before heading to the back while I wish I could dig a hole and bury myself in it. Not the best way to start this out.

It's not thirty seconds before she comes back. "You can sit down. He'll call for you when he's ready." The phone rings, and she answers right away, leaving me with nothing to do but sit in one of the molded plastic chairs lined up in front of the window. A few tables are in use at the moment, but otherwise, the shop is fairly empty. I guess it's a little early for the dinner rush.

Five minutes pass. Ten minutes, twenty. Now the tables are

empty, and it's just me and the girl behind the counter. Whenever I try to catch her eye, she suddenly remembers something she's got to do. I'm pretty sure she wipes down the tables three different times before finally giving up and scrolling through her phone without bothering to acknowledge me.

By four thirty, things are starting to pick up, with the phone ringing fairly constantly and a second girl coming in for her shift. She throws a curious sort of look my way before heading behind the counter, where she and the girl, who seems to hate me, complain about how short-staffed they are. Meanwhile, here I sit, biting my tongue rather than reminding them that I'm sitting here, waiting to be interviewed. I could possibly help out with their problem.

By the time five o'clock hits, I'm ready to call it quits. It's obvious this man has no intention of speaking to me, and as much as I want to barge into his office and ream him out for bringing me down here, I don't have it in me. And who knows? People might talk. My name used to be fairly well-known. I might end up screwing myself out of the opportunity to find a job if word spreads that I caused a scene.

And oh, the way my mother would take it out on me.

I'm about to stand and approach the counter when the door to the office flies open. "Laney?"

"It's Leni," I offer with a faint smile. He only looks me up and down before turning away and heading into his office. Does that mean I'm supposed to follow him? After a few seconds of indecision, I force my feet to move, taking me in the direction of the open door.

He sits behind a tiny desk stacked high with papers and crumpled napkins. "So you're looking for a job here?"

"Yes." Is that a trick question?

"I'm looking back over your application here." He leans in close to his laptop screen, squinting. "You don't really have any experience."

"That's true. I was training for the Olympics, but an injury put a stop to that, so I didn't have the opportunity to get an after-school job like a lot of people do."

"So you don't know anything about point-of-sale systems or food preparation."

The way he looks at me makes my skin crawl, and now I wish I had worn something more than a tank top. His gaze hovers around my chest and doesn't move until I fold my arms. "No, but everybody has to start somewhere, right? I'm a fast learner. And I just spent the past hour observing the girls out there. I can take orders, wipe down tables, and refill drinks. I'm willing to put in the work."

When all he does is stroke his chin, I add, "I really need this job. I'll do whatever it takes."

That was a mistake. I see it immediately in the way his eyes light up. "Whatever it takes, huh? You better be careful. Some managers would take that the wrong way and get the wrong idea."

Tears of rage threaten to fill my eyes, but I blink them back quickly. When I'm in a situation where I can't scream, my body always wants to revert to crying. "Then I guess those aren't the kind of managers I'd want to work for," I grit out.

He pushes back from the desk, shaking his head as he makes a big deal of shuffling papers around. "I'm sorry, but you are not a good candidate. Thanks for coming in."

That's all he wanted? To get a look at me and see if I'd be

willing to put up with his perverted ass? I practically launch myself out of the chair and waste no time bursting out onto the sidewalk, running along the businesses up and down the strip. I need a shower. Two showers. Scalding hot.

Terrific. Now what do I do? I guess I'll go home, though the prospect fills me with about as much happiness as does the idea of working for a pig like the man I just interviewed with. There's a bus stop up on the corner, a metal and glass shelter with benches. I'd rather sit on a bench and wait for the next bus than reach out and ask for a ride. I shudder to think of the hoops I'll have to jump through for that. Besides, it's been way more than an hour since Colt and Nix dropped me off. I'm sure they're done working out by now and are probably home. Not that I particularly care about inconveniencing them, but I'm sure they will care very much and will find a way to take it out on me.

With that in mind, I duck beneath the shelter and take a seat before pulling out my phone to check the bus schedule. The one that runs closest to the house will still have me walking a few blocks, but that's nothing.

"Dammit," I whisper, checking the schedule again to make sure I'm not looking at the weekend version rather than the weekday. No, I'm in the right spot, and according to this, the last bus ran at five o'clock. If the jerk hadn't kept me waiting all that time, this wouldn't be a problem.

I would still rather eat my own tongue than ask for help from either of the Alistair brothers. Well, at least I know my sneakers are sturdy enough to get me home. I get up with a sigh and begin walking.

I should have known the job was too good to be true. The way he reached out to me so quickly, even though I don't have any qualifications. People are always looking for a way to take advantage, it seems. I hate that I even entertain such jaded thoughts, but facts are facts.

I'm about twenty minutes into my walk when the sudden blaring of a horn behind me makes me jump. I look to my left in time to find a now familiar truck speeding by, with Colt and Nix laughing as they pass. I don't know if I want them to stop or if I'd rather they keep going.

As it turns out, it doesn't matter what I want because Nix doesn't so much as ease up on the gas pedal, rocketing them off fast enough that the taillights are nothing but pinpoints in almost no time at all.

I wonder if I could get lucky enough for them to crash that stupid truck.

CHAPTER 6

S taring at the computer screen, I squint my eyes, trying to read the job ads, which keep getting more blurry. How long have I been staring at my computer? According to my eyesight, way too long.

Closing all the tabs, I turn off my laptop and push up from my desk. I grab a book from my nightstand and flop down on my bed. Maybe a good book will put me in a better mood before I go to bed.

At least my mom didn't throw out my novels. I can still get lost in the pages like I did when I slept in that tiny room in the trailer. I still can't believe how my life has changed so quickly.

Two months ago, I was living with my mom at a trailer park, and now I'm in the Alistairs' home. My mom is in the other room, busy with wedding preparations, and my arch-enemies are playing video games downstairs.

I didn't particularly like our living arrangements before, but at least I felt safe in my own home. I slept in my bed surrounded by my things. This house is bathed in luxury, but the sleek design of the house, decorated with pristine furniture and extravagant art, feels more like a showroom than a place to live.

Everything about this house feels off. The rooms feel colder, and I don't mean the temperature kind of cold. I mean, this doesn't feel like a home. In a home, people love each other, happy memories are made, and you don't go to sleep in fear.

I'm not welcome here and don't think I ever will be.

Burrowing into my pillow, I flip open the book and read until my eyelids feel heavy, and each turn of the page takes more effort than the one before. I don't want to stop, though, because when I'm reading, I leave the world around me and dive into a new one. For a few hours, I live someone else's life. For those moments, my problems don't exist, and I can be free.

I'm just about to doze off when a loud banging on my door has me jumping up from my bed, letting the book fall to the floor next to me. "What?" I ask breathlessly, grabbing my chest as if my heart is about to burst through.

"Get ready. We're going to a party, and you're coming," Nix tells me through the door.

What? Did he just say party? He's just messing with me again. One of his cruel jokes.

"Um, I'm okay. I'm in bed already."

"Get dressed, or you're going naked. We're leaving in five minutes."

I look at the alarm clock on my nightstand. It's already nine thirty, which I realize is probably not that late for a normal teenager.

"I'm not going anywhere with you!" My words are barely out when the door flies open, and the two brothers waltz into my room.

My pulse doubles in speed.

"Get out!" I yell, wishing I had wedged my chair under the door.

Both guys ignore me completely. Nix goes to my closet while Colt heads straight for me.

"What the hell are you doing?"

Instead of answering me, he reaches for the hem of my nightshirt and pulls it up in one swift move. I'm so caught off guard that I don't have time to fight him, not that I would have a chance anyway.

He pulls the shirt off my body and throws it carelessly behind him. I'm left standing in nothing but my shorts. I lift my arms and wrap them around my boobs as fast as I can but not before Colt gets a good look. The corner of his mouth lifts up into a mischievous grin.

"Don't flatter yourself. It's not like there's much to cover up."

Not wanting him to see how hurt I am by his comment, I turn away from him, looking for something to cover up with. It's only when I hear the soft gasp behind me that I realize my mistake.

I just exposed the ugliest part of me. My boobs might be small, but at least they're normal-looking, unlike my back. Multiple surgeries on my spine have left me with a large, ragged scar running down the center of my back. I didn't know it then, but the moment I fell, a lumbar vertebrae fracture ended my career. No one has ever seen it besides the doctors and my mom. And I wasn't planning on ever showing anybody. I always make sure my clothes cover my back completely, so no one catches sight of this monstrosity. Now a guy who picks on all my flaws, no matter how tiny, has seen the biggest one of all.

"Here, put this on." Nix's voice booms through the space moments before some balled-up fabric hits me in my shoulder.

Quickly, I lean down and grab it. Without even looking at what it is, I pull it over my body frantically. Only once my skin is covered do I look down and realize he gave me a summer dress.

"See how quick that was. Now, let's go."

"Why? Why can't you just leave me alone?"

"So you can mess with our stuff, go through it while we're gone? You're coming with us so we can keep an eye on you."

"I don't give a shit about your stuff!"

"You really have a mouth on you." Nix grabs my wrist and starts to pull me toward the door. "Maybe we can put it to use later."

"Fuck you," I spit back.

In response, he tightens his grip on my wrist painfully as he drags me down the stairs. Colt is right behind us, following along quietly. I wonder why he hasn't said anything about my scar. Probably thinking about the best way to make fun of it.

"I'm not even wearing sandals, and I need to grab my purse." I don't even mention the fact that I'm still wearing my pajama bottoms under the dress.

"You don't need any of that," Nix tells me as he opens the front door. As if he's in a hurry, he pulls me outside so fast I have to jog to keep up with his large strides.

This time, Colt gets into the driver's seat while Nix opens the back door and literally lifts me inside, throwing me on the bench before closing the door behind me.

What the fuck is going on?

I barely have time to sit up and buckle myself before we speed down the driveway.

"Can you at least tell me where the hell we're going?"

"Pool party," Nix grunts.

"I'll wait in the truck."

"As if we would leave you in our truck. You'll probably steal everything that's not attached," Colt accuses.

"Jesus! How do you come up with all this shit? I've never stolen anything in my life, and I sure as hell don't want anything of yours."

"Sounds like something a thief would say."

"Says the guys who literally just kidnapped a human being."

"God, stop being so dramatic. We're taking you to a party. You should be grateful."

Before I can answer him, he turns his stereo up so loud that the sound makes my ears hurt.

The only thing I'd be grateful for is if this truck would crash. At this point, I wouldn't even care if I was in it as well.

CHAPTER 7

*I*nstead of parking at the front of the house, Colt pulls the truck around and parks in the backyard by the pool. A group of people sits on the deck, hollering as we pull up.

Colt cuts the engine and opens his door. Nix does the same while I remain motionless in my seat. Maybe I'm lucky, and they forgot I'm here.

Nix crushes my hope the next moment when he opens the back door. "Let's go, Leni."

I take one more deep, calming breath before I unbuckle and slide off the seat. As soon as I climb out of the truck, the drunken chattering around the pool dies down.

All eyes are on me as I walk barefoot over the lawn toward the small crowd of people. As I get closer, I recognize most of them. Bradley, Hunter, and Trent used to play football with Nix and Colt. Two other guys I know from my math and science classes.

"What the hell is she doing here?" Deborah's shrill voice pierces through the air.

I glance over at her and immediately wish I didn't. *Piper.* My once-best friend is standing right next to Deborah, staring at me in shock, just like most other people here.

"Don't mind her. My dad made us bring her along. She'll sit quietly by the pool. You won't even know she's here," Nix explains as he shoves me toward the end of the pool.

I gladly follow his request and sit down on the chair far away from the rest of them. Pulling my legs up, I wrap my arms around my knees in hopes of preserving as much body heat as I can. It's not particularly cold tonight, but it's not warm either, and I'm barely wearing anything.

For a while, the party goes on, and everyone ignores my presence, which I am totally fine with. Bored, I watch the pool water move and count the tiles around the edge. I got to over one hundred when I catch someone walking in my direction from the corner of my eye.

"Here, drink this," Nix holds a red Solo cup in front of my face.

I make no move to take it. "No, thank you."

"Why do you have to make everything so difficult?"

"How am I being difficult just because I don't want to drink? I didn't ask you for this. I didn't ask you for anything. You're the one making everything difficult."

"Suit yourself," Nix growls and throws the cup to the ground like a toddler who doesn't get his way. Its content spills over the deck, and ice cubes tumble into the water.

"God, you're such a bitch. He only offered you a drink," Deborah sneers from the other side of the pool. I ignore her, which doesn't sit well with her. She is used to being the popular girl, and all the attention has to be on her all the time. Being ignored is the biggest insult to her. One she is not going to let go.

My heart sinks when I see Deborah walking in my direction. Not because of her but because of Piper, who is following her. I don't want to talk to her. I don't even want to see her. There's too much bottled up inside of me.

Pushing up from the chair, I speed walk around the pool on the opposite side of them. Deborah lets out an angry huff and even tries to come after me, but her four-inch heels are no match for my bare feet.

She yells something after me about not being able to afford shoes. I ignore that part as well as I step into the house, closing the sliding door behind me.

The inside is eerily quiet. So much so that I contemplate going back outside. On the other hand, it is warmer inside, and no one will bother me... or so I thought.

I only take a few steps into the kitchen area when the door slides open behind me. I spin around and see Bradley has come in.

"You know, when girls go inside at a party, that usually means they want to get fucked," Bradley says with a smirk. He walks into the house like he owns it, which makes me realize that he probably does.

Looking around for a way to escape, I spot a hallway with an open door, and the corner of a sink is visible from here. "I'm sorry to disappoint you, but I just had to go pee." I make a beeline for the bathroom, fully intending to lock myself in until further notice. Unfortunately, I don't get far before he snatches my arm, digging his meaty fingers into my skin, and tugs me toward one of the bedrooms.

"Let's go. I'll show you the bathroom," he teases.

Digging my heels into the ground, I manage to twist my arm out of his hold. "Fuck off, Bradley. You're a prick, and I'd never let you touch me."

"Quit being so damn rude. I let you come to my party, so the least you can do is let me fuck you."

Another insult is sitting on the tip of my tongue, but I never get to speak it because Colt's voice cuts through the room.

"Get lost, Bradley. Find some other chick to bother. She is busy... with us."

"You know what, Bradley? On second thought, I'll hang out with you." Anything will be better than spending another minute with Colt and Nix.

Nix shoots Bradley a warning glare, challenging him to go against him without ever saying a word. Like the scared little rodent he is, Bradley scurries away, leaving me alone with the two people I don't want to see.

"Can we go home now?" I step toward the back door, but Nix moves over to block my way.

"We just got here. You should have taken that drink. Maybe that stick up your ass would loosen up a little." He takes a few menacing steps toward me, and I automatically walk backward and hope to get away from him.

I realize too late that all I'm doing is walking farther away from the party and into the dark corner of the house.

Nix and Colt circle me like predators while I'm helplessly caught in their trap. My pulse spikes, and the knot in my throat grows heavy.

"You know we've been really nice to you today. We took you

to a party. I made you a drink. I even followed you inside to make sure you were okay."

"Well, aren't you a saint?" I huff sarcastically, trying my best to downplay the fear festering in my gut.

"I really am. You should show some appreciation." Nix smirks.

"I would be thankful if you had listened to me and left me at home. I don't wanna be here."

"Don't worry, we'll take you home... right after you suck my dick."

I gasp softly before fully processing what he just said. "I'd rather walk home... or nail my hand to the wall."

"Those are not your options. You're either going to blow me, or we're both going to fuck you."

My heart sinks. This has to be a joke. "You're insane. I'm never going to have sex with you in any kind of form."

"I'm about to prove you different. How pleasant this experience will be is completely up to you."

They're messing with me. This has to be just one of their cruel games. There is probably a camera in here filming all of this. Their hyena friends are watching from the backyard, laughing at the way they are scaring me.

"You're going to be a good girl and suck my brother's dick, and if you do a good job, we won't take your virginity tonight."

"Stop it. This is not funny," I grit out, hoping he doesn't hear how my voice wobbles at the end.

"We're not laughing, are we?" Colt comes up behind me and snakes his arms around me. I stiffen, every muscle taut, ready to fight. He pulls my body against him until my back is snug against his chest.

I feel his hard length pressed against my ass, and that's when I realize they're serious. This isn't a joke. Real fear kicks in, and my mouth goes dry.

Colt buries his face in my hair, sucking in a deep breath that makes my skin tingle and sends a shiver down my spine.

"You smell good," he murmurs against my skin before forcing me to my knees, never loosening his grip on me. He kneels behind me, keeping his legs right outside of mine, so I'm completely immobile.

Nix moves in front of me, his crotch directly in front of my face as he undoes his shorts and frees his already hard dick.

"I'm not doing this." I shake my head, strands of hair falling into my face.

"Fine," Colt growls behind me. He keeps one of his arms around my torso like an iron shackle while his free hand reaches under my dress. He grabs my shorts and yanks them down my legs.

"Stop!" I yell so loud that I wonder if somebody hears me outside. Nix must have had the same thought because, the next thing I know, his palm is placed over my mouth.

He gets on one knee, so we're face-to-face. His free hand reaches between us, and his fingers touch my chest softly before he runs them down my body. I try to wiggle away when he brushes over my panties, but that only makes him chuckle, and Colt tightens his grip on me.

Nix cups my pussy, and I whimper into his palm. Tears form in my eyes, making my vision blurry. He shoves his finger between my folds, and even though the thin fabric of my panties is between us, I can feel the rough pad of his finger rub against my clit.

"Last chance, love bug. Are you going to give me the blow job I deserve?"

What he deserves is a swift kick in the dick.

I nod in defeat, and the first tear falls from the side of my eye. It runs down my cheek before dropping onto my collarbone.

He lifts his hand off my mouth, and I automatically run my tongue over my dry, salty lips.

Nix stands up, towering over me while palming his cock. I can't take my eyes off his swollen cock. It's bigger than I expected, long and thick with veins running over the otherwise smooth skin. "Open up."

I don't realize I'm shaking until I part my lips, and my jaw trembles. Nix guides himself into my mouth, the mushroom head of his cock touches my tongue, and panic starts bubbling inside me.

Blinking my tears away, I gaze up at him, searching his face for any hint of compassion I might be able to reason with. There is none. His eyes are hazed over with lust, his jaw set in a tight line. He wants to hurt me and is determined to make me submit.

He pushes forward, filling my mouth with his cock until he comes so close to my throat I gag.

Desperate to keep even an ounce of control, I close my lips around his shaft, hoping to stop him from going too deep. A sinister grin plays on his lips as if he knows exactly what I'm trying to do.

Nevertheless, he goes easy on me, letting me set the pace, at least for a little bit. It doesn't take long for his shallow thrusts to become more frantic, and he takes control completely.

"Relax your throat. Let me fuck it." His voice is rough, unhinged, like he's barely holding on. His hands lift up, and he cradles my head in his large palms, holding me in place so he can use me.

"Breathe through your nose," Colt instructs from behind me.

I squeeze my eyes shut, concentrating on my breathing and not throwing up each time Nix's cock bumps against the back of my throat.

I'm so overwhelmed with everything happening that it takes me a second to realize Colt's hand is sliding under my dress and into my panties. Pressing my thighs together, I try to stop him, but he simply uses one of his knees to force my legs apart.

Now that he has better access, he doesn't waste any time. His fingers dip into my slit, and he finds the small bundle of nerves hidden between.

What the hell is he doing?

Helpless and immobilized, I am trapped, forced to endure whatever the guys have planned for me. My mind is in disarray, and my body is confused by what's happening.

Colt rubs small circles around my clit while his brother fucks my face relentlessly. I'm able to suck in small breaths between, but it's still less oxygen than my brain is used to.

I'm lightheaded, and my body feels weird, almost like I'm about to float away. A warm, foreign feeling builds between my thighs. Colt's finger slides over my skin as if there is some moisture easing the friction.

"You better stop grinding your ass against my dick. I might have to fuck you after all." Colt breathes heavily in the shell of my ear.

I wasn't even aware I was moving at all. My body seems to have a mind of its own. Or maybe it's because my actual mind can't come up with a single clear thought.

I'm so overwhelmed, both my mind and my body. Bombarded with all these feelings, I don't know what to do or think. Spit drips from my mouth, my throat burns, and my core is on fire.

Colt's fingers play with my clit, rubbing, teasing, and pinching it. If he doesn't stop soon, I'll come. Is that his plan? But why? This is so fucking confusing.

"Come for us, Leni. Come while you suck my brother's cock." Colt increases the pressure on my clit, and the pleasure in my core reaches new heights.

Suddenly, I'm hot, and my whole body feels like it's on fire. Nix also picks up his speed, grunting as he fucks my throat fast and hard. I whimper around his length, which only seems to egg him on.

Colt takes my clit between his fingers and pinches it painfully while grinding himself against my ass. A jolt of pain radiates from my pussy to my core. My back arches, and a pained groan forms in my chest.

Then the pain is gone and is replaced with something else entirely. My orgasm slams into me viciously out of nowhere. Every nerve ending in my body is firing off all at the same time. I'm not sure if it's the lack of oxygen or the intensity of the orgasm that has me passing out for a moment.

"Fuck." Nix grabs my jaw, positioning it the way he wants. "Keep your mouth open." He fists his cock, stroking it violently in front of my face.

I do as he says, keeping my mouth open and my tongue sticking out. I expected him to come in my mouth, but I'm still surprised when the warm salty liquid hits my tongue. I'm even more surprised by the bitter taste and by the sheer amount of cum filling my mouth.

"Swallow it," Nix orders. He takes a step back as if he wants to watch me from a different angle now.

I close my lips, but instead of swallowing, I spit out on the floor between us.

Nix's lips curl up in a growl. He looks like a feral animal, ready to rip me to shreds, and for a split second, I wish I had just swallowed his damn cum.

He kneels in front of me again, lifting his hand. I flinch, thinking he's going to hit me, but he doesn't. His fingers wrap around my throat, squeezing it lightly.

"Next time I tell you to do something, you do it." I'm waiting for an or... but it never comes. He leaves a vague threat hanging between us, then releases me with a shove.

Letting my eyes fall shut, I lean my head back against Colt's shoulder. His arms are still tightly wrapped around me, and even though I gave up fighting him a while ago, I never leaned into him like I'm doing now.

For a few seconds, I simply let him hold me. It might only be a moment, but I'm able to forget who he is and what he has done to me. I pretend he is someone else, someone who actually cares about me, who protects me instead of torments me. I'm comforted by his closeness alone, my body blissfully ignorant about the fact that he is one of the causes of my pain.

As fast as that moment came, it leaves even faster.

"Didn't I tell you I'd put your mouth to better use?" Nix's voice catapults me back to reality.

Lifting my head up, I blink my eyes open to look at him. "I hate you."

Colt finally releases me, and I sag to the rug beneath us, barely able to catch myself. I scramble off the floor, wiping my tears away with the back of my hand.

"Maybe. But eventually, you'll thank me for this."

Thank him? "There is something seriously wrong with you."

"Oh, love bug, something is seriously wrong with all of us. You'd do well to remember that."

CHAPTER 8

I'm still on the floor, trying to catch my breath and wrap my mind around what just happened. This doesn't feel real. I must be having a nightmare, and any moment now, I'm going to wake up.

"Come on, get off the floor." Colt grabs my upper arm and pulls me to my feet. My legs are shaky, but I manage to stand on my own.

Looking around, I notice Nix has disappeared into the bathroom. He returns, holding a washcloth in his hand. "You might want to wipe your face before you go back out." He holds the cloth out to me. I stare at it like it's a foreign object.

"Or don't, then you can brag about getting to suck my dick." He shrugs, dropping the small towel to the ground. My eyes follow the wet rag as it falls to the floor and lands in a careless heap in front of me. I don't know what it is about this piece of fabric, maybe the way he discarded it so easily... just like I've been treated.

My brain simply turns off, and my body takes over. Like a

feral animal, I attack, disregarding my own safety. I don't care if he hits me back. All I care about is hurting him, even if it's just a little.

I fling my arms, curling my fingers until my hands turn into claws, and I use them as my weapons. The sharp edges of my nails dig into his skin as I run them down the side of his face. He hisses out in pain and slaps my hands away before covering his face with his arm.

I'm not done with my attack, though. Clenching my hands into fists, I pound them onto his chest as hard as I can. "I fucking hate you!"

"That's enough!" Colt grabs me from behind, pulling me off his brother. He holds me just like he did before, close to his body, with his arms wrapped around my torso tightly.

Nix drops his arm, and I take in his scratched-up face. Four bright red, equally spaced-out scratches run down the side of his face. One of them is so deep that blood drips down his jaw.

He lifts his hand, bringing his middle finger to the deepest scratch. When he looks at that finger and sees the blood at the tip, his shocked expression turns even darker than it was before.

"You're going to pay for this," he promises.

I have no doubt he means it.

"And you'll pay for what you did," I snap back at him.

Shaking Colt off my shoulders, I spin around and push past them. Speed walking through the house, I slide open the back door and make my way over the deck and past the pool. The sound of heavy footfalls following me only makes my legs move faster.

I'm so focused on getting away from the guys that I don't

notice Deborah in the midst of the people I pass. By the time I do, it's already too late.

Her body slams into me, her elbow digging into my ribs as she shoves me toward the edge of the pool. My bare foot slides over the wet tile until there is nothing below anymore.

All I can do is twist my body midair, so I won't face-plant into the water. I hit the surface on my back. Pain radiates from my back through the rest of my body, making me regret turning in the first place. I should have gone headfirst.

Holding my breath as I go under, I curl up in agony. Cool water engulfs me as I sink to the bottom of the pool. Even through the water, I can hear laughter from above, and for a moment, I wonder if I could just stay here forever. I could close my eyes, let the darkness eat me up, and stop breathing forever. Would anyone care? Would someone even miss me?

Fuck them.

Shaking the morbid thought away, I kick my legs and push through the water until I break the surface. I suck in a deep breath and ignore the laughter coming from the rest of the party. I swim to the other end of the pool and lift myself out of the water. Without another look back, I walk to the truck and sit down on the other side of it, where no one can see me.

With my back against the large tire, I wrap my arms around my torso. I'm soaking wet. The thin dress I'm wearing is completely useless in keeping me warm. It doesn't take long for me to start shivering.

I play with the thought of just starting to walk home when I hear Colt and Nix approaching. I push myself up off the ground just as they come into view. I don't need to be on the floor, cowering at their feet when they get here.

Neither one of them says a word. They simply unlock the truck and climb in. I get into the back seat, hoping to ruin the leather with the pool water dripping off me.

We're about halfway home when Nix breaks the silence. "You know if you tell anyone about tonight, all the people at the party will say you're lying."

"Contrary to what you might think of me, I'm not stupid. I already figured that's the whole reason you brought me along."

He doesn't give me an answer. It's not like I expect one, either. We drive home in silence the rest of the way.

Nix parks the truck in front of the garage. He cuts the engine, and I open my door to jump out as fast as I can. I'm still shaking, partly because I'm freezing and partly because I'm so fucking angry. Angry with them and angry with myself for letting this happen in the first place.

I haven't even made it to the welcome mat when the front door flies open, and James appears. "What the hell is going on? Why are you shaking and soaking wet?" He looks past me to his approaching sons. "And what happened to your face?"

"Leni fell into the pool. She freaked out a little, and when I pulled her out, she accidentally scratched me," Nix explains. The lie falls from his lips so easily that if I didn't know better, I would believe him too.

"Is that true, Leni?"

"What's true?" My mom comes up behind James, looking between us in confusion. "God, Leni, why are you not wearing a bra?"

I look down at my dress, realizing the thin material has basically become see-through, the outline of my nipples clearly visible. Even though I'm still cold, my face suddenly turns hot, and I'm sure my cheeks are bright red.

As quickly as I can, I wrap my arms around my boobs. "Can I please just go to my room?"

"Not until you tell us what's going on? Did you really fall into the pool?"

"I..." Shit, what am I going to tell them? My hesitation is enough to spark James's suspicion.

"You two, go to your rooms," he orders his sons. To my utter shock, Nix and Colt obey without a word. They push past James and disappear into the house.

James motions for me to come in while my mom goes to the living room to grab a blanket. I step into the foyer, and James closes the door behind us. My mom wraps a blanket around me, and I pull it tight, trying to get warm.

"Amanda, baby, why don't you go lie down. You need to rest. I'll make sure Leni is okay."

"Yeah?" My mom looks so confused, unsure what to do.

"It's okay, Mom. You can go back to sleep. I'll be fine," I assure her.

"Okay, honey, I'll see you in the morning." She lets out a yawn, rubbing her eye with her fingers before slowly making her way back up the stairs.

"Now, tell me what happened tonight. What did my idiot kids do to you, and why are you soaking wet?"

This is it, the moment I've been waiting for. I have a chance to tell him everything, all the things his sons have done to me, and what they forced me to do tonight.

Yet when I open my mouth, all the words I want to say are stuck in my throat. I can't make my voice work, and I don't know why. I want to tell him. I want to confide in him so badly, but when I try to force the words out, I hit a roadblock.

Maybe it's shame, guilt, or simply fear that won't let me speak. Whatever it is, it makes my whole body clam up, and my tongue feels heavy in my mouth.

I can't tell him, at least not today.

"Nix was telling the truth, I fell into the pool, and he pulled me out. I didn't mean to scratch him."

"Are you sure?"

I nod. The lie leaves a bitter taste on my tongue, but for some reason, that still feels better than the truth.

James doesn't seem convinced, but he is also not pushing the subject. "All right then, why don't you go get some rest? I'll see you at breakfast."

"Okay. Thank you." I force a smile, wondering if I just made the biggest mistake of my life.

CHAPTER 9

*L*ast night feels like a bad dream. I wish it was. I wish there was nothing more to it than something my subconscious cooked up while I was asleep.

No such luck. And even a hot, soapy shower isn't enough to wash away the shame. I know I did nothing wrong and that I had no choice. That doesn't mean I don't feel dirty, used. And conflicted since there's no forgetting the way my body reacted despite my disgust and rage.

It's something I'm still struggling with after I'm dressed, as I go to the door while steeling myself for whatever is about to happen downstairs at breakfast.

"You have got to be kidding me!" The knob won't turn. One of them locked me in again. I can't believe this. When will it ever end?

"Hey!" I don't care about avoiding trouble since it's obvious there's no difference either way. I can keep my head down, keep to myself, and not say a word to either of them. They will always find a way to ruin things, like they're determined to hurt me. So why bother trying to play nice?

"Open this door! This is bullshit!" I pound against the door with both fists and wish it was their faces instead.

The clicking of the lock is both a blessing and a curse. I back away quickly, prepared to fight, and the sight of Nix makes me bare my teeth in a snarl. "I knew it was you doing this. What is your problem? Why are you doing this to me? I never did anything to you!"

"Do yourself a favor, love bug," he mutters before looking over his shoulder down the hall. "Don't start shit around here."

"I didn't start anything! You are the ones who won't leave me alone."

"Damn right. You stay where we tell you to, for as long as we tell you to. And if I ever catch you out of your room at night?" An ugly smile twists his features, making him just as disgusting on the outside as he is on the inside. "Then you'll pay. I'll see to it."

After last night, I can't even take that as an empty threat. I know what he's capable of.

"Why are you doing this?" I didn't want it to come out sounding so pitiful, but it's how I feel. Small and inconsequential and pitiful. "Why do you hate me? I've never done anything to you—and if I have, I wish you would tell me because I wasn't aware of it. I never intended for any of this."

"Why? You want to know why?" He takes one slow, menacing step toward me, then another. I have no choice but to back away until I bump up against my desk. Even then, he leans down, and I lean back until my head touches the wall. "Why does there have to be a reason? I hate you. I always have. I hate you and everything about you. I've hated you since the first time I set eyes on you. Back when you were strutting around like hot shit, like you were somebody special. You're not so special now, are you?"

So that's it? He hates me because I was popular once? All because of what I could do, not because of who I was. It's not like I asked for any of it. "But things have changed now. And I didn't do anything—"

"Just shut up. The sound of your voice makes me sick." His eyes dart over my face, his nose wrinkling like he smells something nasty. "You are a disease. You're a cancer buried deep, and there's no cutting you out."

I knew he hated me, but I didn't know it was like this. So nasty and vile, deep-seated. All I can do is stare at him in mixed surprise and horror, still wondering what I did to earn it.

"So if I can't get rid of you," he continues, "then I'm going to make your life miserable. We both are, Colt and me. Just because he isn't here to agree doesn't mean he feels any differently about you than I do. You need to go. And if we need to make it so you have no choice but to leave, that's what we'll do."

"And if I say anything to your father?"

His eyes narrow into slits. "Go ahead. Give it a try. See what happens. Because if you think last night was rough, you're in for a big surprise." He runs a hand down my side, and I squirm away, making him laugh. "Oh, Leni, it will get so much worse."

The sickest part of all is the way he whistles lightheartedly as he leaves the room and closes the door. At least he's smart enough not to lock it this time, but then I'm smart enough not to test him. No way am I going downstairs now, not when I can't stop shaking and feel like I might burst into tears at any moment.

I've never felt anything like that before. That cold, blatant hatred. I didn't know there were people in the world who didn't bother hiding feelings like that—who comes out and calls somebody a cancer they can't get rid of? It's sick, disgusting. What happened to him to make him this way?

No. I have to shut that line of questioning down immediately. I'm not about to humanize him or bother myself with figuring out how his brain works. I think I'd rather not know.

I go to the bathroom and splash my face, hoping to calm myself down. I'm so alone here. No allies—James might be if I wasn't afraid of the repercussions of confessing everything to him. I don't even know whether he would believe me. All this friendly, fatherly stuff might only be an act intended to placate my mother. If that's true, the joke's on him. I doubt she would care much if he treated me like I was garbage. It could be one more thing for them to have in common.

It's safer to keep this to myself. It would be childish of me to imagine swearing James to secrecy. No doubt he would go straight to his sons, and where would that leave me? In much worse shape than I'm in right now, that much is for sure.

It's a long morning, but at least I have books to keep me occupied and distract me from my empty stomach. Unfortunately, that only works for so long—by the time the clock is closing in on noon, I'm almost weak with hunger. It's enough to distract me, so I can't even enjoy reading. Maybe I'll get lucky, and they won't be home.

Since when does my luck work that way? My heart sinks at the sound of their voices in the kitchen, along with their father's. Anybody who didn't know any better would think they were listening to a happy family, laughing and joking. I doubt anybody could imagine how bad things really are.

It's either face them or starve. When I look at it that way, there's no choice. I wander into the kitchen, careful to make it seem like there's nothing wrong while I grab an apple from a bowl on the counter. The first bite is heaven, crisp and sweet. It's a shame my gaze drifts over to my so-called family, and my eyes briefly meet Colt's. Now there's a sour taste in my mouth.

"Leni." James smiles broadly when he turns to find me. "I was beginning to think you didn't feel well. Is everything all right?"

I feel Nix's eyes boring holes into me. I'm not going to give him away, but I might let him worry for a moment. That's why I take my time before answering. "Sure, I'm fine. Just a little tired." The smug look on both brothers' faces makes me want to claw their eyes out. They think they're so superior like they have me under their thumbs. Not that they don't, but I hate how sure they are of it.

"And what are your plans today?"

It's different, having someone in the house who seems to genuinely care what I do with my time. I almost don't know how to handle it. "I'm not sure. I guess since the job interview at the pizza parlor didn't work out, I'll have to apply for some more jobs. I'm sure there must be something."

Colt passes on his way to the refrigerator and brushes against me like it's an accident—when I know it's anything but. "I can think of at least one thing you could do to make some money." He mutters it so low his father can't hear. A very perverse part of me wants to turn around and ask him to repeat himself. Why would I even think something like that? It would only end up getting me hurt.

"You know, it seems silly to have you running around town,

applying for jobs in these piddly little businesses." James purses his lips thoughtfully. "Do you think you could handle some light clerical work?"

"I've never considered anything like that."

"Maybe you should." An indulgent smile begins to stir his lips. "It just so happens we could use someone to do extra filing and copying down at the firm, maybe answering phones. I have no doubt you could pick it up in no time."

He laughs gently, his gaze fixed over my shoulder. A moment later, I know why, as the sound of Mom's heels hitting the floor reverberates through the air. "I'm sure the apple couldn't have fallen too far from the tree," he concludes. "If you're half as quick a study as your mother, it'll be a breeze."

"What's all this about?" she asks with her brightest smile before leaning in to kiss James's cheek as she passes by.

"It's the simplest solution imaginable, and I can't understand why I didn't think of it before. I could hire Leni to do filing and other clerical work around the firm."

He doesn't see it from where he's sitting, but I do. The way she falters a little, almost stumbling before she reaches up for a glass from the cabinet. "You think that's a good idea, sweetheart?" Her voice is too bright, too energetic. I know where this is going.

"Why not? She's industrious, wants to earn her own way, and provide for herself. Shouldn't she be given the opportunity to do that?" He slides a private little wink my way, like we're on the same team. I appreciate the effort, but he's not going to get his way. She'll see to it.

Our eyes meet for the briefest instant as she swings around to face him. That fleeting glance tells me everything I need to know. Under no circumstances does she want her daughter working in the same office as she is. "I don't know, sweetheart. Are you sure something like that wouldn't make it look like Leni is capitalizing on our relationship?"

"What do you mean?"

She shifts her weight from one foot to the other, shrugging, acting vague and playful when I know she's feeling anything but. "You know how people talk. It's already one thing for us to be together, getting married. Then you bring your new step-daughter in and give her a job, too? I'd hate to see you accused of nepotism."

"It's my firm," he reminds her. "I can do what I want."

"You know what? It's not even an issue." Colt waves a hand back and forth between him and Nix. "We got her a job at the gym already."

It's almost funny how all of us turn to him in unison. "What?" I whisper.

"You did?" Mom coos. "That's so thoughtful and wonderful of you boys!"

I'm too busy being shocked to react. James cocks his head to the side. "What would Leni do at the gym?"

"You know, wiping down equipment, washing and replenishing towels. Basic stuff like that." He won't look at me, no matter how hard I stare at him. Is he for real, or is this all another way of making a fool out of me? Making sure I'm with them as much as possible so they can terrorize and use me?

No way am I doing this. "Uh, I don't know," I murmur.

"It's perfect!" Mom clasps her hands over her chest and almost bats her eyelashes at the two of them. "You are the most wonderful young men. Considering how amazing your father is,

I suppose it's not that big of a surprise you turned out so well." Clearly, she does not know them at all.

Then she turns to me, her smile fixed, her eyes glittering. "Right, honey? And it'll be a way for you to spend more time getting to know your new brothers."

"We'll be sure to take good care of her," Nix interjects. When I glance his way, I find him smirking.

"Sure," I mutter, shrugging. "Sounds great." Because right now, the alternative to spending more time with these two is infuriating my mother, and sadly, I'd rather deal with them than have her find little ways of making my life even harder every day.

CHAPTER 10

"Y*ou* look beautiful, Mom." I stand back from the three-way mirror, where my mother studies her reflection, wearing the wedding dress that some poor seamstress has probably worked herself blind to fit in time for this last-minute wedding. But they did a good job. It fits her like a glove, and she looks regal, classy. Whoever made it must be a magician, in other words.

"So long as I hardly eat another bite in the next two days," she says with a laugh I know is meant more for the store clerk arranging the short train behind her. She doesn't shine that bright, brilliant smile on me.

And it's like she hears me thinking because she catches my eye in the mirror. "Why haven't you tried your dress on yet?"

"Sorry. I got distracted watching you." There's a curtained-off room behind me, and the violet dress is on a hanger, waiting for me to put it on. I step into the little cubby, and I'm glad for a minute's privacy as I strip out of my clothes and lower the dress over my head. It's pretty, and a lot like Mom's, with the sleek, slim cut and soft satin.

All is well until I turn around and look over my shoulder to see the back. "Mom?" I call out, staring at my reflection. "I'm sorry, but I don't think I can wear this."

Before I know it, the curtain flies open, and she gives me a look meant only for me, with everybody else behind her so they can't see how she really is. "What's the problem?" she murmurs through clenched teeth. Yet her brows draw together when she looks in the mirror and sees what I see. "Oh. I didn't think about that." The dress is cut so low that my scar is clearly visible.

"I really don't want everybody seeing it," I whisper. *Please, be my mother for once.*

"Of course, you don't. Neither do I." She wipes away the disgust on her face quickly, but not quick enough that I miss it. She thinks I'm disgusting and doesn't want something so ugly ruining her big day. It shouldn't surprise me by now. Nothing she does should surprise me.

"Well, that's fine," she decides. "I'm sure there has to be something around here you can wear. So long as it's the same color, you should be fine. But there's no time to have it fitted, so you'll have to find something that fits you off the rack."

I change quickly before going out to the sales floor and combing through racks of dresses. I have the original dress over my arm to make sure the color matches, and it looks like there isn't much to choose from in my size. In fact, after checking out every single rack in the store, there's only one dress I end up taking back to the fitting room.

Mom has now changed back into her street clothes and is sipping her second glass of champagne. I guess calories don't count if you're drinking them. "Let's see it on you," she urges, steering me toward the dressing room again.

Right away, I see the problem with this one. Sure, it covers my back, but it barely covers my ass. I tug it as hard as I can, but that's not going to magically add a few inches of material. I'm almost ashamed to open the curtain and show everybody how much of me is on display.

Mom shrugs. "It fits you well. A little shorter than I'd like, but if it's our only choice, so be it."

"Maybe I could wear the other dress, but with like a shawl or something?" I shoot a hopeful look toward the woman who's been helping Mom through this, and she taps her chin with one shiny nail.

"I don't think we have anything in that color, I'm afraid. With a little more time, we could order something."

"Then I suppose this is the dress we're going with." Mom polishes off the rest of her champagne, and that's that. I'm going to spend the entire ceremony hoping nobody is looking at my butt cheeks. Then again, what else was I going to be doing? Gritting my teeth while pretending there's nothing gross about watching her play the happy, perfect wife so glowingly in love with her Prince Charming?

At least this is over now. We leave the store with our dresses safe in their zipped-up bags, and immediately James jumps out of his shiny Mercedes to help us. "Everything go well?" he asks after kissing Mom. "I want everything perfect for my bride."

"Everything already is, honey." I hate the breathy, soft sound of her voice when she talks to him. James takes my dress and carefully lays it out in the trunk along with Mom's.

But when I make a move to join them in the car, Mom shakes

her head. "No, you're not coming with us." When James turns her way, probably because of the shrill way she said it, she quickly smiles. "Your brothers are picking you up. In fact, here they come." Yes, unfortunately, a familiar truck is now pulling into the parking lot. My heart sinks while a bitter taste fills my mouth.

James is wearing sunglasses, so I can't see his full expression, but there's something unhappy in the way his mouth tightens. "I thought the three of us were going to go to lunch."

"I wanted it to be just the two of us, honey." She runs a hand over the back of his head. "I was only thinking about you and me spending a little time together before things get crazy."

"Don't worry about it," I mutter, even though the idea of getting in the truck with the two of them makes my heart threaten to burst out of my chest. I'm sure they're not thrilled about having to spend time with me any more than I am about spending time with them. The only difference is, I'm not the one who's going to use this as an excuse to be a vile piece of shit.

The second I open the door, Colt's voice assaults my ears. "Hurry up. We're going to be late."

Oh, no. If it wasn't for Mom and James watching, I would close the door and head for the nearest bus stop. I have to grit my teeth through climbing in, even though my instincts are telling me to do anything but. "Late for what?" I ask once I'm belted.

"You're starting work at the gym today," Nix informs me. I catch his gaze in the rearview mirror. "Surprise."

"But I'm not ready for this."

"Too bad. That's how it is." Colt's voice is flat as he raises a hand to greet his father before we pull away.

I have to find a way to calm my sudden panic. If it wasn't for them, for knowing how they are, I wouldn't be so nervous. Sure, starting a new job is always going to be a little nerve-wracking, but I'd be able to handle this better if it wasn't for the deep distrust I have for these two. I never even went in for an interview, and somebody hired me? Nothing about this is adding up. There has to be some sort of game here. I am so tired of having to predict what's happening next, always planning my next move and looking over my shoulder.

"You are the one who is in such a hurry to get a job," Colt reminds me without looking over his shoulder.

Yes, because I want to get away from them. "It's just a surprise," I retort. "I'm really glad to have this job." The two of them exchange a look that doesn't bode well for me. What do they have up their sleeves this time?

I don't have to wait long to find out. The sight of somebody I really, truly do not want to see fills me with panic the moment we step through the doors of the gym. And from the look of it, she wasn't expecting me, either. "Leni," Piper chokes out from behind the desk. "What are you doing here?"

"She's working here now, or didn't they tell you?" Nix is absolutely loving this, though Colt doesn't look as amused.

"Right. They told me somebody new was coming in today but didn't say who." She pulls out a clipboard and places it on the counter. I had no idea she was working here. So that's what this is all about. They deliberately set this up so I'd be as uncomfortable as possible.

"We're gonna go work out. Have fun, girls." Nix laughs while Colt only snorts, and the two of them wander off to leave me with my paperwork and former best friend.

"So how have you been?" she asks while I fill out the form in front of me.

"Amazing," I mutter, never lifting my gaze.

"Um, it's pretty exciting, your mom getting married and everything."

"I guess." Is she seriously trying to do this? I can't imagine having the gall. It was her choice to walk away from our friendship, and now she thinks she can act like nothing happened?

"I've been working here for a few months," she informs me, though I certainly did not ask. "It's pretty cool. So long as you know who to stay away from. Some of the guys who walk in here—"

"All done." I slide the clipboard back across the counter. "What do I do now?"

Her eyelids flutter, and her mouth falls open, but she quickly composes herself. "Um, you can work here behind the desk with me. It's not difficult. You sign people in, sign them out, and sometimes you process payments. I can show you how to do that."

Because I want to spend another minute with her. "I think the guys mentioned something about cleaning the equipment? I can do that. Where do I find the supplies?"

Her face falls a little, and I'm glad. It's nothing compared to the way she's made me feel, but it's a start. She points at a small closet across from the desk, where paper towels and bottles of cleaner sit. "I think I can figure this out. Thanks." And with that, I head deeper into the gym, where dozens of people sweat while music thumps from speakers set up in the corners of the room.

At least I don't have to be close to Colt or Nix while I'm doing this. They're both working out with pretty complicated-looking equipment, loading extra weight before sitting on the benches and pushing themselves through their routines.

It's not bad enough I have to be here with my two biggest enemies, but the third on the list is here as well? The worst part is, if she hadn't gone and messed everything up, I could really use her friendship about now. I have no one to confide in, and Piper would have been the first person I went to if she hadn't chosen to turn against me. My heart is sore as I walk through the gym, hustling over to machines once people leave them so I can spray the handles and seats before somebody else uses them. Not exactly the most thrilling job, but it's easy enough. And at least it means I don't have to be alone with these two idiots— there are plenty of people around all the time, all through the first ninety minutes of work.

"Hey. You're new around here."

I didn't notice a man, who looks to be in his mid-thirties, approaching me. He's handsome enough, I guess, though I've had my fill of handsome men. Colt and Nix are gorgeous, but they're evil. Looks don't mean much when you don't have a soul.

So I'm understandably wary as I offer a brief smile. "I just started working here today."

"Oh? Then I guess I'll have more of a reason to show up, won't I?" From the looks of him, he's here a lot, and I can't pretend not to appreciate his muscular build and broad, brilliant smile.

His dark eyes crinkle at the corners when he smiles again, running a hand through his short, sandy hair. And what would your name be?"

"Her name is none of your fucking business." Colt wedges

himself between us, popping out his earbuds. "So why don't you just get back to your workout and let her do her job?"

The older man quickly sizes Colt up and either decides it's not worth the effort or he doesn't feel like getting his ass kicked. He backs off, hands raised. "Sorry. Just making conversation."

"Yeah, well, it's a gym. This is where we work out." Colt waits for the guy to step onto a treadmill before turning to me, his eyes narrowed.

I don't give him a chance to start his shit with me. "What is your problem?" I whisper. My cheeks are burning with embarrassment, and I know there are people paying attention even if they're pretending not to. "I'm supposed to work here, you know? How am I going to keep my job if you do things like that?"

"He's a piece of shit. And you were lapping it up, weren't you?"

"You don't have the first idea what you're talking about. That much is obvious. He was only trying to be nice."

"Would you grow up?" he sneers. "He wasn't trying to be nice. He was trying to get into your pants."

"Oh, and I forgot, didn't I? I have no say in who goes there, either, do I?"

We're still glaring at each other when Nix joins us, covered in a sheen of sweat, though he doesn't seem winded. "Come on. Time to go."

At first, I figure he must be talking to his brother, but then I realize they're both looking at me. "You're kidding."

"Does it look like I'm kidding?" Nix grunts. "We finished our workout, so we're going home. And you're coming with us."

This is all too bizarre. "But I'm working. I can't just walk out."

"Yeah, you can. Since that's the arrangement we came up

with. We know the guy who owns the place. We can pretty much do whatever we want."

That's their entire problem in a nutshell. They've spent their entire lives believing they can do whatever they want with no consequences or thoughts for anyone but themselves. "How am I supposed to earn any money if I'm hardly ever here?"

"Do you ever stop complaining? We're going. That's the deal. Don't worry. You'll get your money." Nix rolls his eyes and turns away, followed by Colt. I guess I don't have a choice but to believe them and follow. If this is all a joke, it's a pretty complicated one, but even Piper looks surprised to see me leave. I can't bring myself to acknowledge her, even to show my own confusion.

Every day, I lose a little more control over my life. How long will it be before I have no say over anything at all?

CHAPTER 11

"*L*eni! Come on, we have to go." My mother's voice doubles and triples on itself as it echoes up the stairs and through the second floor. She's trying hard to sound happy and lighthearted, but I'm not fooled. I'm holding her up, and she wishes she could chew me out for it.

"Be right there!" I call out while taking one last look at myself in the mirror. This is my nicest dress, far nicer than anything else in my closet except the dress I'm wearing tomorrow at the wedding. A light yellow color with a black floral print, it swings around my thighs when I walk and even has pockets. For the first time in days, I feel like myself. Nobody is telling me what to wear or how to be. And that gives me a little bit of courage to face whatever tonight will bring.

I hate that I have to dread what should be a nice, memorable evening with family. The rehearsal dinner is a big event. But I'll be too busy worrying about staying away from the pair who will be my stepbrothers as of tomorrow.

That's not the only thing I'm worried about as I pick up my

purse. My back's been bothering me all day—I didn't do anything to aggravate it, and I don't have to. Sometimes, I happen to move the wrong way, and bam. I'm in at least discomfort and, at worst, pain for the rest of the day. What a time for this to happen. It's not bad enough that I have to smile my way through this little charade, but now I'll have to do it while my back is screaming.

I guess that's what painkillers are for. I don't like using them since they sometimes leave me feeling loopy—and I don't want to feel that way around Colt or Nix, who I know would take advantage of it. At the same time, what's the alternative? Having Mom get mad at me for being a wet blanket, as she puts it? I guess since we're going to a dinner, it isn't like the pill will sit on an empty stomach. I go to my bathroom and pull the bottle down from the cabinet, popping one into my mouth and washing it down with a handful of water from the sink.

"Leni, we have to go. We can't keep people waiting!"

I give myself one last look in the mirror, checking out my makeup and hair before squaring my shoulders and starting for the hallway. Another good thing about these pills: in about half an hour, I'm going to feel happier than I have any right to feel. Kinder, friendlier. I'm sure Mom will be pleased once I'm feeling social.

Everybody is waiting by the front door. Instantly, I know I've made a mistake. Colt and Nix are wearing dark suits, like their father, while my mother is dressed in a white gown not unlike the one she'll be wearing tomorrow. They could be headed out for some red-carpet event, and I'm wearing a dress I bought from Target a couple of years ago. Sure, it's the nicest thing I own, but compared to them?

My mother doesn't seem to notice, so at least she's not going to berate me. "Finally. We can get out of here and not be seen as rude for keeping hungry people waiting."

"You're too hard on her sometimes, sweetheart." James offers a wink that I appreciate, even if I don't love what I know will be my mother's reaction. When he sticks up for me like that, it only makes her angry with me. She'll find some way to take it out on me when we're alone.

It's no secret the guys think I look like crap. If the glance they exchange when I fall in step with them is any indication. "Nice dress," Nix mutters while his brother snickers.

"Thanks," I say flatly.

"Where did you get it? Goodwill?" Nix murmurs as we get into the car. Of course, we're only taking one car, meaning I have to sit in the back between the two worst people I know. Now I wish I was wearing pants since they both insist on rubbing their legs against mine as James pulls away from the house.

This is like one of those nightmares where I show up for school without shoes on, or in my underwear, or something like that. Only there's no waking up from it. I'm an afterthought, and now everybody will know it when they see me standing along-side the rest of my so-called family. For somebody so concerned about appearances, You'd think Mom would have mentioned the dress code for tonight. I could have figured out a way to dress up a little more if I'd had warning.

"Are you feeling cold?" Colt asks, his hand brushing my thigh. "You have goose bumps."

"Stop," I whisper, smacking his hand away while our parents are oblivious in the front seat. Mom won't stop talking about tomorrow, and all the little last-minute details she hopes don't fall to pieces. Meanwhile, her daughter is getting groped in the back seat.

"Loosen up," he murmurs, snickering the way his brother does while once again groping my thigh. "You might actually have a little fun for once."

"Somehow, I doubt that." This time, I dig my nails into his hand, and he doesn't try again.

The dinner is being held at a country club, some big, fancy place with fountains out front and dramatic lighting. Mom takes James's arm once we're out of the car, and they glide into the building like a king and queen. Nix and Colt make it a point to walk in front of me, so I'm bringing up the rear.

Everybody is already here, and it's a lot more people than I expected. They all start applauding when the happy couple enters the room. I'm a few minutes shy from when my pill is supposed to kick in, and I wish it would hurry up because grinding my teeth through this is painful, maybe more so than my back. Everybody's dressed the way the rest of my family is, and I have never felt so out of place. That's saying something since I spent a lot of time in a back brace.

Mom doesn't bother introducing me to a lot of people, which is fine with me, though I get the feeling most of them are from the office. "Hey, Amanda! How come you don't dress that way at work?" one of the men calls out across the room, and she giggles and waves at him while everybody laughs like that was a funny joke.

"And this one cleans up well, too," one of the women murmurs, touching James's arm, but she's not looking at him. She's looking at Nix, and she might as well have the word cougar written across her forehead.

One of the waitstaff passes with a tray loaded with appetizers. I take a few on a napkin, hoping to get some food in my stomach quickly since it doesn't look like we're sitting down to eat dinner right away.

"So Nixon," the cougar purrs, taking him by the arm. "I remember when you were a skinny little boy with braces. You've certainly grown up." It's actually kind of funny watching him pretend to be pleased when it's obvious he's grossed out by a woman more than twice his age. Maybe this night won't be so bad after all.

One thing is for sure: I'm glad I didn't take the job at the firm. These people are so plastic and fake and even a little creepy. Though this is James's rehearsal dinner, and he's getting married tomorrow, half of the women don't stop flirting with him. Maybe it's not such a surprise that he met a woman and got involved with her even though she was his employee. I wonder how many of these women he's been through.

"Champagne, miss?" I'm startled to find a server standing nearby with a tray full of flutes. Sure, why not? It'll help the night pass quicker or at least more pleasantly. My brain is still way too sharp to get through this without revealing how cringeworthy the entire evening is shaping up to be. There's more champagne waiting for us when we take our seats, settling in for dinner.

And I'm going to need it since, naturally, I'm smack dab between my so-called brothers. I know I'm technically supposed to wait for a toast or whatever, but I take a few sips anyway. It helps make everything a little more bearable.

I have to sit through toast after toast, pretending to be happy. I'm glad nobody is paying me much attention. Not even the guys, both of whom are on their best behavior for once. Too many witnesses, I suppose. Besides, Nix is distracted by his admirer, who keeps shooting him looks from the next table. I have to fight the urge to giggle before accepting another glass of champagne. It's not until I finish half of that one that my skin feels a little hot.

Using the napkin, I fan my face with air and take a few calming breaths. My stomach churns, and I reach for the water on the table. No more champagne for me.

"Are you all right, honey? You look a little pale." My mom reaches across the table and touches my cheek. Her concerned demeanor is short-lived and turns quickly into selfishness. "Don't tell me you're getting sick. Not today, and definitely not tomorrow."

"I'm not sick."

"Did you eat anything today? Maybe your sugar is a bit low."

"I don't know, I..." Shit. The pain meds. "My back was hurting earlier, and I took some pain medicine on an empty stomach. It was stupid. But I'll be fine."

"Why don't you head home and get some rest? I need you up bright and early, okay?"

"Yeah, that might be best. I'll call an Uber."

"We can take you home," Colt offers.

"No. You should stay. I don't want to ruin your night." I give him a tight smile. Of course, he knows I don't want him to come with me.

"Don't be ridiculous. We're basically family now. If you don't feel well, we'll take you home and make sure you're taken care of." Nix places his hand on my shoulder, and a wave of oohs and aahs moves through the surrounding guests.

It takes every ounce of self-control not to roll my eyes and slap his stupid hand off my shoulder.

"I think that's a good idea. If you don't feel well, I don't like the thought of you being alone," my mom tells me before turning to the guys next to me. "Thank you for being so thoughtful and taking her home. Leni is so lucky to have you."

Unable to hear another word of this bullshit any longer, I stand up from my seat so suddenly the chair almost tips back. I murmur a quick goodbye to everyone before scurrying out of the restaurant with Colt and Nix hot on my heels.

"What a way to make an exit." Colt chuckles.

"Look. I'm really not feeling well. Can you please just leave me alone?" I hurry past the hostess and push open the heavy door leading to the street. Stepping out on the sidewalk, I suck in a lung full of fresh air, hoping it will clear my head.

Unfortunately, it has the opposite effect. Maybe it's the sudden oxygen increase or the change in temperature. Either way, my head spins, and my vision goes blurry. I feel my whole body sway to the side.

Just when I think I'm going to pass out, four hands are suddenly on me. As those hands grab onto my arm, I'm jolted upright.

"What the fuck did you take?" Nix snaps at me.

"Hydrocodone... it's just for pain."

"That's some strong shit. How much champagne did you drink?"

"Um, two... I think." Closing my eyes, I breathe through my nose, trying my best to get it together. My legs remain wobbly, and I have to lean against something just to stay upright.

"Great. Can you go and get the car. I don't feel like carrying her." Colt's voice is so close, almost like my head is against his shoulder or something.

Nix curses under his breath. I'm vaguely aware of footsteps in the distance, and whatever I'm leaning against starts to move.

"Don't drool on my shirt."

Why would I drool on him? I don't have the energy to say it out loud. My tongue is heavy in my mouth, and my eyes won't open even a little. All I want to do is go to sleep.

Something wraps around my torso, and suddenly, my feet are not on the ground anymore. In the distance, I hear a car door open and close. My body is being moved, and then I'm placed on something flat. I instantly relax, curling up on my side, tuck my hands under my head like a pillow, and let the warm fuzzy feeling pull me under completely.

CHAPTER 12

"Get her zipper." Colt's voice sounds far away, but the way each of his words vibrates against my ear makes me think my cheek is pressed against his chest. I try to open my eyes, but my eyelids are so damn heavy. I only get a glimpse of the inside of my room before they fall back shut.

I try to lift my head, but none of my muscles work. My body is almost paralyzed, trapped in the space between sleep and wakefulness.

Someone unzips the back of my dress, and cool air washes over the skin I usually keep covered up. An odd sense of freedom overcomes me. My back is exposed, and even the air in my perfectly heated room feels cool and unusual on my back. This sensation normally fills me with so much anxiety I seldom let it happen in the first place. Something is different today... today there is no fear, no shame, or embarrassment.

All I feel is warmth.

I'm being put on my bed. The soft fabric feels good on my skin, while the pillow cradles my head perfectly. I try to pry my eyes open once more, just in time to see the outline of someone crawling onto the bed with me. The mattress dips, and a warm body covers me like a weighted blanket.

That same body gently pries my legs apart and settles between my thighs. Only then do I realize I'm completely naked. Something is wrong.

A surge of panic zaps through my body, making me squirm.

"Relax..." A male voice says before placing a soft kiss on my lips. I'm so confused by his actions and the way he tries to calm me that I don't recognize Colt's voice right away.

"Colt?" My voice is nothing more than a soft whisper. So low I'm surprised he hears me at all. "Colt, please."

"Please, what?"

What am I asking again? My head feels like it is stuffed with cotton, and I have to dig each of my thoughts out.

"Please... don't hurt me."

"I wasn't planning on it. At least not tonight."

I don't know if he's trying to be funny. I don't know what he's trying to do. I can't open my eyes all the way, and it's so frustrating. I can't control myself at all. "What are you doing?" I murmur when he doesn't get up. I go stiff with a gasp when his lips brush against my cheek, then move down my jaw before brushing against my throat.

"Just relax. Let me take care of you."

This can't be happening. It can't be Colt touching me the way he is, so gentle and sweet. It can't be Colt kissing my neck until I shiver and goose bumps cover my skin. I have to be dreaming. That's the only explanation.

"You're so beautiful," he whispers before planting another kiss, this one against my collarbone. "So perfect." I would thank him, but my tongue is too thick and heavy. Besides, what does it matter? This is all a dream, anyway. You don't have to thank somebody in a dream, do you? Even my thoughts aren't making any more sense than what my body is feeling. And what it's feeling is something deeper and more intense than anything I've ever known. There's wetness pooling between my thighs, and my pussy is aching for attention.

I've had some sexy dreams before, but not once did they include Colt, though. Normally, it's some stranger, a sweet guy I met at a coffee shop, maybe. Then there is usually a part where I get frustrated because I can't get off, not understanding that everything happening is only happening in my head.

Not so this time, when the sensation of Colt's hand cupping one of my breasts while gently sucking the other is so intense, so real. "Oh god," I somehow manage to moan. It doesn't come out clearly, but I guess that doesn't matter in a dream, either. He understands, and he chuckles a little before turning his attention to the other breast, gently sucking on my nipple, rolling his tongue around it in slow, sensual circles that make me lift my hips and grind against him.

"Let's see if you taste as good as you look." The next thing I know, I feel his lips on my inner thigh. I want to reach down and push him away, but I also want to spread my legs wider because that feels incredible. Featherlight kisses that make my nerves dance and sizzle, pulling moan after moan from me. I'm sinking deeper and deeper into the blissful sensations, and why not? Why fight it? Don't I deserve to feel good, even if it's only in a dream? It's been so long since I've felt good, and never at Colt's hands, that's for sure. I don't even know why I'm having a dream about him, of all people.

His breath is hot against my sensitive skin. "Such a pretty pussy," he whispers, almost too soft for me to hear, but just that burst of air makes me shudder. It's like my whole body is tuned into his every move, every touch, every word.

And then something warm touches my bald lips, and I almost lose myself to the intensity of the pleasure rolling through me. I can't help but reach down to touch the back of his head and run my fingers through his hair, and he seems to like that because he moans, and the vibrations feel so good. It's all so good. Whatever he's doing or whatever I think he's doing, there needs to be more of it. Much more.

"Yes... Colt..." It's so good, and I want to feel good, even if none of it is real. Maybe it's knowing it isn't real that lets me let go and focus on the way my body is acting, the way it feels like I'm floating down a river of warm honey, sweet, washing over me with every lap of Colt's tongue.

"You taste so sweet. Like honey." Wasn't I just thinking about honey? Of course, he's saying the words I'm thinking. It's my dream, after all. I wonder if he knows what I'm thinking now when I grind my hips, desperate to get to the finish. I'm so close, the familiar tension building, growing until it's ready to consume me. I'm ready to be consumed.

And then he flicks his tongue across my clit over and over, lightning fast, and I explode. My thighs tighten around his head, and I ride it out, wave after wave of bliss rolling over me until my body finally relaxes and goes limp again.

Only it doesn't stop. I expect to wake up or at least for the dream to end and move into something else, but instead, I feel his lips against my thighs again, then moving up over my stomach, my breasts, and my throat. "I love making you come," he whispers in my ear before kissing my cheek, then covering my mouth with his. I even think I taste some of myself on him as he kisses me over and over, his tongue probing my mouth, exploring. He's reigniting my hunger, stirring the fire that was starting to go out, bringing it back to life.

"Let me inside you," he whispers between kisses, groaning helplessly when our bodies brush and his hard dick rubs against my leg. "I want to be inside your pussy."

"Yes," I whisper, spreading my legs wider to make room for him as he settles between them.

"Do you want me to fuck you?"

"Yes, Colt..." I don't know what's happening anymore. I don't care. I don't want it to stop, even if it is all in my head. Not when it feels like my body is like a wire being pulled tight, so tight I'd snap at the slightest touch. I need that release again. I need to feel filled, whole.

The pressure from him nudging against my pussy is intense —but it's nothing compared to when he pushes himself inside me, stretching my channel so wide that, for a moment, all I can think about is the pain.

I somehow manage to lift my hands to his chest, feeling his skin under my palms. "It hurts," I whimper, making him stop.

"Shhh, you're doing good," he soothes, peppering featherlight kisses across my face. "Just relax, and I promise it won't hurt after this."

He moves slowly, the way I need him to, in and out, and that delicious friction makes me moan while he breathes heavy against my neck.

"See. The pain is already over. Now you can enjoy the rest."

Everything about this—the feel of him, his weight pressing

me against the mattress, the heat of his breath, his soft grunts each time he sinks as deep as he can—is all so overwhelming. Thoughts and sensations overlap, fighting for my attention. All I know is it feels good, so good I don't want it to ever end. I don't want to ever wake up from this. Not when my body feels so alive, not when I feel so free.

"Leni..." He sounds nothing like the Colt I know, who would never whisper my name so helplessly like he's just as lost as I am. This is the dream version of Colt, the Colt I wish he was.

"Yes, Colt. Yes." He starts to move faster, and I want that, too, and I moan my encouragement. The heat is building again, the tension, and my pussy starts to tighten with every deep, driving thrust. I have no choice but to give myself over to it, to focus every fiber of my being on what's about to happen.

"Come for me," he grunts. "Come for me again." There's no way not to do what he says because my body is already so close to the edge, a little closer every time he grinds against my clit, and every time he fills me up. I couldn't stop if I wanted to, and I don't want to. Even if it's only happening in my head.

"I think... I think I'm... oh god!" And then everything explodes, and it's unreal, the way wave after wave of unbelievable bliss rolls through me, starting at my core and rippling out until my entire body sings with pleasure. I want to hold him close, but I still can't make myself move much—not that it matters because, a moment later, he pulls away and comes across my stomach.

Whatever happened to make me dream that, I want it to happen again. "Wow," I whisper. I think I hear him chuckling softly but can't be sure. I'm already sinking back into the darkness, and I don't want to. I want to savor this. I want to ride out the sweet aftershocks for as long as I can. I don't want it to go away.

My eyes are forced open when I feel something warm on my stomach again. He's standing over me, looking peaceful. Satisfied. Mirroring my own feelings. He's even smiling a little, his sexy dimples showing as he wipes me with a washcloth. I lick my parched lips and try to find the words, but I don't know what to say. I don't know how to feel. I have no idea where this is coming from. Why would my mind make this shit up?

"Now you go to sleep," he whispers, draping a blanket over me, covering me up to my shoulders. I think I feel him stroking the hair back from my face, but I'm not sure. That can't be possible. None of this is possible. I'm so lonely and so desperate for kindness that I've resorted to dreaming about it.

"Why can't you be this nice to me in real life?" I whisper. My eyelids are so heavy I can't keep them open anymore.

"Don't worry about that, love bug. Just sleep." Something warm and soft brushes against my forehead.

Did he just kiss me? It feels like it, and I could laugh at myself for being so pitiful, so needy. Instead, I give up struggling to make sense of what just happened in favor of allowing myself to let go and drift away.

CHAPTER 13

*D*amn. I feel like a truck ran over me. My eyelids are so heavy I can barely lift them. It's like somebody put scotch tape over them. When I do manage to get them open, the light streaming into my room only makes me flinch as my head starts to pound. I quickly squeeze my lids shut again.

Note to self: no champagne with painkillers. Maybe no champagne anymore, ever. That might be a smarter idea.

Shit. Today is the wedding. I'm not going to be able to lie around in bed much longer. I'm surprised Mom hasn't already come in and demanded to know why I'm still in bed. I had better get moving before she does because I'm not sure I could handle her shouting at me when my head already feels like it's in a vise.

I start to throw the blankets back, an old trick I learned for getting my ass out of bed back when I was training both before and after school, sometimes waking up as early as four in the morning to make it to the gym. I don't miss those cold, dark mornings, but they taught me a lesson. The sooner I'm not so comfortable, the less reason I have to burrow deeper in the bed and fall asleep again.

Only there's a problem, a big one that reveals itself as soon as the blankets are off. Why am I naked?

I yank the covers up around my neck, eyes bulging, my heart taking off at a sickening pace. Why am I naked? Wait. How did I get to bed, to begin with? Why can't I remember?

Why can't I...

Oh. No.

I don't want to do this because I don't want the confirmation. I reach down between my legs and confirm how sore I am. What happened last night wasn't a dream.

I had sex with Colt. Or rather, he had sex with me while I was too out of it to know the difference between reality and something my drugged-up brain had concocted.

And now I'm going to throw up.

Once the wave of panic-induced nausea passes, rage quickly takes its place. He knew I wasn't in my right mind. That was the whole reason I had to come home in the first place. I was totally out of it, but he had sex with me anyway.

Headache forgotten, I jump out of bed and hurry through getting dressed before marching down the hall. I'm going to kill him for this. After everything he's done to me, this is the worst. How could he take advantage like that? How could he use me?

Unfortunately for him, he's in his room with the door cracked, sitting at his desk with his back to me. I wish it was as easy as sneaking up on him from behind and, I don't know, plunging a knife into his back or his neck or something like that. But then again, no, I wouldn't want it to be quick. I'd want it to be slow, and I would want him to know it was me.

Turns out, he already knows that. "Are you going to come in all the way, or are you going to stand there and watch me like a stalker?"

The smug prick. How dare he even have the nerve to speak to me? I fling the door open and storm across the room, folding my arms when coming to a stop beside his chair. "How could you?"

He swings around in his chair, and I see he's wearing an easy smile. "How could I what?"

"How could you fucking rape me last night? Don't act like you don't know what I'm talking about."

His eyes widen in a mockery of surprise. "Rape you? Is that what I did?" He even touches a hand to his chest like he's shocked.

"Well, I wasn't in any position to say no. I didn't even know what the hell was going on. I thought I was dreaming!"

"It must've been a pretty nice dream. You sure seemed to enjoy it when you creamed all over my cock."

I had an orgasm? Yes, now that I think about it, I remember coming. A thousand showers couldn't wash off the filth I feel all over me. The way he's looking at me doesn't help. The way he smirks, like now we have a secret between us, one he finds extremely funny. "You're sick."

"And you begged for it."

"What? I could barely speak. I couldn't even string two or three words together."

"Let's go to the recording, shall we? It might clear up a few things for you."

"You have a recording?" This is getting worse by the second. "A video?"

"No, I'm sorry to say because I would've liked to watch that. But the sounds are enough to help me remember the magic." He takes out his phone and pulls something up, then places the device on the desk before hitting play.

Suddenly, the room is full of the sound of soft but rapid breathing. "Colt..." It's a moan, and it's coming from me. I know the sound of my own voice. A humiliated flush creeps up my neck and floods my face. "Yes... please."

"Does that sound like I forced you?" he asks, lifting an eyebrow. "Because, to me, that sounds like a girl who's about to come."

"Stop it," I whisper, my skin crawling as the sound of my moans grows louder.

"Oh, Colt, yes... yes, so good..."

Colt rubs a palm over his crotch. "I'm starting to get a little hard just listening to it." He smiles triumphantly before stopping the recording. The silence that replaces it is somehow more chilling.

"Like I said, you know I didn't know what was happening. You saw the condition I was in. I was half unconscious most of the time."

"Not when it counted, or do you want to listen again to be sure?"

"I'm going to go to the police."

He sits back, looking me up and down, narrowing his eyes. "You think so?"

"I know so. I don't need to be screaming the word 'no' for it to be rape. I'm sure there are still traces of narcotics in my blood, and anybody at the party last night would have seen me drinking champagne. I even left because I wasn't feeling well."

I don't know what I expect. An apology? I should know by now that will never happen. I could hold my breath until I dropped dead without hearing a single apologetic word. "You know what? Go to the cops," he decides with a shrug. "Tell them what happened. Tell them you were out of your mind and not yourself. But if they come to me, and I play them this recording, who do you think they'll believe?"

Now I feel filthier than ever. Used and discarded. "What is wrong with you?" I whisper. After everything I've seen from him, after everything he's done, this is by far the worst. He's evil. Not even the slightest bit sorry for how I'm feeling now.

"You knew I was a virgin. How could you do this to me?" Most of the anger has left my voice, and sadness and denial have taken its place. "How could you take this away from me?"

Colt loses his smug smile. His expression turns somber, and something like empathy flashes over his pale-blue eyes. For a fraction of a second, I think he might actually apologize. That must have been wishful thinking.

"Be glad this was your first time. You should be thanking me for providing you with such a pleasant experience."

Because I can't pummel him to death with my fists, and I don't want him to see me cry, I run back to my room and slam the door hard enough that the walls shake. That's not enough. I want to tear the place apart. I want to break every piece of furniture in this room and then throw it through the windows, so they break, too. Same thing with the bathroom. I want everything shattered, in pieces, the way I feel inside.

How could he do that? How could I let him? He stole my virginity. Yes, stole like a thief. It was mine to give, mine alone.

And nobody will believe me. I don't even think my mother

would. She'd blame me for mixing alcohol with one of my pills —if she believed me at all that Colt used me, which I doubt. Colt would never play that recording for her, and that's the only real proof anything happened last night. He could just as easily say it's something I made up in my head.

No, I'm not safe anywhere—with anyone. And in another few hours, we're going to be family.

"Leni. What the hell is going on up here?" Mom is already berating me before she's even opened the door. She's wearing a white satin robe, her face devoid of makeup, her hair freshly washed and still damp. "Here I am, expecting you to come down to meet with the hair and makeup people, and you're slamming things around. Have you forgotten what today is?" She snaps her fingers close to my face, something I've always hated. It's not easy resisting the impulse to slap her hands away.

"I was about to come down in another minute or so."

"Well, you had better. We have a schedule to keep."

"Wait a second, please," I blurt out when she turns away.

She sighs heavily before turning back around. "What?"

"Something bad happened. Something I need to tell you about. I swear, I didn't do anything to bring it on. But it happened for sure, and I didn't want it to."

She holds up her hand, closing her eyes. "For God's sake, please, could you let something be about me for once? Why do you insist on making everything about you?"

"I wasn't trying to, I swear."

"Right. Tell me another good one."

"Please, please listen to me." *For once, be my mother. Care about me, love me.* I can't say any of those things, of course. She would probably laugh at me if I did.

"This is my day. Do you hear me? My day. For once, I will not let you make this about you. I'm sorry if you have a difficult time handling that, but that's how it is." She runs a hand through her hair, scowling. "It's bad enough I'm going to have to explain to everyone why my mother didn't see fit to come to my wedding. I won't have you screwing this up for me, too, just like she has."

My shoulders slump, and I look at the floor, dejected but not surprised. "You can tell me about it later, okay?" she adds, but I know better. She'll conveniently forget all about this. "But it's going to have to wait until my big day is over. Now come on. We have a lot to do and very little time to do it in."

What else can I do? I can't make her care. I've spent my whole life trying to make her care about me, to really care about something other than what I can do for her. She'll never let me live it down, all the money she spent on my training, conveniently forgetting the fact that she was the one pushing me, always on my back, insisting I be the best.

So even though my heart is aching, and I would rather do anything else than face the world today, I follow her down the stairs, where sure enough, an entire team of hair and makeup artists waits for us. Now she's every bit the happy, blushing bride, accepting a mimosa that one of the makeup people offers.

They offer me one as well, but I shake my head. "No, thank you. I had a little too much at the rehearsal dinner."

I wish more than anything I could blink and magically be transported to tonight after all this is over.

Instead, I take a seat and let the professionals get to work on me. With Mom chattering on and on in her excited way, at least nobody will expect me to join in the conversation. I can sit here and be miserable alone—which in the end, is not so different from my normal life, anyway.

CHAPTER 14

"*C*an you believe I'm nervous?" My mother laughs softly while checking herself out in her compact, adding a little more powder to her nose as she talks. "James is the one thing in life I've ever been completely sure of, but I'm still jittery."

I'll try not to take that personally. "You look beautiful. And you know he loves you. You have nothing to be nervous about."

"I just want everything to go off without a hitch. For once, I need everything to be perfect."

"It will be." I'm not even thinking about what I'm saying anymore. The words flow out of me like I'm a robot. I feel numb more than anything else. I'm still angry, but it's cooled to a simmer. It has to since I can't spend the entire day full of fiery, murderous rage. I'm still going to have to play nice and pretend to be part of a happy family today.

"This is it. This is the start of our new life. Finally, I'm going to get what I deserve." I turn away from her, looking out the car window as the driver takes us the rest of the way to the venue. I know better than to correct her. Besides, she didn't make a mistake. She's only thinking about herself, as usual. She doesn't care about what I deserve.

At least I have an excuse to separate from her once we get inside, where guests are already filing in through the front door while we sneak in through the side. "You'll sit up front," she tells me before pausing so the photographer can get a shot of her—without me in it, of course.

"I'm not walking down the aisle in front of you?"

"No," she says with a laugh, looking at me like I'm out of my mind. There I was, thinking I was her bridesmaid or something. There I go again, assuming the best from her. "You'll sit in the front row, but you're not going to stand up with me. Nobody is going to steal the focus from me today." If anything, this is preferable to standing up in front of everybody so they can see me, the girl who got raped by her stepbrother last night.

And here he is, taking a seat in the front row across the aisle separating us. He and Nix both look impressive in their fancy tuxedos. They might even be able to fool people into thinking they're decent. I won't let myself look at them. I won't give them the satisfaction.

As usual, I have no choice in the situation. "Ew. Look at her. She's barely wearing anything."

My body goes stiff, my blood turns to ice, and my skin pebbles with goose bumps. I would know Deborah's voice anywhere. "She can't even help but be trashy today of all days. I can't believe you were ever friends with her. I swear, sometimes I still wonder about you, Piper."

She's here, too? I slide a look to my right from the corner of my eye, and my stomach drops. Deborah and Piper are my stepbrothers' dates. Unbelievable. It's like every aspect of their lives has to ruin mine somehow. The girls are wearing beautiful dresses, both of which are a normal length compared to mine. When Piper winds her arm through Colt's, I know she's his date. If I thought it would make a difference, I'd tell her what he did to me last night, but she would only find it funny.

Again, I have to call upon the part of my mind I toughened up for competition. They can't get to me. They're nothing, people with no lives at all. I would like to think if I was popular and came from a wealthy family, I would be a little nicer to people.

Today is about Mom and James, anyway. When the music begins, and we all rise, it gives me an excuse to turn my attention in that direction.

She glides down the aisle, her eyes sparkling with tears, both hands wrapped around a bouquet of enormous white roses so fragrant their aroma wafts my way before she's anywhere close to me. She hands me the bouquet and, strictly for show, leans down to kiss my cheek before taking James's hand—he's handsome as always, beaming at his bride.

It's a very nice ceremony, pretty heartfelt. Mom only breaks down crying twice, giving James the opportunity to give her his handkerchief so everyone in attendance can swoon a little. I know she must be loving this. She'll be riding this high for ages.

It's a short event, at least, and before I know it, James and Mom are kissing, and Mom is outstretching a hand to take her bouquet back. I clap along with the rest of the guests as they pass, though unfortunately, my gaze brushes against Colt's, and an icy chill runs through me, thanks to his knowing sneer.

There's no escaping them when we head upstairs for the

reception, either, even though I try to lose myself in the crowd. The seats have already been assigned, and I have the misfortune of sitting with my family, of course. Meaning I have to sit with the girls, too.

"You're here alone, Leni?" Deborah asks with an edge to her voice. "Wow, I'm so surprised. You're usually so popular."

I ignore her, taking my seat across from where she's sitting. This won't last forever. It's only a few hours. And so many people are around. What's the worst she could do to me? All right, maybe I don't need to ask myself that question.

"Congratulations! Your father looked so happy." I don't know the person standing next to Colt's chair, but she's gushing like she's never been to a wedding before.

"Thanks, it's been a great day," he replies with an easy smile.

"Is this your girlfriend?" she asks, gesturing toward Piper. Her cheeks flush, and she lowers her gaze, giggling. "So pretty. You make a beautiful couple."

"What about us?" Nix slings an arm around Deborah's shoulders, and she laughs uproariously while leaning against him.

"I'm blinded by the beauty at this table." The woman shields her eyes, and everybody laughs at their shared joke. Then she glances my way, frowns, and walks off. Mom hasn't taken her seat beside me yet, so maybe it's not clear who I am, but still. How rude.

Now that I think about it, does anybody here know who I am? Did anybody bother learning about the bride and her family? More importantly, did Mom bother to tell anybody she has a daughter? Deborah shoots me an evil look from across the table, and I pointedly look away, glad to see waitstaff coming out with trays full of food. If we're eating, we are one step closer to this being over. Mom and James take their seats, having been busy getting their pictures taken.

Though, even as everybody's dining, there's no end to the visits from other guests. Everybody gushes over the guys, how grown up they are, the sort of small talk people make at events like this when they don't know what else to say. Since nobody knows who I am and none of my family goes out of their way to introduce me, I sit silent, eating my food and minding my business.

A hush falls over the room when someone gets on a microphone and announces the first dance is about to begin. "Ladies and gentlemen, it's time for the bride and groom to share their special moment." Immediately, dozens of cameras are lifted into the air so everybody can capture this.

There's so much happiness all around me, so many smiles, even a few tears as James expertly guides my mother across the dance floor. She's beaming, obviously in heaven. I want to be happy for her. I really do. Maybe once she's happy and feeling secure now that she's Mrs. Alistair, she'll ease up on me a little. There won't be as much of an excuse to resent me. I find myself welling up with hopeful tears by the time the song's over, and James treats Mom to a deep dip that leaves the crowd gasping and applauding in appreciation. It's a perfect moment, like something out of a movie. I know she's living it up.

Now that that's over, the floor is open for anybody who wants to dance. The plates are being cleared away, and many of the guests are getting up to enjoy the open bar. I can't help but sigh in relief when Colt and Nix take their dates to get drinks, even though we're all underage. Things like that just don't matter when you're in their position, I guess.

"Sitting here all alone?" James is smiling as he approaches, one hand extended. "That hardly seems fair."

Yikes. As nice as he is for offering, I don't know if I want the attention. "I'm not much of a dancer," I admit, even though the DJ chose another slow song. That can't be too difficult, swaying back and forth.

"Do you want to know a secret?" He leans down a little, eyes twinkling. "Neither is your mom. But I made her look good, didn't I?" It has the desired effect, making me laugh and loosening me up. "Come on. It'll be fine. There's nothing to it." I can almost believe him as I place my hand in his and stand, allowing him to lead me onto the floor.

"You know," he murmurs as he drapes an arm around my waist while taking my right hand in his left. "It's not always going to be like this. The awkwardness. I see it—I didn't want to bring it up, is all. But I do see how uncomfortable things have been for you, and I'm sorry. I've been quiet about it up until now because I didn't want to rock the boat before the wedding. I'm sure that everything will loosen up now. It just takes time to adjust."

I can almost believe him. I want to. Who wouldn't? I hate what my life has become. It was one thing when I lived only with Mom and had to avoid her for fear of her temper and the ugly things that came out of her mouth. But now?

I almost want to tell him what happened last night, but I wouldn't dare. Not here, not now. "I'm sure you're right," I murmur.

"Besides, brothers are supposed to make their sisters a little crazy. But don't you worry. If they ever cross the line, you can always come to me. I'll always be here for you. I want you to know that."

"Thank you. That means a lot."

He is a very good dancer, surprisingly graceful and light on his feet. He almost makes me believe I'm good at this. "You know, you do look very lovely tonight. Almost as lovely as the bride herself."

"Not hardly." Mom looks like a princess, a queen, seeming to glow from all the way across the room where she's snapping photos with guests.

He smiles across the room at his bride. "We're finally going to be one big, happy family. I believe that with all my heart."

I'm glad one of us does. It's obvious he doesn't know who his sons truly are. I would hate to burst his bubble and ruin his illusions.

When the dance is over, I excuse myself to go to the ladies' room. It's funny—even though nobody is really paying me any attention, I'm still overwhelmed and want to be alone for a few minutes, at least. It's quieter in here, secluded, even cooler without so many bodies heating things up. I take advantage of that by sitting on a stool in front of a long mirror spanning the wall opposite the sectioned-off toilets. Maybe I can stay in here all night, pretend to be an attendant. I'm sure nobody would know the difference, anyway, since I hardly exist.

"I thought I saw you crawl in here." I look up from where I'm rubbing my feet to see Deborah entering, a glass of red wine in one hand and an ugly smirk etched across her face.

"Can you please give it up for just one night?" I ask. "This isn't the time or the place. I want to keep things nice for my mom."

"Then you should have stayed home. Nobody wants to see your ugly face around here."

"Whatever you say."

Clearly, that isn't enough for her. She wants to watch me break down. Nothing short of that will satisfy her. "So you agree? You're ugly, and nobody wants to see you around?"

"Deborah, it's not that I'm normally in the mood for this, but I am especially not in the mood right now. I don't know what you want me to say besides we're not in high school anymore." You'd think she'd act more like an adult. I know we're only eighteen, but geez, we're not twelve.

"You could say goodbye."

I stand, sliding back into my shoes and facing her. "You want me to say goodbye? Fine. I'm leaving the room."

"No. That's not quite good enough."

I can't help but gasp in horror when she tosses the entire content of her glass at me. The red wine splashes onto my dress, and crimson immediately soaks into the light-colored fabric. The cold liquid seeps into my dress and my skin before dripping down my legs and onto my heels.

"What the fuck is wrong with you?" I whisper, looking down at myself. It's ruined, there's no getting this out, and I can't imagine sitting through the rest of the night looking this way. Mom is going to have a fit.

She giggles, shrugging when I look up from the disaster she caused. I already feel the wine soaking through the satin and onto my skin. "I guess you'll have to go home. Trust me, it's better this way for everybody." She even pats me on the arm like she's being sympathetic before strolling out of the bathroom and leaving me stained and sticky.

I guess she's getting what she wanted. I can't stay around here like this. I doubt anybody will notice I'm gone, anyway. I pull out my phone to order an Uber, which thankfully isn't far from the venue. I only have to wait a few more minutes, trying in vain to dab away the worst of the stain before ducking out, almost running for the door before anybody sees me like this.

And as I go, the sounds of music and laughter follow me. Everybody else is having the time of their lives while I slink away, embarrassed. I don't think I've ever felt this alone.

CHAPTER 15

It's eerie how quiet the house is now. I feel like I'm walking into a mausoleum when I enter. It isn't my heartache and embarrassment causing me to feel that way, either. There's something about the coldness in here, the lack of warmth or charm. Some people might call it elegant or tasteful. I think it's a waste of money. I'd rather live in a comfortable, slightly cluttered house where I feel at home.

My footsteps echo off the floor as I walk to the stairs, then climb them slowly, exhaustion finally settling in and dragging me down. There's only so much a person can take. After that face-off with Deborah, I'm waving the white flag. I'm done for the night. So what if my mother finds out I left early? I doubt she'll miss me. She might be glad I'm gone, come to think of it. This can be my wedding gift to her.

It feels great to get out of this sticky dress and wash up in the shower. I wish I could wash everything off, all the dirtiness I feel deep down inside, but soap can only do so much. I know in my heart it's up to me whether I choose to give in to the depression and despair Colt and Nix clearly want me to sink into. It's up to me whether I feel dirty and used. I'm not going to let them break me.

Though it's probably easier said in my own head when I'm here alone. I can breathe freely for once without the fear of somebody walking in on me or finding some way to make me miserable.

Nobody's here.

Which means nobody would know if I...

Nope. I need to shut down that line of thinking right now before it takes root.

I shouldn't. I'm only asking for trouble, aren't I? I shake my head at myself, determined not to stir up more problems than I already have. Sure, everybody is at the wedding, and I'm positive they'll be there for hours—things had hardly started by the time I left.

That doesn't mean I can sneak around, nor does it mean I should.

Yet by the time I'm finished putting on my pajamas, curiosity is threatening to kill me. There has to be something I could use against them, something I can hold over their heads the next time they want to hurt me. Obviously, the threat of going to the police means nothing, especially thanks to that little recording Colt made. Could I find something just as damning? I can't be the only girl they've hurt this way, and I can't be the only one they've recorded for posterity.

There's only one way to find out, and the longer I spend fighting with myself, the more time I waste. That's why, even though the house is dark and quiet, I run down the hall on tiptoes and enter Colt's room.

There's a laptop on his desk, and since it's the only thing sitting around that looks even remotely useful, I open it in hopes of being able to access some of the files without needing a password. Maybe luck is finally going my way since a swipe across the trackpad with my finger opens up the desktop. A tingling sensation rushes over me, and my heartbeat picks up. I listen hard for any signs of someone coming home early, but the only thing to reach my ears is silence. This is as good a time as any.

Is he this stupid or simply so full of himself that he doesn't think to cover his tracks? There's a folder right there on the desktop with my name on it. What could he possibly have? Maybe a copy of the audio file from last night? Not that I want to hear it again, but it would be good to know they have a backup sitting around.

The folder contains a few items, the first of which is a video. I can't tell much from the thumbnail, so I click on it, hoping against hope it's not anything too disgusting.

I guess my luck can only run so far since, instantly, I'm transported back to the night of the party. The night they both forced me to suck Nix's dick. I want to turn my eyes away from it, but I can't stop watching. From this vantage point, it's even more disgusting. The way I so obviously struggle, and the tears in my eyes. The gagging, choking sounds I made while the brothers only laughed at me.

The cold, nauseating sensation of being helpless washes over me and makes me shake. How dare they? Who do they think they are?

Before I can click on the second icon, the lid to the laptop snaps shut, and suddenly I'm face-to-face with none other than Nix himself. "Bad girl."

"I..." *Shit.* How the hell am I getting out of this?

"What? Snooping through my brother's shit or just strolling down memory lane, thinking about getting off to the memory of having my dick in your mouth?"

"No, no, that's not what I want," I somehow whisper, even though I'm close to hyperventilating.

"Don't you know what happens to little girls who can't keep their hands off other people's things?"

Not only is he here—in my face and obviously bitter—but he's also drunk. I smell it on him, on his breath. Even his sweat sends the scent of alcohol wafting my way. His speech is a little slurred, but his eyes are sharp when they narrow on me. "What are we going to do with you? You little snoop. Can't be trusted home alone."

"I was only—" Anything I might have offered to defend myself melts away when I swivel around in the chair to find Colt standing in the bedroom doorway.

And not only Colt, either. "You never know when to give up, do you?" Deborah demands, disgust dripping from her voice. "It's like you're begging for everybody to hate you. Maybe you have a mental problem or something."

They're all drunk; that much is obvious. She's leaning against the wall for support while Colt looks as sloppy as I've ever seen him. They must have done a lot of hard drinking, very fast. It hasn't been all that long since I left the reception.

"Fine, you caught me. I just wanted to see if there was anything you guys had on me—and I see there is," I add, my voice shaking in spite of my attempts to sound strong. "It's disgusting what you have there. How can you live with yourselves?"

"Oh, now she's all high and mighty," Deborah announces with a laugh. "But then she's used to that. Always thinking her shit didn't stink."

"Not so fast." Colt stops me before I can escape, locking an arm around my waist and pulling me away from the door so Nix can close, then stand in front of it. "You're not going anywhere."

I'm going to be sick. These are the last three people in the world I need to be alone with. "Please, I was only trying to—"

"God, does she always whine like that? How do you keep from throwing her ass down the stairs?" Deborah steps up, getting in my face while the guys laugh. "Whiny little bitch. So pathetic. Maybe if you had stayed out of here, this wouldn't be happening. Ever think about that?"

"Now, why would she mind her own business? That's too much to ask." Colt leans in, breathing on my neck. "She would much rather act like a victim and whine and cry about how mean everybody is to her. You got yourself in this situation. Only you."

Like they wouldn't have found some other reason to get on my case even if I had stayed in my room all night. "I get it, okay?"

"No, not okay." Nix sits on his desk chair, straddling it, arms crossed over the back. "What do you think we should do to her as punishment?" he asks Deborah.

Her eyes light up, and my mouth goes dry. This is going to be bad. "I don't know. There are so many possibilities." She snaps her fingers, beaming. "I know. We strip her naked, shave off all her hair, and leave her in the middle of nowhere."

Nix and Colt burst out in hysterical laughter while I fight for every breath, thanks to my growing panic. "That's a good idea,"

Nix decides. "I like the naked part, too. The rest of it, though? We'd have a hard time explaining it to the parents."

She lifts a shoulder. "Then let's start with the naked part."

Nix jumps up, eyes flashing, his smile reminding me of a wolf. While Colt holds me still, Nix tears off my pajama shirt. The cool air makes my nipples pucker, and I could die of embarrassment. I could just die. The last sound I hear will be Deborah's hysterical laughter.

"I have an idea. Hold her still." Deborah goes to the desk and grabs a black marker. No matter how I try to pull myself free, I doubt I could escape from one of the guys, much less two of them. Not when they're this determined to humiliate me.

"Now hold still, bitch." She narrows her eyes, concentrating hard on scrawling the word SLUT across my chest. Every letter she completes makes my stepbrothers laugh harder, louder, until they're practically howling by the time she's finished.

She's only finished with that word, though. She has more to do. Starting from between my boobs, she works her way down to my navel. "W... H... O... R... E."

"Nice work." Colt laughs, and all I can do is whimper. "What do you think, Leni? Do you feel more like your true self now?"

"After all." Deborah smiles in my face like she's the happiest she's ever been. "We already know who you are. Now, the rest of the world will know, too."

Then she looks at the guys. "Turn her around. I'm not finished yet."

Maybe it's the chilling flatness in her voice when she says it, or it could be the idea of her seeing my scar and how much worse she'll make my life once she does. Whatever it is, gives me the strength I need to break free. They're probably too drunk, their reflexes are slow, and I use that to my advantage.

"Hey!" But that's all Deborah gets out before I fling myself at her, knocking her against a dresser and out of my way. I fly to the door, throw it open, and run like hell down the hall. I fling myself into my room and slam the door before wedging the chair underneath the knob.

"Come on, Leni!" Deborah calls out, her voice getting louder as she approaches. "We just want to have fun! Don't be such a pain in the ass!" Either Nix or Colt says something to her in a low voice, and she giggles. The sound fades away as she retreats to their room. I don't have to imagine what's going on in there. So long as they're leaving me alone, I really don't care.

Once I'm sure they're not going to do anything like try to kick the door in, I allow myself to turn away from the door and head back to the bathroom. The shower walls are still dripping, but I'm about to get them wet again. There are tears in my eyes and a lump in my throat as I turn on the water and step in, grabbing my mesh sponge and soaping it heavily before I begin the task of scrubbing the marker off my skin. It's not easy, but then what is? This is my life, after all. Nothing about it has ever been easy.

My tears mix with the hot water as my skin gets redder and redder the longer I work. I'm not getting out of this shower until my skin is clear. I don't care if it takes all night and I run out of hot water. I will not allow those hateful words to live on my body.

I will not let her win.

CHAPTER 16

*T*ime is ticking away. I have a decision to make.

The idea of being in this house alone with my stepbrothers while Mom and James are on their honeymoon is unthinkable. One of the only things that kept me going last night was knowing that, eventually, James would come home. Mom? I doubt she would care either way. But he at least gives me hope. He's the only one around here who's kind to me. I need to believe that kindness will make a difference. I need him to believe me and stick up for me. Somebody has to because I'm not getting anywhere by myself.

This isn't like me. I'm not the kind of person who runs around squealing on people. I doubt either of my stepbrothers would believe this, but I would rather mind my own business.

That's what I'm fighting with as I wander my room, my conscience and my sense of self-preservation fighting it out as one crucial minute after another ticks by. They're leaving soon. I don't have much more time to make up my mind.

I can either spend the honeymoon locked in this room,

afraid to step foot outside even to get something to eat, or I can tell James what's happening. At least he might warn them to stay away from me. He'll be on my side. He has to be, especially when I tell him there's proof on the laptop. It's the only chance I have left.

That's that. When I look at it that way. When I consider how many awful things they could do to me while it's just the three of us, it's obvious I have no other option. I open my bedroom door, take a deep breath, and prepare to track him down before he leaves.

As it turns out, I don't have far to go. He's carrying a bag over his shoulder, fiddling with his sunglasses on his way down the hall. A smile lights up his face when he sees me approaching. "There she is. I haven't seen you all day. You made a quick escape last night. Were you feeling all right?"

"Yeah, I had an accident with some wine, so I figured it would be better to come home and get changed than walk around in a stained dress all night."

"That's a shame. I'm sorry you missed so much of the party."

I can't say the same. "Anyway, it seemed like you two were having a good time, and that's what matters."

"What a sweet thing to say. If I've told your mother once, I've told her a hundred times: you are a wonderful kid, and she did a fantastic job of raising you."

I have to say it. I have to say it before I lose my nerve. "Can I have a minute? I know you're probably on your way out, but I need to tell you about this before you leave. And believe me, I don't want to do this. I've been trying all day to come up with a way not to tell you about this."

"Not to tell me about what?" He reaches out and touches my arm, frowning. "What's happened? What can I help with?"

"I know this isn't going to be easy for you to hear, but Colt and Nix..." Oh god, I didn't think about how humiliating it would be to repeat all of this. But I have to get through it.

"What about them?"

"I'm sorry, but they hate me."

"Remember what I told you last night about the awkwardness—"

"It isn't awkwardness. It's so much worse than that. I wouldn't say anything like this if it wasn't true and if I wasn't afraid. But they do hate me. And..." I rub a hand up and down my arm, looking at the floor. "They force me to do things. They have forced me to do things recently. I didn't want to do them, but they made me."

"What kinds of things?" He hasn't blown up yet, so that has to be a good sign. I knew this was the right thing to do. He's the only sensible person in this house.

"One night, they forced me into... performing oral sex on Nix." I glance up at him, wishing I could crawl into a hole, wishing he would stop looking at me the way he is because I feel so sick and dirty.

"They forced you into that?"

"Yes. I'm so sorry to have to tell you about this. I know they're your sons, and I'm sure you don't want to believe anything like this about them. That's not all of it, either. It gets worse than that."

His head snaps back a little, eyes narrowing as he scans my face. "Are you sure this isn't some sort of misunderstanding?"

My heart sinks, but I can't give up. Of course, that's the first thing a parent would think. They wouldn't want to believe the worst about their child—well, unless they were my mother. "Believe me. I'm sure. There was no room for misunderstanding."

"You didn't all have too much to drink, lose track of yourselves?"

"No. No, not at all. And like I told you, that's only one example of many. But it's constant, and I don't know what to do about it. That's why I had to come to you. I'm so scared of being alone in the house with them while you're gone. Please, can you help me? I don't know what else to do."

He sighs, his shoulders slumping a little. "Leni, it isn't that I don't believe something happened to you, but I know my sons. I know they aren't perfect, but what you're describing... it's all too much to believe."

"I know it is." This is the hardest part of all. This is the part that's really going to kill him. "But there's a video."

His eyebrows lift. "Excuse me?"

"There's a video on Colt's computer. I found it last night. They took it while I was... you know. On my knees." My voice shakes, and tears are in my eyes, but this is worth it. I have to push through. "If you can't help me, I'm going to have to tell somebody else and show it to them. I'll go to the police if I have to."

And then it happens.

I can pinpoint the exact moment I see him for the first time. The real James.

His pupils dilate, eating up most of the color, turning his soft blue eyes that usually look at me with fondness and concern into an icy, dark blue.

One second, the James I danced with last night, who's been the only kind person in this house, is in front of me. The next second, he is gone, and the man in front of me now raises his lip into a snarl like an animal about to attack. He is the predator, and I'm the deer, literally frozen in the headlights.

I'm a flash, his hand is around my throat, and he's slamming me against the wall. The force knocks the air out of me, and the tears that were already filling my eyes instantly spill over as the pressure in my head builds.

He leans in, his face swimming in front of mine now that my head is spinning and my vision is blurring. "James!" I croak, fighting against his hand, fighting to pry his fingers away. It's like trying to bend iron.

"You listen to me, you little slut." His spit hits my face while I strain for air that never comes. "If you ever so much as mention going to the police again, I'm going to make you regret it. You'll wish you had never even thought of it." He pulls me an inch or two away from the wall and slams me against it again, hard enough that my head bounces off it. "I will come to your room, fuck you bloody, and I will slit your fucking throat from ear to ear. Do you understand?"

I only understand I'm finally facing the biggest devil of them all. And he's not interested in playing. "I said, do you understand?" He gives my throat another squeeze as if he could force the words out of me. I push up to my toes, hoping to relieve a little bit of pressure on my throat, but it's no use. My lungs burn excruciatingly, begging for air that's not coming.

Oh my god, I'm dying. He's killing me. I beat weakly at his arms, but he just won't let up. A rattling noise comes out of me, and even that isn't enough to make him let go. I feel myself drifting away. I feel the life leaving me, and he's not stopping. Why isn't he stopping?

Something warm runs down my leg, and it takes me a moment to realize that pee is running out of me. The warm liquid trickles down the insides of my thighs, soaking into my jeans.

"That's what I fucking thought," he grunts, his face almost touching mine. I don't even have the strength to try to pull his arm away anymore. My body is going limp. My body is letting go...

Darkness consumes me, and I sink into it. I have no other choice.

When I open my eyes, I'm on the floor. I'm not sure how much time has passed or what's happening to me. I'm dizzy, I feel like I'm going to throw up, and every time I move my head, my vision swims. I feel like I'm underwater, but wouldn't my body feel light if I was? Not like lead, the way it does now.

A pair of legs appear in front of me and whatever part of my brain is still working reacts. I try to push them away, but my arms are so heavy. I'm so weak.

Did that really happen? I can't make it make sense, any of it.

It isn't James standing in front of me, crouching and taking me by the arms. It's Nix. Nix, whose expression is blank, who doesn't say a word as he helps me to my feet. I'm soaked, and I stink like pee, and I'm so fucking weak.

Somehow, though I know it should matter, none of it really does. It's like I'm floating above myself, watching Nix trying to help me down the hall. My legs are too weak and eventually give out on me—all he does is scoop me up and take me to his room.

I don't have it in me to fight him. I don't have it in me to do anything but go limp in his arms.

That didn't happen. It couldn't have happened. Not James. The things he said. He almost killed me, didn't he? I felt myself dying. How is this possible?

Nix closes the lid on the toilet in his bathroom, then sets me down on it before reaching into the shower to turn the water on. There's nothing snide about him, nothing cruel or nasty. He only takes off my clothes one piece at a time, moving efficiently. All I can do is try to help him along as much as I can, but I'm useless.

Once I'm naked, he leads me into the shower. It almost seems strange that he doesn't follow me—isn't that the point of this? No, all he does is place me under the water and soap up a washcloth, which he gently but quickly runs over my body.

The entire time, he never says a word. He doesn't even look at me. I lean against the wall, still too wiped out to do much else. James. How could he do that? I can't even put it all together in my head. It all feels like something that happened to somebody else. Not to me. Not from James. If it wasn't for the water hitting me and the scent of the soap, I might think this was all a dream. After all, Nix is being nice to me. That's the opposite of normal, too.

Once he decides I'm clean enough, he turns off the water and pulls out a towel from the wall closet. I just stare at it for a few seconds when he holds it out to me. Shaking his head, he wraps a towel around me and guides me out of the shower. He's just as gentle as he dries me off, and it never occurs to me to do it myself. It's hard enough for me to stay upright.

I could have died. I almost died. And he left me there, not caring.

Nix hangs the towel on a hook, then takes me by the hand like it's the most normal thing in the world and leads me into his bedroom. I'm naked and shivering, so lost. What do I do now?

He goes to the dresser and comes back with a T-shirt, which he even helps me into. It falls almost to my knees, but it's soft and clean.

Once he's finished, he places his hands on my arms again, and I lift my head to look into his eyes. They're flat, without even the light that usually enters them when he's having fun with me. How is he so detached? It's almost like his feelings are turned off or worse, he is so used to this, it's normal to him.

"Did you see?" I don't have to explain what I'm talking about.

"I did. Heard it too." His words are so nonchalant as if seeing his dad choking and threatening to kill me is an everyday event.

"But you're not surprised."

"He's my dad. I grew up with him. You don't think I know this part of him?"

A shiver works its way through my body, and this time it's not from the cold. Instantly, my mind goes to Colt and Nix being helpless children in a house trapped with James.

"Go to your room," he murmurs in a voice that sounds nothing like his. "You need to forget this ever happened."

Without waiting for me to reply or to ask exactly how that's supposed to be possible, he goes to the door and opens it, then leads me out into the hall before closing the door on me. There's nothing for me to do now but go to my room, lie down, and try to do what Nix said. It isn't like I want to remember anything that just happened anyway.

But how am I supposed to forget?

CHAPTER 17

"*N*o... no!"

I'm half out of my bed by the time I fully wake up, one leg thrown over the side, almost sitting up. Like I was in the middle of dreaming about running away from something. I don't remember my nightmare clearly, but the fear is fresh and vivid, like I'm in real danger.

The worst part: I am in danger. It's not like a normal nightmare that will eventually fade away to nothing as the day goes on. I can't get away from it. I still feel his hand around my throat, thanks to the ache he left behind. That will fade, sure, but the memory will come back every time I look at him.

After a minute, my heartbeat slows to something more regular. Less like my chest is about to explode. I had to leave a light on before finally settling in to go to sleep. No way was I about to lie here in the dark, and now I'm glad for the little lamp burning on my nightstand. That nightmare was bad enough without waking up in the dark, where anything could be hiding.

The chair hasn't moved from under the doorknob, not that it

would without my knowing about it. No way is it moving without the door getting kicked in somehow. That would have woken me up. It's my only peace, that chair. The only thing protecting me. How pathetic.

It's the growling from my stomach that makes me check the time. It's past four in the morning—no wonder I don't hear any TV, music, or video games coming from elsewhere in the house. Even my stepbrothers are quiet at this time of the day. Maybe I should start keeping a schedule opposite to theirs. Stay awake overnight, and sleep during the day. Less chance of seeing them.

It was the threat of seeing them that kept me up here all night, even through dinner. I never ate. I was too afraid to step foot into the hallway. Now I regret it. I'm wide awake, so I cannot ignore my hunger by going back to sleep.

I might as well see if the door's locked. I always assume it will be now. It saves time.

I couldn't be more surprised to turn the knob. They left it unlocked. Now's as good a time as any to run down to the kitchen and grab some food. The guys are bound to be asleep. I'm too hungry to worry too much longer, anyway.

When I make it to the kitchen without running into anybody or finding evidence of either of them hanging around, I head straight for the refrigerator. There are small yogurt smoothies on one of the door's shelves, and I grab one, uncapping it quickly and gulping half of it back before coming up for air. There are packages of turkey and cheese in the drawer, and I take both of them, along with mustard and mayo. I have time to make a sandwich, and maybe I can find protein bars or something to take up and store in my dresser in case there are times I can't make it down here.

"Sneaking food now?"

Everything in my arms ends up on the floor when I jump. The mayo rolls away, and Colt bends to pick it up. He's smirking when he straightens and plops the jar on the counter. "You're jumpy, aren't you?"

"I guess that has something to do with people sneaking up on me in the middle of the night." I gather everything else together but don't know what to do now. Make the sandwich? Walk away?

"Go ahead," he murmurs, passing me on his way to the fridge. "I'm not stopping you. Just try to leave some for us."

"I don't think I could eat a whole pound of turkey at once."

He seems to be in a decent mood, but I know better than to think that will last.

"You didn't come down to eat last night, so you must be hungry."

My hand shakes a little, but I steady it before he can see when he closes the door and turns toward me. "Why are you paying attention to me?"

"I have no idea. But I noticed."

"I wasn't hungry then." My body stiffens, and it's hard to breathe when he closes the distance between us, reaching over me to grab a few slices of turkey. "Excuse me. I'll be out of your way in a second."

"You're not in my way. Right now."

I pile turkey and cheese on a slice of bread, throwing it together sloppily to get back to my room. The only place I feel safe. "I'll stay out of your way as much as I can. I usually do, anyway."

"Yeah, yeah. So you say. But you still can't seem to stay away from me. Why do you think that is?"

It's no use. He won't stop talking in circles. "I know this is fun for you, even if I can't understand why. It's not for me. I only want to get some food and go back to my room. Can I do that, please?"

He rolls up a slice of turkey and takes a bite before chewing thoughtfully. "You know, you might get a lot further along in life if you'd be a little nicer."

"Nicer? Next thing, you'll be telling me I should smile more." Before he can do that, I speak over him. "I'm not the one who started this. All I'm interested in is keeping myself safe from the two of you."

He stares at me for what feels like a lifetime before nodding slowly. "Don't let me stop you. Take your sandwich. Keep yourself safe from me."

I can't honestly believe he thinks he isn't a threat. Not after the way he's treated me all this time. Not after what he did to me.

"I will keep myself safe from you and your crazy family." I'm not sure how yet, but I'll find a way.

"Nix told me. My dad finally showed you his... other side."

I was wondering if Colt knew. I guess I shouldn't be surprised that Nix told him. Thinking about that situation has me reaching for my neck. James left some nice finger-sized bruises on the tender skin under my ears. I gently rub the spot, wondering if Colt can see it in the dim light.

"Is that what you call that?"

"What would you call it?" His eyes zone in on my neck before they darken. His jaw ticks, and his lips pull up in a tiny snarl. Is he mad that his dad touched me? More likely, he is mad that he wasn't there.

"I guess the other side fits... deranged, insane, and unstable would work as well."

"I don't care what you call it. It is what it is, and there is no changing it."

It is what it is? What kind of bullshit answer is that?

"We'll see about that." I make a grab for the food and stop just short of running down the hall, walking as fast as I can and jogging up the stairs. I keep an eye on the hall but don't see him emerging from the kitchen before I reach the second floor. I guess he's in the mood for a brief truce.

I hope he doesn't think I'm going to let my guard down.

CHAPTER 18

*a*t first, I don't know what pulled me out of a deep sleep. I only know I woke with a start, my head leaving the pillow, and my heart in my throat. The chair is firmly in place in front of the door, so it's not that.

Another round of pounding against the door makes me sit up. So that's what woke me. This time, it's not enough to bang. "Hey! Let's go! You're holding us up here," Colt barks.

"What are you talking about?" I throw my legs over the side of the bed, fuzzy-brained the way I normally am when I'm ripped from sleep.

"Let's go! You've got work! And you're going to be late."

Work. Yet another thing I have no control over. How am I supposed to know when these two want to go for a workout if they don't tell me beforehand? How can he accuse me of running late when I don't operate on a schedule in the first place? This is too bizarre.

There's no time to argue about that right now, not that I would. This job is all I have at the moment, and even though I don't understand the circumstances, I don't want to ruin things. That, and I'd rather not give my stepbrothers another reason to make me miserable.

"I'll be right there!" I grab for the first clean things my hands fall upon in my dresser, then rush to the bathroom to brush my teeth and wash my face before running a brush through my hair. The whole process can't take more than five minutes, but the way Colt and Nix act when I run downstairs, you would think I kept them waiting for two hours.

"Sorry. I didn't know you wanted to go this morning."

Nix rolls his eyes and pushes away from the door, where he was leaning as he waited. "You can assume we're going to go most days."

"Could you maybe give me the heads-up the night before so I know what time to be ready? I don't want to hold you guys up," I add before they can blow up at me.

"Whatever. Let's go. You already have me behind schedule."

I know better than to ask exactly what schedule he's talking about. I don't think I've ever met two such self-important people.

It's mercifully quiet in the truck, almost eerie. The guys have their little muttered conversation, but it's not about anything important. I think they're talking about sports, something I have very little interest in. They can talk about anything they want so long as it's not me.

During the whole way, I have to fight to keep from staring at the back of Nix's head. He'll know I'm staring, and it will only make him mad. Nothing about his attitude toward me reveals anything about what happened yesterday. Maybe in his mind, it never happened at all. I can't believe anybody could just forget something like that, no matter what he says.

It's easy for him to say. He's not the one who saw his life flash before his eyes. I have to take a few deep breaths to slow the sudden panic threatening to grip me. Every time I so much as brush up against the memory, my body reacts like I'm back in the moment.

I couldn't be more disappointed to see Piper standing at the front desk when we arrive at the gym. She's talking to a muscular middle-aged man who lifts his chin to greet Colt and Nix before turning to find me standing behind them.

"Oh. You must be Leni." He extends a hand and gives me a firm shake. My boss, I suppose? His name tag tells me his name is Chad. "I was explaining to Piper how I'll need some help in the storage room today. We just got a lot of supplies shipped in, and they need to be unboxed and accounted for. Think you could help her out with that?"

Exactly what I want. Time spent one-on-one with my ex-best friend. The two of us in a storage room with nothing to do but talk. At least I know there's a time limit. It seems like the guys work out for an hour and a half, maybe two hours. I can handle a couple of hours with her, I guess.

"Come on. I'll show you where it is." She waves me along behind her, and I follow silently. I don't dare look, but I wonder if either of my stepbrothers notices me walking with her. I'm sure they'd think it was funny. For all I know, this is the entire reason they got me a job here. Knowing I'd have no choice but to face the person who betrayed me worst of all.

It doesn't take long to figure out what Chad was talking about. Stacks of boxes are lined up along one of the walls in the cramped room. Shelves lining the other three walls are covered in all kinds of items—towels, bathroom supplies, and cleaning products. And it looks like whoever's been charged with keeping things organized and decluttered has been sleeping on the job since there's empty packaging lying around, and the shelves are in disarray.

Rather than stand around and discuss what to do first, I grab a trash bag from a roll sitting on a shelf and start gathering up shrink wrap, packing tape, and things people have left lying around. Piper hesitates but soon follows my lead and straightens up the supplies left on the shelves. The sooner we get this over with, the sooner I can get out of this room.

"So the wedding was really nice. Your mom looked so happy."

Ugh. She's still trying. I don't know if it's obnoxious or pathetic. Maybe both. Rather than acknowledge her, I open one of the boxes waiting to be unpacked and start pulling out shrink-wrapped pairs of spray bottles full of cleaning solution. Rather than leave them on the shelves this way, so somebody will cut away the shrink wrap and leave it lying around, I separate them and line them up on the shelf. I might not have a typical job here, but I'll still do it right.

"I heard why you left early," she offers. "And I'm sorry she did that. I don't know why she does those things."

"Don't apologize for her," I warn in a flat voice. "You have no idea how it sounds. And it makes me feel sorry for you."

"You feel sorry for me?"

"I do." I still don't want to look at or speak to her, but now that she's the one who started this conversation, I'm not going to hold back. If she doesn't want to hear it, she should leave me alone. "You know what she's doing is wrong, and you know it deserves an apology, but you won't stand up to her and tell her to quit it when she's in the middle of being awful. So yeah, it's really sad to listen to."

"You don't know how it is."

"I think I do. But it doesn't matter. You made your decision, and that's fine. But you can't change your mind and act like the past never happened. It did. And it hurt."

"I'm sorry," she whispers. "I really am."

What good has that ever done? It doesn't erase any of the pain she's caused. All the time I spent wondering what I did wrong, why it was so easy for her to turn her back on me.

I can't pretend it doesn't feel good, though, hearing her apologize. Still... "That's fine, but it doesn't change anything. You betrayed me, and you were the one person I thought I could count on. We're never going back to the way things used to be."

She works silently for a few moments, and I think I might hear her sniffle once or twice when she's facing away from me. "Okay, so it can't be the way it used to be," she finally murmurs. "But can we at least talk? Like, when we're here together. We might as well talk, right?"

"Honestly? I have nothing to say to you. We're not going to be friendly, so let's just get the job done."

Part of me expects her to argue, and I'm ready to be firm—or to flat-out ignore her if it comes down to it. But she doesn't argue, only sighing before stacking rolls of toilet paper and paper towels on the shelves when I hand them over to her. For the first time in days, I feel good about myself. I put my foot down instead of giving in and accepting the little scraps of friendship she's willing to give me now.

So this is what it means to set boundaries, the way I've

always heard. It might be something worth doing again. I can think of a few people who need boundaries.

But no, because the other person needs to be willing to honor those boundaries. I don't think Colt or Nix know the meaning of the word. Even if they do, they don't care. If anything, they get off on knowing they're crossing my boundaries.

It's easy to lose track of time when I'm this busy, and by the time we've finished breaking down the boxes we unpacked, the door to the supply room opens. Chad looks around, eyes wide. "I have to admit, I didn't think you'd be able to get this much work done so fast. I figured the two of you would be in here gossiping the whole time."

I almost have to bite back a grin when I see the way Piper's face falls. For once, it feels like I have the upper hand, and I don't think anybody could blame me for enjoying it a little.

"What can I do next?" I ask, deliberately excluding her.

"No need for that. It's time for you to go home, anyway."

Here I was, looking forward to getting this over with quickly, and now I'm disappointed because I was kind of on a roll. "You know," I venture, "I don't have to leave with them. I can stay for a full day if you want. I'm more than happy to do that."

He only shakes his head. "That's not how this is going to go. We have an arrangement. You are here when they are." Exactly what did they do to come to this arrangement? Why is so much of my life a mystery to me?

It's pointless to argue. I have no choice but to walk out through the gym and into the lobby area, where my stepbrothers are waiting impatiently. Just when I was starting to feel good about myself, they had to go and remind me of the lack of control I have over my life.

Nix sends a smirk my way as we walk outside. "How was your shift?" I know he's thinking about me being forced to spend time with Piper, and he obviously finds it hilarious. Again, I have to wonder how it's so easy for him to forget everything that happened yesterday. He was almost kind to me afterward. Where's that version of him now?

"It was fine. I got the supply room organized."

"What an achievement," Colt mutters, and the two of them laugh as we climb into the truck.

All I can do is bite my tongue and keep to myself, remembering how good it felt to put my foot down with Piper. I could get used to feeling like I'm calling the shots in my life.

And if that's what I'm going to do, then there's something I need to look into right away. I need to get a real job. Not only to get away from Piper but to get out from under my stepbrothers' thumbs. I can't stand living on their schedule and jumping whenever they tell me to.

CHAPTER 19

"Thank you so much for your help. I didn't think he'd ever get the hang of what they're trying to teach them in these math classes, but his teacher said he's already improving from where he was this time last week. He finally gets it."

I lean closer to the webcam at the top of my screen, smiling at the woman chatting with me from her home. Her son ran off like he was on fire the moment our lesson was over, but it gives me a few minutes to catch up with his mom. "I'm so glad. Trying to pick up new concepts is not always easy. Especially when you're in summer school. Nobody wants to be there."

She grimaces. "I'm sure if he had somebody like you explaining these things during the school year, he wouldn't have needed summer school. Is this the kind of thing you're only doing over the summer, or do you think you'll be able to provide tutoring during the school year?"

That's a good question, one I hadn't considered yet. I've only been doing this online tutoring thing for a few days, not enough time to settle down and come up with a plan. "I might be able to fit the work in," I decide. "But I won't know for sure until I start my classes. It will only be my first semester in college, so I'm not sure exactly how long it will take to adjust."

"What are you majoring in?"

"I want to eventually be an elementary school teacher."

"Perfect," she assures me with a wide smile. "Let me tell you, you are worth every penny and then some. I know my husband agrees with me—name your price, and we'll happily pay."

I'm almost too pleased to speak. "Thank you. That means a lot." A moment after we end the Zoom call, I check my PayPal account and see she's already paid the invoice I sent out.

Could it really be this easy? All I did was post in a few parent groups online that I'm available for math and history tutoring over Zoom. I didn't know there'd be parents jumping at the opportunity to get their kids tutored over the summer—a few students was as much as I hoped for. Now, my schedule is pleasantly full as I check my calendar to make sure none of my appointments overlap.

It's almost funny, in a way, how good it felt to receive a little praise just now. It goes to show how long I've gone without it. Not that I'm hungry for it or desperate for approval, but the fact is, I used to get it a lot more than I do now. When I was training and competing. To go from that to being ridiculed and belittled on a daily basis... that's a long way to fall. Only now, with money in my account and praise ringing in my ears, do I know how badly I've missed getting recognition for the things I'm good at.

And once the school year starts, I'm sure there will be more students. More parents eager to part with their money if it means giving their kids a leg up. Considering I'm only tutoring middle schoolers, maybe it won't be too much to juggle this on the side while I study for my own classes. Lots of people work during college, and not from the comfort of their room, either. I can handle it.

In the meantime, I'm going to save every penny I make and put it toward moving into the dorms when school starts. One good thing about having a scholarship for college: it'll let me put my money toward surviving rather than spending it all on tuition. Even though it's only the local school and not some big, expensive place, it means being able to get along for a lot less money than I would otherwise. I've done the math, crunched the numbers, and even considered how much I'll have to buy to furnish my room. It feels good to have a plan and a way of meeting my goals. Another few weeks of tutoring, and I'll already have enough saved up for the first semester. I really wish I had thought of tutoring sooner.

One added bonus: I can look forward to never having to go to that gym again. And once I'm out of this house, I won't have to deal with Nix, Colt, or James again, either. At least not on a daily basis. Maybe not ever. I doubt I'll be missed come holiday time.

This is starting to look like my salvation.

The thought of my stepbrothers makes me tune my ears to any sounds coming from the rest of the house. I haven't heard much from them today. In fact, they've pretty much left me alone the past few days, ever since I announced I was going to start tutoring. They haven't even given me a hard time about not going to the gym with them.

I wish I could relax and believe this means we've reached a truce of sorts. I wish I didn't have to wonder what they're cooking up.

The problem with using my desk chair for its intended purpose is leaving my door unprotected. It's a risk I have to take, and within minutes of my call ending, I'm reminded why I should have gotten up sooner and wedged it under the knob when the door swings open behind me. I brace myself, gritting my teeth and hoping whatever they want, they lose interest fast.

"Look at you. The little wannabe teacher." I find Colt reflected in my screen, slouching against the doorframe with his arms folded.

"Is that supposed to be an insult? Because yes, that is what I plan to be, eventually."

"Life at the gym not good enough for you?"

"I think this job makes more sense," I explain as nicely as I can. I don't want to turn this into a fight. I can't give him an excuse to mess with me. "It's good experience."

There's no pretending I don't know why he smiles the way he does as he pushes away from the frame, entering the room. "You want experience? I'll give you an experience."

My skin crawls at the implication, not to mention the fact that he's already given me an experience I would rather not go through again. No matter how much I felt like I enjoyed it at the time. I wasn't in my right mind. I didn't understand what was happening. He's managed to ruin that for me, too. I can't even remember coming that night without feeling used and dirty.

"I mean the kind of experience that will look good on a résumé."

He perches on the edge of my desk, overwhelming me without hardly trying. His physical presence alone is enough to make my body go stiff, ready for whatever's coming next.

"So what? You just sit here on the computer and tell kids

how to do their homework?" Could he sound more dismissive? Because organizing storage shelves is so much more important?

"Something like that."

"And people pay you for that?"

"They pay pretty well, actually." I can't help but feel proud of that. "Lots of parents want to make sure their kids are at the head of the class. There's a lot of pressure out there."

"That makes sense. Though I can't imagine why they'd pay you for that."

He's only trying to get a reaction, and I know it, but that doesn't stop my irritation from bubbling over until I have to say something. "I'm actually pretty good at math, and history was always my best subject."

"You're such a nerd." It's funny, though. He doesn't sound as nasty as usual when he says it. I'm under no illusions here. We're not friends. But at least he's not being cruel. It's amazing how little I've come to expect.

"Yo, what are you doing in here?" Nix shows up out of nowhere, and the entire energy between us changes. If I didn't know better, I would think some of Colt's posturing and cruelty is due to his brother's influence. I'm not going to fool myself into believing that. I know I can't trust Colt; he's proven it to me. But I can't pretend there isn't a difference in Colt's expression now that Nix is standing beside him. He's harder, colder.

Nix sneers down at me. "Hard at work? I guess if you don't have any friends, there's not much else to do."

"She's too good for the job we got for her," Colt reminds him, wearing a nasty smirk. "You can't even be nice to some people."

"And that's why you don't have any friends," Nix decides. "Because you don't know how to be grateful."

"I'm sorry, but a job at the gym isn't going to look as good on my résumé as tutoring."

"You're such a fucking loser." All things considered, I've heard worse from him. "Don't get used to it."

"What does that mean?"

"It means things are going to change around here again once the parents get back."

I don't like the way he says it. The barely veiled threat under his words. "How?"

Rather than clue me in, he elbows Colt. "Come on. We've got shit to do." Strange, but I can almost feel the expectation in the air when Nix stares at me. "Well?" he demands.

"Well, what?"

"Don't you want to know what I'm talking about?"

"Not really. Have fun, whatever it is." But I don't turn away, back to the laptop. I'm not turning my back on them.

"Come on. She's not worth it." Colt pulls Nix away, and once they're in the hall, he mutters something that makes him laugh in a way that sends a chill down my spine. Are they planning something? Or do they only want me to think they are, so I sit here worrying myself half to death?

Psychological warfare. That's what they are doing to me.

What they want most is for me to react, and I'm not going to give them that satisfaction if I can help it.

Instead, I'm going to sit here and wonder what Nix meant about things going differently once our parents get home. There's still another ten days before that's supposed to happen, and I've been secretly dreading them coming to an end. I don't know what is going to happen with James or how things are going to change. Whether he's going to go back to the way he was before, which I can only guess now, was all an act. The more time before I have to face him again, the better.

But I can't imagine anything I'm doing right now that I couldn't do once life goes back to normal. I'm making money and want to get out and take care of myself. What's so wrong with that? No matter how I try to come up with a reason for somebody to get in the way, I can't come up with anything.

Then again, I never imagined James doing what he did, either. Even now, it feels more like a nightmare than an actual memory. The way he changed so suddenly, going from the nice guy I thought I knew to someone dark and violent. It's enough to make me worry about Mom, and that's saying something. Very rarely do I worry about her since she doesn't seem to care much about me unless it's about the way I make her look or about the way I ruined her life. Has he ever treated her the way he treated me that day? I can't imagine since why would she have married him?

The answer to that question is pretty simple, actually. Just looking around my bedroom is answer enough. It's practically the size of half our old trailer. She's been desperate to get out of that life. Is she desperate enough to marry a psychopath?

I stare out the window, lost in my worries. Wondering if my mother is somewhere alone with somebody who could suddenly lose his temper and do to her what he did to me...

CHAPTER 20

*I*f I'm grateful for one thing, it's my books. My only way of escaping for a little while. When I'm reading, I'm not worrying. I'm not dreading or remembering. I can exist in another world, someplace where things make sense. Where people don't hurt each other for no reason, where they apologize for the things they've done—and if they don't want to apologize, they end up paying for it in the end. I think that's the part I like best. Knowing the bad guys are always going to get what's coming to them.

Sadly, real life isn't that simple. I certainly know that for a fact.

I'm so deep in my latest favorite read that the knock on my bedroom door startles me. I've been up here all day. Glad nobody has bothered me since that strange conversation earlier before the guys left the house. I took advantage of that at the time, going down to grab something to eat when nobody was around to bug me. That was hours ago, and now it's dark outside the bedroom window. Time sometimes slips away when I'm deep in a story, and that clearly happened today.

My heart sinks as I slide back into reality. There's another knock, louder this time. "Did you fall asleep in there?" Colt barks.

And if I did? Would that be a crime? "No. Just busy."

"If you're hungry, come on down. We brought dinner back."

Immediately, I feel defensive. They brought dinner, and they're going out of their way to get me to come down to eat with them? There's got to be something else going on. "I'm not hungry right now."

Since it doesn't seem like he's going to go anywhere, I get off the bed and go to the door. He's wearing a pretty neutral expression when I look up at him, but I'm not fooled by that. "Come on," he grunts. "It's just dinner. Figured you might want to eat at a normal time instead of waiting until the middle of the night."

I wish I could trust him, either of them.

"Last time, it was just a party." I make air quotations with my fingers in front of his face. "And you ended up forcing me to suck your brother's dick."

"I made you come too. Don't forget that part."

"I'd like to forget that whole night, actually. We don't always get what we want. Which is happening to you right now because I'm not coming down for dinner."

What the fuck are they up to this time?

"All right, let me rephrase the question." Colt raises his hands and mirrors my air quotations as he speaks. "Get your ass downstairs. We are having dinner together like a fucking family."

My molars grind together so violently that there is a one in three chance I'm about to crack a tooth. "I'll be down in a minute," I grit through my teeth. Fucking asshole.

It's almost surprising when he doesn't demand I follow him right away. He only saunters off, hands in his pockets.

What are they doing? There has to be something behind this. I hate how paranoid I've become, but I have to be. Not that it's ever gotten me very far, though.

It would be foolish to accept this at face value, so I don't. I'm on my guard as I walk down the stairs. Nix and Colt are talking, and I hear what sounds like paper bags rustling on my way to the kitchen. I can't help but imagine opening a container full of maggots or a dead rodent or something. That's how far they've sent me spiraling.

But no, it's the aroma of garlic and tomatoes I pick up as I draw closer to the kitchen. By the time I get there, the guys are already taking seats around the island in the center of the room. "I wasn't sure what you'd want," Colt explains. "But you seemed to like it that one night when we had chicken parmesan for dinner, so that's what I ordered for you. Pasta, garlic bread."

Nix grunts with his mouth full, gesturing to the other containers strewn across the island's surface. "There's other stuff here, too. Sausage and peppers, eggplant. Some salad."

And it looks completely normal. My stomach is growling, my mouth is watering, and I wish I could enjoy this wholeheartedly. "Thanks for thinking of me," I murmur sarcastically as I take a seat, grabbing for plastic utensils and napkins.

"We're assholes, but we're not complete assholes," Colt assures me. I cut into my chicken, keeping my eyes lowered. We clearly have very different ideas about that.

"So you were saying earlier that you want to be a teacher?"

I glance up at him and nod, swallowing. Is that really how we're going to do this? Simply make small talk like nothing ever happened? When Colt keeps staring at me, expecting an answer, I decide to play along. "Yeah, that's the idea."

"Do you have your classes set up yet for this semester?" Nix asks.

I can't figure out how such seemingly innocent questions could be used against me, but that doesn't mean I'm ready to take any of this at face value. "Yeah, but right now, it's your basic core classes. Math, psychology, stuff like that."

"I'd want to get all that stuff out of the way." Nix spears a sausage link from one of the containers and takes a bite without bothering to cut into it. "I hate math."

Colt snorts, and it almost sounds like he's about to choke on his food. "Maybe Leni should give you some tutoring."

The very thought sends a chill down my spine. "So long as it's elementary or middle school level. When you start getting into trig and calculus, I have a little bit of trouble, too."

"I always hated algebra," Colt grumbles. Nix mutters his agreement.

Is this really happening? It's almost like we're three people having a normal conversation.

"Elementary education is sort of generalized, but if I had to pick a focus, I think I'd want to be a history teacher," I decide after taking another big bite of the chicken. It's delicious, cooked perfectly, and the pasta is al dente. Sometimes, I don't like pasta from takeout restaurants since it can be overcooked and watery, but this is delicious. I'm glad I came down now.

"History is just, like, memorizing stuff. Dates and whatnot."

"It can be," I agree, nodding to Nix. "But I like being able to piece events together. Like this war happened because of this and that from a hundred years earlier. When you look at it that way, it's actually really fascinating. Getting a feel of the big picture. I'm sure kings were out there making decisions they couldn't imagine would lead their country to war in a hundred years, you know?"

"What did they care? They'd be dead by then, anyway." Nix always has a way of cutting to the heart of something.

"That's true." Just like how in a hundred years, nobody is going to care that I've been repeatedly hurt and humiliated. My food doesn't taste so great all of a sudden, but I know that's just my thoughts coloring my feelings. I need to stop thinking that way. I wish I could enjoy simple things like this without always being afraid.

"So what did you guys do today?" If they are in a friendly mood, I might be able to squeeze some useful information out to use against them later. "You said you had things to get done."

"Oh, you know. Errands, stuff like that. We went to the gym." The way Nix stresses that last word tells me he's still bitter over me refusing the job.

"Am I really going to have to start working there again once our parents are back?"

"We were only trying to do you a favor," Colt insists.

"And that's really nice, but I felt like I was getting paid to do nothing. I want to feel like I'm actually earning my money."

"Do you ever get tired of trying to do the right thing all the time?" Nix grumbles. I'm actually glad he did it, even if Colt shoots him a dirty look. I need to remember who I'm dealing with here. They might want to call a temporary truce, but that doesn't change anything in the long term.

"No, I actually don't. Maybe you should try to do the right thing sometimes."

"Meh." Nix shrugs. "Maybe you should try to be bad."

Ignoring his comment, I turn my head back to Colt.

Plus," I continue, "it's good experience for me to work with kids. I can learn how to identify what their needs are. Not everybody learns the same way. It's probably much better practice, figuring that out now than waiting until I'm in front of a classroom of twenty or thirty kids."

"Like getting thrown in the deep end," Colt muses, nodding slowly. "That doesn't help the kids who really need it."

"That's right. That's exactly it." I'm almost pitifully relieved that he agrees with me, that he gets it. This food is delicious, but what I really need to sustain me is being understood, being seen. That's what I'm starving for. Colt is probably playing on that, knowing the kind of predator he is. He finds a weakness and preys on it.

"It's been a long time since I had something that good," I admit, desperate to change the subject.

"That doesn't surprise me. No offense, but your mom isn't the best cook. I mean, she tries." Nix grimaces, and the three of us chuckle together.

"We really didn't have much to work with for a long time," I remind them, even though he's absolutely right. But I do feel like somebody should defend her, at least in front of them. If I was talking to a friend, my response might be different. "And she only wanted to impress you guys, I'm sure. She went a little overboard."

"She didn't have to waste her energy." I can't tell if that means it wouldn't have mattered either way because she was never going to impress them or that she didn't need to try so hard because they like her. I'm going to go with the first one since I find it hard to believe these two could like anybody. I doubt anyone could ever live up to their expectations.

"I hope you didn't fill up too much for dessert because we got cannoli. Their cannoli is excellent." Nix gets up and goes to the refrigerator, where a small box sits. He takes it out and opens it, leaving it in front of me. They really do look good.

"What the hell? You only live once, right?" I take one and sink my teeth into the sweet cream and crispy shell. "Oh, yeah. This is great." I set it aside after a few more bites, figuring I can eat it later while I'm reading. Though, right now, I feel kind of tired. It must be all the stress I've been under. Maybe I'll call it early tonight and try to get some sleep. I'm sure all the pasta I just inhaled isn't helping.

When the doorbell rings, my head swings back and forth between them. "Are you expecting anybody?" I ask, already halfway off the stool.

"Oh, yeah. We invited some people over."

My feet hit the floor—soon followed by my knees. I grab for the counter to try to hold myself up, but my legs are like jelly. "What the hell?" I whisper, looking down at my useless legs. They seem too far away for some reason. And why is the room spinning?

Colt walks past me without so much as a glance, and before long, I hear a lot of voices overlapping. Excited voices, laughter.

Someone crouches in front of me. My head falls back when I try to look up at them, and through my blurry vision, I see Nix grinning. "You didn't think it would be that easy, did you?" he asks, shaking his head. "You're so fucking gullible. Like we give a shit about what you're doing in school. Please."

I can barely keep my eyes open. "I don't understand..."

"Yeah, that's pretty obvious. But don't worry. You'll be out cold during our party, so we won't disturb you." He laughs when I try and fail to speak. "You were right about one thing, though. You made a pig of yourself. I didn't think you'd eat the whole container, or I wouldn't have put so much in your food."

So much of what? I can't ask, my tongue thick and useless. What did they give me? Why did I trust them?

Colt reappears, followed by a handful of guys I vaguely recognize from school. They were on the football team, weren't they? And they're carrying cases of beer and paper bags full of bottles that jangle together. "You're not going to get in the way tonight," Colt says as his friends spread out around the kitchen.

All I can do is close my eyes and give up, letting the darkness overtake me. It's not like I have a choice.

CHAPTER 21

*O*h my god.

I'm afraid to move. I don't want to open my eyes. I don't even want to turn my head from one side to the other on my pillow.

I'm pretty sure I got run over by a truck at some point. There's no other explanation I can come up with for how absolutely awful I feel. I should go back to sleep—I must have picked up something, a bug, maybe. That would explain why it feels like I'm dying right now. Even trying to roll over in bed makes my stomach churn, and my head threatens to explode.

What the hell happened last night? I feel like something did, something I should remember, but I can't come up with anything. Not that I'm trying too hard to think. Concentrating is too much work. Everything is too much work. Maybe I really am sick. Or maybe there was something wrong with my food.

Shit. My food.

Now I understand everything, and it doesn't do much to

make me feel better. No, I feel even worse because I realize now that I was unconscious during a party full of football players.

And my stepbrothers, who I highly doubt would stop anybody from doing anything awful to me.

With my eyes closed, I run a hand over myself under the blanket. I'm fully dressed, thank god. It doesn't mean they couldn't have put my clothes back on me, but it does seem like a lot of trouble. And besides, I'm starting to understand how these two think. They'd much rather I wake up naked, asking a hundred questions, ready to die of shame.

What was it they were saying to me before I passed out? How they wanted to keep me out of the way? I think that's what Colt said—and maybe that's all it was. They wanted me drugged, unconscious, unable to ruin their good time or to tell anybody else about it after the fact, which is probably more along the lines of what they were actually concerned about. I doubt they're allowed to have parties here when their father is out of town. Maybe he told them not to. They probably figured I would rat them out. As if I get a flying fuck about what they do as long as it doens't involve me.

Fuck. What if this did involve me?

Before I know it, my mind is conjuring up the worst possible scenario. Did Colt and Nix do something else to me? Or did they let their friends do something to me? Like I wasn't already nauseous enough just from being conscious. Maybe they only like recording terrible things they do to people, not the things they let their friends do. I can hope, anyway. If there's a video out there somewhere of me having stuff done to me while I'm unconscious, I don't think I could live through it. I really don't.

But everything feels okay down there, too. I'm not sore the way I was the day after Colt took advantage of me.

The rest of me seems to be in good shape. Aside from my head feeling like it will fall off and roll across the floor if I try to get up, plus my shaky stomach. But the rest of me seems fine. I should probably try to go back to sleep.

I might be able to if it wasn't for the nagging sense that I'm forgetting something, overlooking something. I can't imagine what it could be.

Whatever it is, it's enough to keep me from settling back into sleep. Instead, I pry one eye open just far enough to find a bottle of ibuprofen and a glass of water on my nightstand. It looks like one of them felt guilty enough that they left me something to help me get through the worst of it. I reach out and struggle my way through opening the bottle with my eyes closed, then shake out a couple of tablets before washing them down with the tiniest bit of water. I don't trust my stomach enough to drink more than that.

Why do they have to be such assholes? Why do they have to do this to me? I wouldn't have bothered them. I wouldn't have stepped foot out of this room—and considering there were a bunch of football players downstairs, I would have wedged my chair under the doorknob, and that would have been it. I don't know where they got this idea about me that I'm always looking for ways to ruin their lives. All they've done so far is ruin mine every chance they get.

It isn't until I roll onto my back after struggling through the simple act of taking painkillers that I feel something strange. Something that shouldn't be there. A stinging sensation like a bug bite or something under my clothes. My lower back—no, closer to my butt cheek. What the hell? Every time I try to move, it only feels more irritating. I guess I shouldn't go back to sleep until I figure out what it is. I'd probably be more comfortable in actual pajamas, too, not the jeans I slept in all night. It means prying my eyes open again and being assaulted by sunlight.

"Good morning, sunshine."

I almost jump straight up out of bed at the sound of Nix's voice. "I thought you would never wake up."

I slowly raise myself into a sitting position, eyeing him warily. He's sitting in my desk chair, legs spread wide, hands folded over his stomach. "What did you do to me?" I whisper.

"You don't remember? I guess it sort of wiped out your memory a little bit, huh?" Oh, he is so smug, so proud of himself. This is all a big joke to him. I don't have it in me to scream the way I want or call him half the names running through my pounding head.

"What did you give me?"

"A mild sedative. No big deal. But like I said last night, I didn't think you'd eat the whole damn meal. I guess that's why you hit the ground so fast."

"How fucked up do you have to be to think that's an acceptable thing to do to somebody?"

"Hey, no harm done. You'll feel better in a few hours, and I bet you got a good night's sleep."

"Go to hell."

"Whatever you say." He stands, grabbing something off my desk I've never seen before and tossing it onto the bed. "Anyway, before I go to hell the way you think I should, I figured I would give you this. You want to take care of that—keep it clean so it doesn't get infected. And use this on it."

I can barely even focus my eyes, much less read what's on the bottle he dropped on the bed. "What are you talking about?" Even saying those few words is enough to exhaust me. He needs to leave the room so I can lie back down. I don't trust him enough to do it now, but he's still standing here.

"It's lotion. For aftercare."

"Aftercare for what, though?"

He tilts his head to the side, smirking. "You mean you really don't remember? I thought for sure. Don't you feel it?"

Dread begins tickling the back of my mind, spreading its way through my brain. "Remember what? Feel what?"

"The tattoo you wanted. You asked for it and everything."

"Just stop fucking with me, please? That's all I want."

"You think I'm fucking with you? You'll feel differently once you look in the mirror. It's pretty nice work, actually. I'm almost jealous."

A tattoo? No way would I ever ask for a tattoo—and I wasn't even conscious. He's just trying to scare me. I'm not going to make it that easy.

On the other hand... Wasn't that the whole reason I was going to get up in the first place? The feeling that something was wrong, something I needed to check out?

I forget about the way my head feels, tumbling out of bed and stumbling toward the bathroom. No way. They wouldn't do this to me. I go in and close the door, then lower my jeans and turn around.

Tears spring to my eyes at the sight of it. A small heart over my left butt cheek, low enough that it's hidden by my clothes but most definitely there. I squint my eyes and move closer to the mirror. Even though it's backward, the word is clear. Alistair. They had their last name tattooed on my ass.

Frantic, I rub at it, but it only hurts, and the ink doesn't move. It's a real tattoo, not something they drew on in pen to mess with me. A helpless, hopeless little whimper works its way from my throat. I can't believe this. Just when I think I've seen it all from them, they go and remind me how much worse things could be.

"You asshole." I fling the bathroom door open, buttoning my jeans, prepared to give him hell. But he's already gone—and, big surprise, he locked the door. I pound my fist against it as loud as my poor head will let me, but there's no sound from the other side. Not even laughter.

Fuck this. I am sick to death of the way they're treating me. I have a little money in the bank now—I need to go somewhere, anywhere. It'll mean digging into my savings, but that's still better than being stuck here with them, afraid to leave my room even when they decide to unlock the door.

A plan is already forming in my head by the time I sit down to put on my sneakers. I can't get out through the door? Fine. The window will do. I didn't spend all those years training to not be able to climb out a window and make it to the ground safely. Sure, I'm on the second floor, but a downspout runs alongside one of the windows, and I can shimmy down.

I open the window and lean out, testing it. It's firmly attached to the side of the house. I grab my phone and tuck it into my back pocket before sitting on the windowsill, swiveling my body and ducking my head and shoulders out. It's a little scary at first, especially since I'm still shaky from whatever drugs they gave me, but muscle memory is an amazing thing. I reach out with my right hand and foot and grab the metal tube, finding the closest bracket used to hold the spout in place. It's attached to the wall and doesn't budge when I put weight on it, so I brace my foot against it before swinging out the rest of the way and gripping the pipe like my life depends on it. Now that I'm out, it's easy to climb down, almost like a ladder, my feet finding the rings screwed into the wall as I lower myself closer and closer to the ground. Finally, I hop the rest of the way down and wipe my hands on my jeans. No sweat.

Next step: getting an Uber out of here. I pull up the app on my phone, careful to duck under any windows I pass while walking alongside the house. I didn't go to all that trouble for Colt or Nix to see me out here. Either I'm good at sneaking around, or they're not paying attention. Either way, I make it to the driveway with no trouble and start walking down, glad to have the house behind me.

I don't know what's going to happen. All that matters right now is putting distance between us. I never thought they would do anything that cruel. What am I supposed to do with a tattoo on my ass?

It's the sound of an approaching car that catches my attention first. My head snaps up from the phone. No. It's impossible. I can't be seeing this.

The car pulls to a stop in front of me, and the driver's side window rolls down. "What are you doing out here?" James asks once he sticks his head out from inside.

No. No, no. I had over a week. Why is he here? "I was taking a walk," I lie, closing the app.

"Well, surprise. I'm home early." The way he smiles is the way he used to, back when he was pretending to be a normal person. It's even more chilling than if he flat-out acted like a psycho.

"And Mom?" I ask since I don't see anybody in the passenger seat.

"She's still at the resort. It's all paid up after all, and it's not her fault I had to come back early for an important call that came up out of nowhere." He lifts a shoulder, chuckling. "Some people, right? No respect for a man's honeymoon."

He's back. Alone. Not that I would trust my mother to protect me, but I figured there'd be less chance of him hurting me while she was here. He'd want to keep up appearances, right?

"I know the guys will be happy to see you. I'll be back in a little bit." Nothing in the world has ever been more important than getting away from him, from this house, from all of it.

"No. You're not going to do that." The smile is gone and replaced by a scowl. "You're going back to the house, and that's where you're staying. Right now. I'll follow you the rest of the way up." He rolls the window up but doesn't move the car, staring at me from behind the wheel. Like he's challenging me to go against him.

There isn't just one red flag waving in front of my eyes right now. There are about a hundred. So many red flags that it's basically all I can see. *Red*.

I can't believe this. I can't believe I have to turn around and walk up the driveway, but what else am I supposed to do? My feet are heavy but nowhere as heavy as my heart. I could try to run past him, down the driveway, and toward the road. If I'm lucky, I'll get to wave someone down before he catches me.

James taps against the glass, pointing toward the house. I give him a tight smile before turning toward the direction he wants me to take, only to spin around all the way before sprinting down the driveway toward the road.

My feet pound against the pavement as I run like my life depends on it. Pushing my legs as fast as I can go, I race toward freedom while the sound of the engine revving up behind me breathes new panic into me. My lungs burn, and my muscles ache, but none of that stops me from forcing my body to keep running.

Unfortunately, it's not enough.

Before I ever reach the driveway, James's car speeds past me, just to come to a sudden halt in front of me. The car is barely in park when the door pops open, and an angry James heads toward me. I dig my heels into the ground and stop a few feet in front of him.

"I'm going to pretend you didn't just try to run from me," he sneers. "Don't be stupid, Leni. I'm trying to be nice here, but if you behave like a brat, I will treat you like one." Just like in the hallway, his voice has no amount of humanity. It's almost like he has a split personality. I don't have to be an expert to know that this side of James is dangerous, unpredictable, and utterly terrifying.

I thought things were bad with my stepbrothers, but something tells me the worst of it has yet to come. For everything the guys have done to me, I'm still more scared of James.

I was too blind to see it before, but now I'm certain James is the biggest monster of all.

CHAPTER 22

"*H*ello! Where is the rest of my family?" James's lighthearted question echoes through the house, bringing to mind nothing more than a sense of doom. At least to me. He walks past me down the hall, and for a second, I think I can run upstairs to my room. That idea dies a quick death for two reasons. One, I imagine the door is still locked, so I won't be able to get in.

Two, James notices I'm not following him and turns, giving me one of those wide smiles I now know hides something very dark. He's even darker than his sons. "Come on. I would like to have the three of you together."

I don't even know what that means, exactly, but there's an undercurrent in his voice that tells me it can't be anything good. He's loving this, that much is clear, smiling brilliantly as he strolls into the kitchen where his sons are making protein shakes in the blender.

I reach the room only a moment after James. If the guys were surprised, I would see it on their faces. They aren't. Did they know he was coming back so soon? Or do they know better than to put anything past him by now?

They don't even look surprised that I'm down here with them. I'd expect a question about how I managed to get out of my room, but I get nothing. There doesn't seem to be any confusion over where Mom is, either. As a matter of fact, I'm the only person confused.

"How was the trip?" Colt asks while Nix pours the shakes into two bottles. I guess they're on their way to the gym. For the first time ever, I actually want to go with them. I'll clean the bathrooms if I have to. Whatever they need.

"It was fine. Amanda stayed behind. You know me, there's no getting away from work."

"We'll stay out of your way," Colt murmurs. He won't look at me. Neither of them will look at me.

"I was thinking just the opposite," James offers in the same jovial way.

Nix shares a glance with Colt. "What do you mean?"

"I wanted to take the opportunity to spend the day with my kids. Including Leni, of course." He shines his smile on me, and my skin crawls like I just touched something slimy.

I finally find my voice. "I have work scheduled. I've been tutoring kids online and—"

"You can reschedule. Believe me, if a man in my position can reschedule a call, you can reschedule a tutoring session with some kid."

"Didn't you say you came home early because of a call?" I blurt out.

That might've been a mistake. The boys stiffen, and James's smile slips a little. "I can do what I want." It's the flat determination in his voice that makes me shudder. I wonder what else he's talking about. What else does he want? What else is he going to do? Because he is definitely not talking about work.

He blinks rapidly and seems to shake himself. "Why don't we watch a movie? We haven't used the movie room in much too long. It just sits there, ignored."

"I didn't know there was a movie room," I whisper, looking at the guys for understanding and getting nothing.

James throws his hands in the air. "See? That's what I mean. I spent all that money getting things put together, and we hardly ever use it. That ends today. I declare this Family Day." He gestures to his sons, waving a hand back and forth between them. "Pop some popcorn. Grab some drinks. I would love chips and dip if we have any."

Then he turns to me. "Come on. Let me show you the room. It's down in the basement." I wasn't even aware the house had a basement. How much don't I know yet? How much is he going to show me?

"I can help the guys with the snacks," I offer, once again looking at the guys. Yes, I don't like or trust either of them, but I'd rather be with them than alone with James. Colt actually looks like he is about to agree with me, but James is on top of it.

"No." His voice is stern, leaving no room for an argument. He only says one word, two letters, yet the tone of his voice and an evil glint in his eyes make the threat very clear. If I don't come, things will be worse.

I don't want to go, but I don't feel like I have a choice. Either I follow him and keep him happy or things get really bad. I don't ever want to go through that again.

He steps up to the wall running beneath the staircase and

presses a hand against it, seemingly at random. Like magic, a door springs open. I had no idea it was there. It blends into the wall that well. He makes a grand sweeping gesture with his arm, so I step through the door and walk down the stairs.

"You know, Leni, I was hoping the two of us could have a minute alone together. I've done a lot of thinking about the way we left things."

We? The way we left things? So it was my fault? I almost stumble but quickly regain my balance.

"I'm sorry for losing my cool before I left for the honeymoon."

My hand tightens around the banister mounted to the wall as the memories come rushing back. He's even wearing the same cologne. It's amazing the things a person remembers.

"I didn't mean to scare you. You just took me by surprise, and I panicked a little. That's not going to happen again. I promise."

We reach the bottom of the stairs, and I offer a tight smile because what else can I do. Tell him I know he's full of shit? Because he is. You can't get more textbook than that. *I didn't mean it. It will never happen again.* I don't have many years under my belt, but even I know enough to see straight through him. A person doesn't act that way out of nowhere, and it certainly wasn't the first time he's ever hurt a woman. I would bet my life on it.

Unfortunately, I'm afraid that's exactly what's at stake here.

We're standing in a fully finished basement, and even with my growing dread threatening to choke me, I can't help but be impressed with the setup. "I had no idea this was here," I murmur, looking around, pretending to study everything when really, all I want to do is keep from looking at him. Unfortunately, it doesn't mean I can avoid the weight of his stare. He watches my every move, and I can't help but wish I had escaped only a few minutes sooner. I could have gotten away before he reached home.

One thing is for sure: he spent a lot of money down here. Large couches are arranged in a U-shape with reclining seats and cup holders between them like in a movie theater. If this were any other situation, I might even look forward to curling up on one of them under a blanket to watch a favorite movie on the enormous TV that spans most of the wall. Speakers are set up in the corners by the ceiling. "You could charge money to show movies down here," I offer with a faint smile.

"You're probably right. Now, we can enjoy it as a family, the way it was always intended." He fiddles with the Blu-ray player in a cabinet under the TV. What am I going to do here? I guess there's no choice but to sit and watch the movie, keep to myself as much as I can, and pray it's over soon. Just being in the same room with him brings back all those terrible, panicky feelings, the fear, the certainty that I was about to die. My chest is so tight it takes a conscious effort to breathe. Am I going to have to spend the next hour and a half like this?

All things considered, that might be the best possible outcome. I'll be lucky if all I have to struggle through is discomfort and fear.

"I even got a chick flick with you in mind." He steps back from the Blu-ray player, wearing a look of satisfaction. "*Fifty Shades of Grey.*"

My stomach drops, and a cold, sick sweat begins to rise along the back of my neck and my temples. Not exactly the kind of movie I want to watch with him, much less his sons.

Footsteps on the stairs make my heart lurch, and a moment later, I find my stepbrothers coming down to join us. Along with them comes the aroma of popcorn, something I usually enjoy. Now? There's no way I'm going to touch it. Who knows what they've put in it? What seemed like a sick, childish prank last night now has a much more sinister feel to it. I can't trust a single person in this basement.

"Come on. Let's all sit down and get settled in. I haven't had the chance to see this one yet, but I've heard it's pretty good." I drag myself over to the sofa facing the TV and sit in the corner, making myself as small as possible. At least James doesn't try to sit close to me, so that's a relief. He's on the other end of the sofa while Nix sits to my left and Colt to my right on sofas of their own. In the center is a big coffee table now covered with popcorn, chips, dip, and sodas. I tried to catch Colt's eye, but he either doesn't notice or refuses to look at me.

James picks up the remote and starts the movie, and the best I can do is stare at the screen and wait for it to be over. I've never seen it, either, but I know enough about the series to know this is not the kind of material I want to be watching in this company. It would be bad enough if this were any normal family, but there is nothing normal about these people.

As soon as we get to the first sex scene, my cheeks go deep red. I stay as still and silent as possible, eyes focused squarely on the screen. I'm afraid of what I'll find if I look around. One of my stepbrothers leering at me, thinking about how they've used me? Or so much worse—my stepfather looking at me that way? God, anything but that. No matter how I look at the situation, it's a perverted nightmare.

Somebody starts breathing a little heavily as the action picks up, and I wish I could crawl out of my very skin. It's so embarrassing. At least I know it will have to come to an end eventually, and then I'm going to beg off with the excuse of work again. The man has to have at least a grain of sense—how could he have gotten so far in his law firm if he didn't? I can't disappoint my clients. Maybe I'll add something about wanting to build a big business the way he has. Soften him up a little bit. I'm so desperate that I would resort to heavy-handed flattery if it means getting away from this situation.

Nobody says a word for the most part except to ask for the popcorn bowl or a napkin. This changes around the time the end credits begin rolling, and I'm gathering my courage to make an excuse and flee this room. James finishes his soda and leaves the empty bottle on the table before sitting back and sighing. "You know, I've been giving a lot of thought to that video you told me about, Leni. The one of you servicing Nix on your knees."

Oh my god. Adrenaline starts pumping through my system as panic sprints through me all at once. What's he trying to do? Get me killed?

No. As it turns out, what he wants is much worse than that.

"I've been thinking that I would like to see it." He turns his body toward mine, staring at me through half-lidded eyes. "In real-time. Now. In front of me."

My body freezes in shock and horror. It's not possible. This can't be happening. I'm stuck in some ugly nightmare. I have to be. This can't be real life. Things like this don't happen in real life. My eyes dart around, landing on Colt and Nix, back and forth. One of them is going to burst out laughing any second now. Then all of them will start laughing. They'll tell me this was all a joke, a way of humiliating me a little further. I wouldn't even be upset. I just want this to be a joke.

Instead, Nix nods. "Fine."

"Yeah, sure." Colt still won't look at me, but he nods.

No way. No freaking way.

There's deep satisfaction in James's voice. "Good. I would hate to have come home early for no reason."

CHAPTER 23

*C*olt stands, waiting in front of me. If anybody wants to start laughing, now would be the time to do it. I'm still waiting, still hoping, even though every passing moment makes it less likely that I'm getting out of this.

"Get up." His voice is flat, like he's left every ounce of humanity behind. He takes me by the arm when I don't move fast enough and hauls me to my feet. I'm expecting somebody to yell gotcha and laugh at me. Why aren't they laughing?

James unbuckles his belt and takes his time about sliding it free before handing it to Nix, who stands behind me and takes my wrists in one hand. I guess I'm too deep in shock to try to fight. All I can do is stand still, frozen in terror, disgust, and disbelief. This is actually happening. They are really going to go through with this, aren't they? Nix cinches the belt tight enough that I grit my teeth against a pained gasp.

"On your knees." Nix doesn't wait for me to move. His hands are on my shoulders, shoving me down onto my knees. The sound of Colt's zipper being lowered catches my attention, and from the corner of my eye, I see him taking himself out of his shorts. He sits down, and Nix sits beside him, also freeing himself.

But it's James's zipper that makes my blood run cold, the thought of him being part of this. Bile rushes up and fills my throat, and I'm afraid I'm about to throw up all over myself. Maybe if I do, they won't make me go through with this. It's almost tempting enough to make me let loose—though I might end up being punished for that in some humiliating way. Which would be worse?

"Come on, now," James murmurs. "Give me a good show. Be a good girl and suck those cocks, and maybe I won't have to fuck your face myself."

Oh no. Not that. Anything but that. I'd rather go through with this than give him an excuse to do that. There's not so much as a sliver of sympathy in the eyes of either of my stepbrothers, both of them stroking themselves in front of me.

"Get to work," James mutters. I don't dare glance his way. I don't want to see what he's doing. I would rather pretend he isn't here.

Nobody would believe this if I tried to tell them. I know that for sure. Because this is unimaginable.

I'm sure nobody would believe I was unconscious when I got their name tattooed on my ass, either. No, they've set me up beautifully, haven't they? I'm completely under their control now. And it looks like I have a job to do, or else the nightmare is only going to get worse.

I shuffle forward on my knees and position myself between Colt's spread thighs. He's closest to me, so I might as well take care of him first.

There are tears in my eyes as I lean down, catching the tip of his dick with my tongue. He sighs softly, still stroking, directing himself to my mouth. Feeding himself to me. I lift my eyes and meet his gaze for the first time since this started, but there's no reading what's going on behind those eyes. His expression is blank and detached. If I didn't know any better, I'd say he doesn't want to be here. But he is certainly hard enough—which means this can't bother him too much, if at all.

"Get to it," James grunts. "Suck that cock. Show me how much you love it."

I open my mouth a little and take him inside, lowering my head until my lips touch the base of his shaft. Colt sinks a hand into my hair, groaning as I lift my head before plunging down again. I just have to get through this, that's all. I can't think about it. I just have to do it and get it over with.

"That's right. Take it all," James grunts. His breathing is already starting to quicken as he jerks off to the sight of me going down on his son.

I increase the pressure from my tongue, hoping it will get this over with faster, but Colt pulls my hair a little in response. "Slow down. Not so hard." So much for that.

"She's eager," James observes with approval in his voice. "She can't wait to drink your cum. Give it to her."

Oh god. I want to die.

"That's right," Colt whispers, moving his hips in time with my movements. "That's nice. Suck it."

"Don't be so fucking greedy." Nix takes me by the throat and lifts me away from Colt, pulling me closer to his own hard, dripping dick. "Remind me how good you are. Don't act like you didn't like it the first time."

I do as he says, totally detached now, forcing myself through the motions of bobbing up and down, swallowing back my saliva, doing everything I can to ignore the grunts and groans and the way James mutters his approval while he watches.

I don't know how long it takes, going back and forth between them, letting them use me. I only know it's a relief when Colt clamps down on the back of my head and starts jerking his hips, fucking my face—not brutally, but forcefully enough that tears roll down my cheeks. I brace myself for what I know is going to come, and it's almost a mercy when it does, when he explodes and shoots his load down my throat. I swallow it as fast as I can, struggling to keep up but managing to catch it all before he slides out of my mouth with a sigh.

"Good, very good," James whispers, breathing fast. "Finish Nix. Make him come like a good little girl."

Nix wastes no time thrusting into my mouth. I want to pull back. I want to push away from him but can't with my hands behind me. All I can do is try to brace myself on my knees while he takes me hard and fast, fucking my face with no consideration, no care about anything but his satisfaction. All I can do is fight to hold on, fight to keep from choking on him as he hits the back of my throat again and again.

James's strained breathing fills the room. "That's right. Fuck her face. Make her feel it." Tears roll down my cheeks, and a strangled sob stirs in my throat, but he seems to like that, too, groaning louder than before.

"You ready for me?" Nix pants, and I barely have time to register the question before he shoves me down hard, grinding my nose against his base and cutting off my air an instant before filling my mouth and throat with cum. There's so much going on at once that I can barely keep track—I can't breathe. I'm choking. I'm gagging. I'm going to throw up. *He won't let me breathe!* My muffled, panicked groans make James breathe harder than ever, and I can hear him grunting in the final moments before he comes, too, with a growl that echoes in my ears, even over the sound of my pounding heart.

It's a relief when Nix lets me up for air. I'm still choking and gasping, but I did it. I made it through. And now it's over, thank god. And I want more than anything to stand in the shower for the rest of the day, even though I know it will do nothing to erase the filth all over me.

James groans before chuckling, patting me on the head like an obedient dog. "Good girl. You made Daddy very happy."

Without saying another word, James stands, whistling softly as he walks up the stairs. I slump a little, my head hanging low, my shoulders heaving as I fight to regain my breath. I barely register the guys getting up and walking around me. One of them releases my wrists before running their fingers over the tender skin where the belt cut into it. I don't know which one because I don't want to turn around. I don't want confirmation that we just shared this experience.

We stay this way for a moment, silent until finally, I whisper, "Let me go. Please. Let me walk out of here. I will never come back. I swear I won't tell anybody about this because I just want to forget it. You can't force me to stay here and do this. You want to be rid of me? Here's your chance. Let me go."

When they don't shoot me down right away, a glimmer of hope sparkles in my chest. Maybe they'll actually listen. Maybe they'll actually give me what I'm asking for.

Who am I kidding?

"It's too late for that now," Colt informs me in a flat voice. "This will be easier if you do what we want."

"You're not going anywhere," Nix confirms.

How can they do this? How can they stand here on either side of me and say this without even sounding sorry? There's nothing normal about any of this, not a single thing, but the way they make it sound, it's inevitable. Like it was always going to be this way, and I'm only finding out about it now. Is this how it always is around here? What the hell has my mother got me into? And would she even believe me if I tried to tell her?

My heart aches when I consider that question, mostly because I already know the answer. Unless she were to see it with her own eyes, she would never believe this because she wouldn't want to. Who would? No, this is it. This is my life now, and I have no say over it at all. All I will ever be able to do is dread the next time it happens and hope I can get through it. That's all. That's as much as I can look forward to now.

Nix takes me by the arm and pulls me to my feet. "I'll take you to your room." Sure, because I'll have to stay in my cell, won't I? Unless I'm wanted. My chin quivers, but I won't give them the satisfaction of crying in front of them. I'll wait until I'm alone, in my room, and then I'll let it out. But not now.

Between the way I was already feeling after last night and the events of the past couple of hours, I'm almost limp with exhaustion. Wiped out, body and soul. My feet are heavy as I climb the stairs to the first floor, then again as we continue up to my room. Nix doesn't say a word, walking silently beside me, then escorting me down the hall. It isn't until we're halfway to my room that I notice a high-pitched, squealing sort of noise. I identify it as a drill a moment before coming to my open bedroom door and finding James attaching screws to my windows.

He holds the drill in his hand as he turns, wearing an easy smile. "Can't keep you too safe, can we?" He doesn't wait for an answer, instead fixing the last screw in place. He tests the window and nods, satisfied. "There. All done. Wouldn't want you falling out of the window one night, would we?"

I don't even care. I can't muster up the energy to think, much less look toward a future where I'm locked in this room with no chance of getting out unless one of them decides they want to play. At least he leaves the room, but Nix stays, following me to my bed. I crawl in, not even bothering to get changed before curling into a ball.

I close my eyes and stay very still, but Nix remains where he is. Jesus, what is he thinking? He's not going to...

He leans down, and I flinch, squeezing my eyes more tightly shut, unable to suppress a whimper. I turn my face toward the pillow so he can't kiss me, but he doesn't try. "He doesn't have a key," he whispers before straightening up, and a moment later, the sound of the door locking tells me he's gone. I'm alone.

At least I don't have to fight back the tears anymore.

CHAPTER 24

J'm trapped. No matter how I look at this, no matter how many different angles I try to approach it from, I'm trapped. There's no other word for it.

I can't get away on foot, that's for sure. They won't even let me out of this room unless they want to, and I doubt I'll be left alone at any point. Now we all have a secret we share, and they're going to want to make sure I don't tell the wrong person. I can't tell anybody. All I have ahead of me is a string of days behind a locked door, being used, being hurt.

How am I supposed to accept that?

What's the alternative? I know it will only get worse if I try to fight back. I can't do this on my own. I can't get away on my own.

And who would help me if I asked for it? Not Mom, I know that much. She would never believe me, even if she gave me the chance to tell her what's happening, which I doubt she would do in the first place. She wouldn't want anything to disturb her perfect little life that she finally managed to score for herself. I would only ruin things, which would make her hate me even more. I'm not going to kid myself into thinking she would be on my side.

It's close to dawn when an idea forms in my head. It's my only shot. There's only one other person in the world who gives a damn about me. And even then, my grandmother is hardly more interested in me than Mom, but at least she doesn't actively dismiss or ignore my problems. She's all I have to rely on. She's my only shot here.

Waiting until morning is torture, but I don't want to call her in the middle of the night and freak her out even worse than I'm sure I already will. As much as I hate waiting, it gives me time to think about exactly what I want to say. I need to make her believe me. I need to drive home the point that she needs to come and get me immediately. Because this will only get worse.

Finally, around seven o'clock, I can't wait any longer. This is around the time she normally wakes up. At least, it was while I was there a few weeks ago. How has it only been a few weeks? I'm a different person now.

I dial her number and cross my fingers. *Please, please, believe me. You have to believe me.*

"Hello?" She sounds put out, but at least she answered. I could cry from relief already.

"Grandma? It's Leni. I'm in trouble and need your help. It's urgent."

"Lenora? Slow down. You're talking too fast. What are you saying?"

"I'm in trouble," I repeat in a whisper. "Please come. I need your help."

"What kind of trouble? Where are you?"

"I'm at home, the new house. Mom is still away. Something

really bad happened, and I can't stay here anymore. Please, please, come and get me. I'll give you the address. But I can't get out on my own."

"You're speaking too quietly. I can barely hear you. What's happening?"

"I can't get into details, but..."

Three short beeps signal the call ending. I pull the phone from my ear, cursing softly, prepared to call her back. How could she hang up on me?

As it turns out, she didn't hang up on me. I no longer have a signal. I don't have Wi-Fi, either. I turn the phone off, then turn it on again, but that doesn't change anything. I might as well be holding a toy in my hand. It's useless.

What is this? What's happening? No way did the bill go unpaid since my account is connected to Mom's, and she would never let her cell phone get cut off. What, then? Of all the times for something like this to happen. Hopeless rage bubbles in my chest until I have to press my face to a pillow and scream or else risk shattering into a million pieces.

The unlocking of the door startles me. I assumed everybody was still in bed, but it's only Colt. Since when am I relieved at the sight of him? Oh right, since his father got home. Nothing in his expression reveals anything of what happened yesterday. There's no acknowledgment in his glance, no embarrassment or guilt. "Dad wants to talk downstairs."

I frantically blink back the tears that spring to my eyes before following him out of the room and down the hall. I was hoping I wouldn't have to look at him today. At least, not this early. What will it be this time? How will he humiliate me this morning? How will he use me? I might as well be on my way to my execution. Part of me wishes I was.

James and Nix are already sitting at the dining room table, though there isn't any food laid out. I take a seat at the far end, as far away from James as I can get, and he doesn't seem to care. He, too, looks just the same as ever and sounds just the same. Like nothing truly evil took place yesterday.

"That wasn't very nice of you," he murmurs, folding his hands on top of the table. "Calling your grandmother."

How the hell does he know I did that? What, is he tracking my phone somehow? I don't even know how it's possible, but it has to be, or else how would he know? I was speaking so softly that Grandma couldn't hear me. How could he? This is a wealthy, powerful man. For all I know, he installed something on my phone before the wedding. He might even have done it through our account with the phone company. I don't have the first clue.

"Our business is our business," he continues, speaking over my internal questions. "That means what happens behind these walls stays here. It does not leave this house. Do you understand?"

Do I? I certainly understand why he wouldn't want me telling anybody about what goes on, but that doesn't mean I understand why it's happening. He's waiting for an answer, so all I do is nod, staring down at the tablecloth rather than look at him.

"Have you ever heard of a conservatorship?" he continues. "I have already spoken with your mother on the topic. I would like to apply for one in order to take control of your future going forward."

That surprises me enough that I look up at him. "Wait. I don't understand. What does that mean?"

His indulgent smile turns my stomach. "It's all a bunch of legal mumbo jumbo," he explains, "I wouldn't expect you to understand all of it. Suffice it to say, a conservatorship gives me control over your finances, your educational decisions, everything. Every decision you make would instead be made by me. Where you live. Whether or not you work and where you work. All of your healthcare decisions, as well. All of it would be overseen by me. You would make no decision without my consent."

I would be completely under his control. Why is he doing this? Why me? "You don't have to do that," I whisper. "I'm not unstable or anything like that. I won't do anything harmful to myself. I've never even been in trouble. Why would you—"

"Because I said so, that's why. Because I said that's what I'm going to do, and your mother didn't seem to have any problem with it." No big surprise there. I'm sure she would agree to anything he suggested, so long as she gets to enjoy the privileges of being his wife. Does she know? Does she suspect anything? Even if he showed her who he is, I'm sure she would still deliberately turn a blind eye. Anything, so long as she lives the life she thinks she deserves. She would even hand her daughter over to him. I would put nothing past her.

"You can't do this," I whisper. I know it's probably not true, but it's what I'm thinking. "You can't. Why would you do that?"

"Because I can. I most definitely can. You had a tough few years. It's hard on someone mentally, you know?" I do know, but this? Fuck. "You forget, one of us is a lawyer, and it isn't you. If I need to manufacture a reason, I will, but I don't need to. I would advise you against telling me what I can and can't do, Leni."

"You can't do this." I repeat, but this time my voice is weaker and trails off at the end.

"But cheer up," he continues. "Things don't have to be that bleak. I'm ready to make a deal with you."

"What kind of deal?" This can't be anything good.

And it isn't. "For the next few days, you will do what I want. Everything I want. You will submit to me, be available to me whenever I desire, and you will offer no resistance."

I don't need to ask what sort of submission he's referring to. He's already shown me.

"You do this until your mother returns, and you can go to school." Oh, fuck me, I didn't even consider my education to be in jeopardy here. I didn't imagine he would go that far. I should know better already. "I'll even pay for everything. Your dorm room, fees, books, whatever your scholarship doesn't cover. I'll take care of it. But only if I have your full participation between now and your mother's return."

What do I do? Say no? And what happens to me after that? I don't want to think about it, but I'm pretty sure my future would involve nothing but humiliation, being forced to do whatever he wants, and living under his thumb while he makes every single decision about my life. Where I go, what I do, who I see. I won't even be able to go to the doctor on my own without him having a say in it.

He's got me where he wants me. And the smug bastard knows it, smiling wide, pleased with himself. "What's it going to be?" he prompts when I can't squeeze a single word out of my tightened throat. "It's up to you."

"Okay," I whisper as his face goes blurry, thanks to the tears I can't hold back.

CHAPTER 25

$\mathcal{I}$ might have agreed to James's offer—which really wasn't an offer, more like an ultimatum—but that doesn't mean I get free run of the house. "You were still a bad girl," he reminded me after we finished our little meeting this morning. "Bad girls have to be punished."

That means no phone and no internet. Somehow, he shut that down, too. Whether it's just my machine that's affected or the entire house, I don't know. I find it hard to believe the guys would be okay with having their internet taken away, though.

But if it meant making me feel even more like a prisoner? Maybe they'd put up with it.

Do they have any say once their father decides what he wants? I don't honestly think so. But that's something I can't figure out. I'm not even sure I want to. The whole thing is so twisted I'm afraid I'll start to lose it a little if I give it much more thought. Because James doesn't want to just use my body; he wants something more twisted and sinister than that. He wants to humiliate me, take me apart into small pieces, until I'm nothing but a puppet in his hand. James is the puppetmaster, and his sons are his strings.

They've shown me a level of depravity I didn't know existed until now. I can't help but turn it over in my mind, trying to make sense of it. I think James wants to own my soul, break my mind at the very least.

Now the question is, am I able to cut the strings? They don't exactly seem like excited, enthusiastic participants, but they don't refuse him, either. Are they into this, or is he forcing them the way he forces me? Has he put them through a lifetime full of this sort of depraved sickness, or am I making the mistake of trying to humanize them? Even now, I'm so desperate to think I might have an ally around here I would stoop to thinking of my stepbrothers as unwilling participants. They sure were willing enough when they were coming down my throat, weren't they?

No, facts are facts. They're just as guilty as he is. They probably share some genetic sickness, the three of them.

I have no way to reach out to my new clients and tell them I can't tutor them anymore. Somehow, that brings me more pain than almost anything else about this situation. I was proud of myself. I had a plan laid out. I was going to do this for myself, earn a little independence. There was something I was good at, and people appreciated me for it.

Shouldn't I have known it would be short-lived? Every good thing in my life seems to be. The clicking of the lock leaves me bracing myself. What's it going to be this time?

It's only Colt, holding a plate with a sandwich on it. "I figured you would be hungry. You never did have breakfast."

"You care about that all of a sudden?"

"Yeah—and I don't have to." He leaves the plate on the desk, but I'll be damned if I take a bite.

"You must really think I'm stupid," I mutter, eyeing the food.

"What's that mean?"

"I mean, what's it going to do to me this time? Knock me out? Again?"

He seems to get the message, but that doesn't change anything. "Whatever. Eat it or don't." He lifts his shoulder and turns away like he's about to leave.

I can't let him do it. I have to at least try. "You know, I had a tutoring session scheduled for fifteen minutes from now. I really hate to miss it. Please, I can't lose everything here, you know?"

"Seems to me that isn't my problem."

"Please, Colt. It really means a lot to me." My words fall on deaf ears since he leaves the room without a backward glance. I'm barely able to stifle a whimper as tears fall onto my cheeks. How can they be like this? What happens to a person to make them this way? I never did a damn thing to deserve this— nobody deserves this. I don't care who they are.

It's not another few minutes before the door opens again. He's back.

And he's holding a laptop. "Here. My internet still works. Can you do your work from my computer?"

"Yes! Thank you." It's kind of gross, thanking him after every- thing he's done to me, but I can't afford pride right now.

"Of course, I'm not going to leave you alone. I'll be here the whole time, so don't get any ideas." The sad part is I hadn't even thought about that yet. I'm sure I would have eventually, but I'm too busy relieved that I can keep my promise.

"Okay, whatever. Just, you know, don't interrupt."

He rolls his eyes. "Yeah, I'll do my best." After setting down the laptop, he eyes the untouched sandwich. "Fuck it. If you're not going to eat this, I will." He takes a bite, then another before leaving it on the plate and settling on my bed.

Now I know it isn't drugged, so I greedily eat the rest in only a few bites. I didn't realize how hungry I was until I saw it sitting there.

Before getting on the session, I go to the bathroom and wash my face, trying to make myself presentable. I've done a lot of crying in the past day alone. I hardly look my best, but at least nobody's going to think the worst the second they set eyes on me.

With Colt stretched out on my bed, out of sight of the camera, I log in to my Zoom account and force myself to smile when the twelve-year-old who needs help with his history logs in. "Hey, Zach," I offer with a wave. "How's it going? How did you do on the quiz you had?" It's easy to forget Colt's presence after a few minutes now that I have something else to focus my attention on.

A half-hour passes much too quickly, so quickly, in fact, that we run overtime. "I gotta go," Zach suddenly announces. "I've got practice." I don't know what kind of practice. I only know I want to tell the kid to skip it today, anything, so long as I don't have to end this call. "Mom said she'll pay you as soon as the invoice comes in." Then he gives me a quick wave, and that's it. I'm back to being isolated.

For the first time in more than thirty minutes, Colt speaks. "You did a good job."

I barely keep from rolling my eyes when I turn in my chair to face him. "Aren't things already bad enough? You don't have to make fun of me."

"I wasn't trying to. You covered well. And you actually seemed like you gave a shit about what the kid was talking about."

"I do give a shit. That's half the reason why it was so important to show up for this session."

"What's the other half of the reason?"

I meet his gaze, unflinching. "It's either that, or I sit here and go crazy." I mean, why mask the truth? There are no illusions between us anymore. I'll be damned if I'm going to spare his feelings by trying to sugarcoat things. "How do you do this? How do you just walk around the house and go on with your life while holding me prisoner?"

Without missing a beat, he answers, "You get used to it."

Dumbfounded, I stare at him with my jaw hanging open. What the fuck? "What does that even mean? I'm supposed to get used to this? Or are you used to having prisoners? Oh god, am I not the only one you have done this to?"

"You think too much into the shit I say."

"That doesn't answer my question."

"No, we've never held anyone else prisoner, and no, I've never forced my cock down someone else's throat... unless they asked for it, of course."

"You are unbelievable." Every time I think there might be a tiny bit of a good person in there, he crushes that thought like an anvil would crush a daisy.

"Anyway, I'll be taking this back now." He gets up, snatching his laptop away from me and any hope of my reaching the outside world along with it. It isn't easy to hold back my emotions, but I manage it.

Before he can leave the room, I murmur, "Thank you. You didn't have to do that. It meant a lot."

"Don't thank me," he mutters as he closes the door. "You don't know what is planned for you tonight."

A t seven o'clock on the dot, the lock clicks. It's showtime.

Nix opens the door. "Come on. Dinner is ready." I stand up, shaking, almost wishing we didn't have to go through the farce of sitting down and having a meal together. Like we're some kind of normal family. I've never exactly been part of one, but I know this isn't it.

Instead of leading the way, Nix walks beside me on the stairs. "Listen," he murmurs. "There's nothing in the food if you're worried about that. But if I were you, I would have a glass of wine with dinner."

"Why is that?"

"It'll help relax you a little. It will take the edge off. And I know what you're thinking," he adds when I snort. "There is nothing in the wine, either. The bottle is unopened. You can watch me open it when we get to the dining room."

I don't give a shit about the wine right now. There's only one thing I care about. "Colt told me there are plans for tonight. Is your father going to join in this time, or will he just watch like before?" I need to know what I'm in for since the obsessing I've done since this afternoon hasn't helped much.

"He won't touch you himself." That's all he has time to say before we enter the dining room.

"I hope you don't mind, but I ordered in." James is every inch the gracious host as I take a seat. He reminds me so much of the way he was when I first arrived, practically falling over himself to make sure I have everything I want. It isn't like I didn't already know that was merely a lie to mask his true personality, but seeing it now drives the point home. Nothing about this was ever real. Meanwhile, my mother is having the time of her life at a spa, sipping drinks on a beach when she isn't getting massages and facials and whatever else people do at places like that.

At least the food looks good, even if I don't have much of an appetite. Something tells me he won't like it if I don't eat, though, so I make a point of taking some roast chicken, potatoes and vegetables. Nix uncorks a bottle of white wine and rounds the table to pour some in my glass. Our eyes meet for a single moment, and he pauses like he's waiting for me to pick up the glass. I don't. I won't. He clicks his tongue, turning away before shaking his head like he can't believe me. Vice versa. I can't believe him, either.

All through this, Colt hasn't said a word, pushing food around on his plate. Not exactly a comfortable situation on the whole. Not that I expect it to be any better.

"So Leni. I've been wondering." James gestures toward me with his fork. "Now that you aren't in gymnastics anymore, has it left a hole in your life?"

"A hole?" It's almost a normal question. I'm surprised.

"You know what I mean. You spent so much of your life laser-focused on one thing, and now it's gone."

"It was a lot to adjust to," I admit in a soft voice, picking at the chicken while I speak. It's good. What a shame I don't feel like eating it.

"I imagine it was quite a blow, your injury."

"Yes, it was. And it was a lot for Mom to handle, too." I don't know why I feel like I should bring her up. Maybe as a reminder of his wife, the woman he married, the woman whose daughter he's now holding captive.

He doesn't seem to notice, or else he doesn't care. "Do you miss it? Gymnastics, I mean."

All of a sudden, yes, I do. I miss it very much. With all my heart. Not because I miss competing but because I very much miss having some semblance of normalcy in my life. Even if training the way I did was anything but normal.

What I wouldn't give to go back to being that person. Somebody who knew what she was doing, what was expected of her. Even though it was grueling, I wasn't afraid the way I am now.

All eyes are on me, waiting for a response. I don't know why it matters so much. "To tell you the truth, I sort of fell out of love with it after a while. When I was younger, I used to really love it. Pushing myself, seeing what I could accomplish. But then it got so serious. There was so much pressure. I couldn't enjoy it anymore."

I glance around the table, shrugging. "By the end, I think I was doing it for my mom. She had invested so much and was hoping so hard that I would succeed. I felt like I owed it to her. But it wasn't because I loved it." And this is the first time I've ever admitted that to anybody. It's pretty sad that it has to be these three, my tormentors, my torturers.

"It is difficult when we feel we aren't living up to our parents' expectations," James muses.

I don't want to talk about this anymore. I don't like the feeling of my life being dissected, especially not by these guys. "What about your mom?" I ask, looking across the table to Colt. "Did you ever feel like you couldn't live up to her expectations?"

It was an innocent question. I didn't mean anything by it. I was only hoping to change the subject away from me. They don't really talk about their mom, so I was hoping... I don't know what I was hoping. To make conversation, I guess, rather than sitting here in silence. Maybe if we could relate on something, they might be less likely to hurt me?

Either way, it backfired. James slams his wine glass onto the table hard enough to send liquid sloshing over the rim. "What the fuck is that supposed to mean?" he barks.

"Don't you ever speak of her," Nix warns, his eyes slits.

"I'm sorry. I didn't know—"

"No, you didn't know, but you had to go and run your stupid fucking mouth anyway," James growls. "You're not the one asking questions around here, understood? We are. Don't ever, ever mention her again."

"Don't talk about things you don't understand," Colt snarls.

"I'm sorry. I didn't mean to upset anybody. Nobody told me—"

"Why the fuck should you have to be told?" James demands. His face is red, and now he's breathing heavily. I remember him looking this way, sounding this way when he was choking the life out of me. My body goes icy cold, freezing solid.

And there's a knife in the man's hand. Oh god. Is this it? Is this when he snaps?

I don't know if I'm relieved or disappointed when he lowers the knife to his plate and clears his throat. "Obviously, things got off track here. Let's go downstairs now and forget any of this ever happened."

Is that supposed to make me feel better? Because all it does is make me tremble in fear as the three of them stand, staring down at me.

CHAPTER 26

*N*ow, I wish I had drunk the damn wine. A lot of it. While I don't want to give anybody more of an excuse to use me, I also don't want to be aware of what's about to happen. Now that I'm on my way down to the basement, with the three men following me, I wish more than anything I had a way of disconnecting from this.

But now, it's all fresh, the fear and the disgust already fighting to see which one will win out. It might end in a tie.

What are they going to do to me this time? I shudder to think, but I'm sure they won't keep me waiting long. Nix told me his father wouldn't touch me. Is that true, or was it only something he told me to keep me in line? I guess I'll find out soon enough.

Just like before, James takes a seat on the center sofa, the one facing the TV. He makes no effort to pretend this is about something it isn't—right away, he begins rubbing himself through his slacks while his sons take their seats. I stand in the middle, the coffee table now pushed out of the way to make room.

James is staring at me, eyelids lowering as he slouches in his seat to make himself comfortable. "Take off your clothes. All the way down to your skin."

Looking at either of the guys for help would be a wasted effort, so I don't bother. As sick as this is, I go through the motions without asking questions or hesitating, wanting to get it over with.

"Somebody is in a hurry," James observes, chuckling. "She can't wait to get some cock inside her, the little slut." My hands shake as I unbutton my blouse, but I manage to open it, then slide it over my shoulders and down my arms. I turn my back to him as I unhook my bra and let it fall at my feet. Maybe if he sees my scar, he won't want to go through with this. It's my last hope.

He doesn't react, at least not negatively. "Bend at the waist," he grunts when it comes time to take off my jeans. "Let me see that ass. Go slow." There are tears in my eyes, and my chin won't stop quivering, but I do as he instructs. His breathing has already taken on a rasping quality as he gets more excited. When I bend to slide the jeans down around my ankles, he groans softly. "Look at that ass. Begging to be fucked." I close my eyes and bite back a whimper at the thought. I'm so mortified, I almost forget about the tattoo. James doesn't say anything, which means he knew about it. I store that information away for later.

A moment later, I'm completely naked, and I slowly turn around with my hands folded in front of my pussy. "No. Hands at your sides. Don't try to hide yourself from me." I look at the wall over James's head rather than stare at his dick while he strokes it as he studies my body. "That fresh pink pussy. Just dying to be filled. It'll get filled tonight."

"Get on your knees in front of me," Colt says, and already he's pulling himself out of his pants. He's hard, and I can't understand how. It takes a certain kind of person to become aroused in a situation like this. A sick person.

But the sooner I do this, the sooner I get it over with. I lower myself to my knees between his spread thighs. At least my hands aren't tied this time.

"Play with her tits," James whispers, so Colt reaches out with both hands to cup them. My nipples are already hardening, thanks to being out in the open air like this—and it's humiliating, the way they harden further at his touch. His warm palms rub over my skin, massaging and kneading while my arms hang awkwardly by my side.

I focus my gaze on a picture hanging on the wall. It's some kind of movie poster from the fifties. At least, judging by the bright red convertible, that reminds me of the movie *Grease*. Maybe I can imagine sitting in that car somewhere at a beach far away from here.

"Look at him," James orders, forcing me out of my fantasy. "Don't be rude now. Give him the attention he deserves."

Dragging my eyes from the poster, I meet Colt's hooded gaze. He stares at me as if he is trying to be somewhere else too. For a fraction of a second, I feel this connection between us. As if we are not enemies but on the same side.

Then it's gone.

"Now, you're going to suck his cock just like you did before. You treated it so well." James's voice has taken on almost a hazy sort of quality, like he's already lost in the moment. "Colt, she's a little shy," he muses. "You might have to ease her into it. Take her by the back of the head and rub it over her mouth."

Colt does just that, taking a handful of my hair to hold my head in place before running the head of his dick over my mouth. I stare at his chest, unwilling to look him in the eye again.

"Lick it," James grunts.

I extend my tongue. Colt groans softly, and something salty hits my taste buds. I do my best not to react like I noticed anything.

James grunts his approval. "Now, feed it to her. Make her take it all the way." Colt lowers my head, guiding himself between my lips, pushing me down until my nose touches the hair along the base. He surges in my mouth, crammed against the back of my throat, and I struggle to keep my throat relaxed so I don't start gagging. Too much food is in my stomach. It wouldn't end well.

I'm not here. I'm far away. This isn't happening.

I repeat it over and over in my mind, wishing that I could believe myself.

"Nix. Don't just stand there. Get her pussy ready for you." I tense up all over when I realize the plan. Nix is going to take me from behind while I suck Colt off. And all the while, their father is going to direct the action like his own live movie.

"Come on, Leni," he murmurs in a tight voice. "Give me a little moan. Isn't it good having all that cock in your mouth? Won't it feel so much better when you have another one up your cunt?"

Colt's hand tightens, tugging my hair, stirring me to react the way his father instructs. James's dark chuckle turns my stomach.

"Nix, get her nice and wet." I shudder in disgust when Nix's hand cups my pussy, massaging it. "Drag your cock up and down her slit. That's right. Tease her a little. Make sure she's good and hungry for it." Hungry? I couldn't be more disgusted. There's no way I could get wet over this. Not with them. Not with him watching.

"Spread her cheeks. I want to see her asshole." A tear rolls down my cheek while my head bobs up and down. Cool air touches my most intimate places, and I want to scream, but all I can do is take it. The humiliation.

"How does that feel?" James asks. "Knowing you have all these men looking at you, wanting you? Knowing you can get our dicks hard the way you do. I bet that's the kind of thing that keeps you up at night, isn't it? Wondering how you can tease and tempt us. Now you'll have this to remember when you touch yourself. Moan for me." When I don't do it right away, again, Colt tugs my hair. I moan around his dick, and James groans like he's pleased.

"Now, Nix. Fuck her good and hard."

I barely have time to register the pressure at my entrance before Nix fills me all at once, not bothering to take it slow. Just the way Daddy told him to. He pushes me forward before taking me by the hips to hold me in place. I can barely keep track of what I'm supposed to do. There's so much happening, so many sensations, so many thoughts. So much screaming in my head.

"That's right. Give it to her. Fuck that pussy." To Colt, he says, "Get her hair out of the way. I want to see her face while she sucks you off." Colt sweeps my hair away from my face like he's told. "That's right. Suck it good, baby."

With one hand, Nix strokes my back, and I flinch when he runs his hand over my scar. But that doesn't seem to bother him. No, he's fucking me at a strong, steady pace, breathing hard, balls slapping against me. I don't know why, but it loosens some of the tightness in my chest when he does that. Like he isn't disgusted by me, even if I'm disgusted by him.

"Grab her tits. That's right, play with the nipples... pinch them," James orders. I suck in a pained breath through my nose, but he only groans his approval. I hear him, his labored breathing, the *thwap-thwap-thwap* as he strokes faster, faster.

"Harder," he tells Nix, who digs his fingers into my hips and begins pounding mercilessly. Now I can't help but grunt every time he slams his body against mine, which seems to please all three of them. "Colt, fuck her face. Come down her throat before your brother fills her cunt."

All I can do is hold on for dear life and hope he doesn't try to smother me the way Nix did. A quick glance up at him from beneath my lashes shows his eyes closed, his head thrown back as he thrusts upward in a quickening pace that soon dissolves into wild humping before he finally lets out a strangled groan and fills my mouth with his seed.

At the same time, James mutters, "Nix, turn to the side a little. I want to see you going in and out. Faster, faster. Make her ass jiggle." Colt is still in my mouth, and I'm whimpering, gagging, tears flowing down my cheeks and soaking into his shorts, thanks to Nix's merciless pounding. I'll be lucky if I'm able to walk by the time he's finished, which is exactly the point, I'm sure. They're both panting, both eager to come, and I pray it happens soon.

"You ready to finish?" he asks Nix, who grunts his wordless response. "Do it inside her. Fill her up."

No! I want to fight. I want to stop him, but there's no stopping this. It's not going to end until James gets what he wants. Nix's thrusts turn into mindless rutting, his grunts and moans landing on my ears as painfully as every thrust from his dick. He drives himself home one last time before a rush of warmth tells me he's emptied his balls inside me. He falls against me a little, breathing hard, moaning.

"Pull out, pull out," James says breathlessly. "I want to see. Let me see that cum... dripping out... running down..." He's losing himself. He's almost there. All it takes is Nix's softening dick falling out of me and the sight of the warm cum I feel dripping from my hole. He gasps, the sound of skin on skin quickening until he groans, loud and deep. "Fuck, yes. Oh, yeah... fuck!"

Though he doesn't make me watch as he comes, the sound of it is enough. His satisfaction. I hate knowing I'm the cause of it. I hate knowing he gets his way.

"Very nice," he finally announces once he's caught his breath. I'm still on my hands and knees, with Colt zipping up in front of me, and Nix doing the same behind me. Nobody has bothered to help me up or even acknowledge me at all. I'm just a series of holes to fill now. I stay on my hands and knees, awaiting instruction. Jesus, they've already broken me that much. I'm afraid to make a move without being told to.

"This was fun." From the corner of my eye, I see James standing. "Take her back to her room." He won't even acknowledge me directly. I might as well not be human.

I gather my things quickly, not bothering to put them back on. What's the point of modesty now? Colt waits until I pick up the last piece of clothing, then I follow him up the stairs. I keep my head down, my eyes on the floor. I just want to be alone.

Soon, I'll be in my room, and I'll be alone. It's the only thing keeping me from falling apart.

And then what? I get to relive this all night? All the while anticipating what happens tomorrow? I can only believe it will get worse from here.

I doubt it will be enough, having his sons do this. Eventually, he's going to want to do it himself. No matter what Nix says, no matter what James told them. Soon, it's not going to be enough.

A single word from Colt might make it better, but he doesn't speak. He doesn't make a sound or crack a smile. He doesn't do anything besides opening my door and stepping aside so I can enter the room. I haven't yet turned around before he's closed it again, locking it as I expected.

Dropping my clothes, I make a beeline to the shower. There's not enough hot water in the tank to make me feel clean. Nothing ever will again. But I might spend a while trying.

CHAPTER 27

*T*here's pounding at the door.

I wake up in the dark, and immediately, my heart's in my throat. I break out in a cold sweat when somebody pounds against the bedroom door again. They fight with the knob, turning it—or trying to. All it does is jiggle a little, but there's no opening the door while it's locked.

"What the fuck is this?" Again, more pounding, more jiggling of the knob. "Motherfucker! Is this a fucking joke?"

I clutch the blankets close to me, my fear exploding and threatening to pull a scream from my throat when I realize it's James. He's trying to get in.

He goes silent for a moment, and I think he's given up—until the pounding turns into a solid thud. Then another, another. I bite down on my fist to quiet a scream I can't hold back. He's trying to break the door down. He's going to break the damn door down!

"Motherfucker..." *Thud!* "Think you can..." *Thud!* "Keep away from me?" *Thud!*

But it's no use. The lock won't give, and the door's too strong. At least now I know how impossible it is to break the thing down, but only now that it's locked against him.

He doesn't have a key. Nix's words come back to me, and now I understand what he was saying. James doesn't have the key to the door. Why not? Why do they have it?

He's not giving up, and eventually, something will break, and he'll get in. I look around in a panic, my eyes combing the darkness for something, anything I can use to fight him off. I can't let him hurt me. I can't, I won't. A bookend on one of the shelves catches my eye, and I tumble out of bed, running forward and clutching it to me. Prepared to use it, and use it again, and keep using it until he's dead. I would rather kill him than let him touch me.

The silence is even more terrifying, maybe because of how suddenly it comes on. All at once, he seems to give up the fight. I don't even hear him walk away. Naturally, that means it's impossible for me to relax. I tiptoe to the door, holding my breath, listening hard. Is he out there, still? Trying to come up with a plan, maybe? There has to be another key around here somewhere. Or maybe he'll attack the hinges next. My heart pounds wildly at the thought, and a cold, sickening certainty settles into my bones. He's not going to stop. He's never going to stop until he gets what he wants.

I don't know how much time passes, but it isn't enough to keep me from gasping when the lock clicks. No, this is it. He found a key. Oh, my god, what am I going to do? I have to protect myself. I have to, no matter what it means.

Yet instead of James appearing, it's Nix. He slips into the room and closes the door quietly, then inserts what looks like nothing more than a small metal pick into a tiny hole on the knob. He tests it, trying to turn it, but it's locked again. Son of a bitch. How did he do that?

Then he turns to me, looks me up and down, and seems to understand the situation all at once. "It's all right. Everything is fine now. Go to bed."

As if my life could get any more absurd. He stands there as if he is the hero, saving me from the bad guy. It's so comical, I almost laugh. Then I realize something even more ludicrous is the fact that I am relieved Nix is here. But that's only because Nix is still the lesser evil.

"With you here?" All he does is stare at me. I can't see him very well in the dark, but I get the feeling he doesn't appreciate the question. And now I'm afraid of what will happen if I challenge him. Just because he's not his father doesn't mean I'm with a friend right now.

I set the bookend down on my desk, then go back to bed like he said. I don't even know whether I should thank him since I don't know if what's happening now is any better than what would have happened had James broken the door down. It's not like Nix has ever held himself back from doing whatever he feels like doing to me.

And when he climbs into bed, I let out a moan of pure despair that even pressing my face to the pillow can't muffle. "Relax," he whispers. He settles in with a good foot or two of space between us, his body on top of the blanket I'm lying underneath.

I wait, my back to him, fear freezing my muscles. He doesn't say a word. He doesn't move an inch, either. Is this all he wants? To lie here next to me?

He's not trying to protect me, is he?

I push that thought away all at once because it's dangerous, not to mention pathetic. He's done absolutely nothing to protect me through all of this. He's never even raised the slightest objection to his father's demands. He's getting just as much out of this as James is.

Though he did try to comfort me when he told me his father didn't have a key. Or was he only giving me the facts? I don't know what to think anymore. I'm too tired, too beaten down, and confused.

Somehow, while I know the danger isn't over for good, I feel a little safer knowing he's beside me. It's enough that I'm able to close my eyes and drift back to sleep.

It's still dark. I'm alone again.

The instant I register Nix's absence, I jump out of bed and run for the door to test the knob. Relief loosens me, and I slump against the door when I find it locked. I never thought I'd be this relieved to know I can't get out of the room. But now I know there's a danger out there much worse than either Nix or Colt, or even both of them put together.

It's barely five o'clock. The sun won't rise for at least another hour. I should try to go back to sleep, but something tells me it would be a waste of time. Too much adrenaline is pumping through my veins.

That's a shame, too, since sleep is pretty much the only time I get a reprieve from this.

It's funny how I immediately look at my laptop when I

wonder what I'm supposed to do with my time. It's not like I can get online.

No, but I can still do something. I don't know what puts the idea in my head or why my brain latches onto it so suddenly, but I find myself opening the machine and sitting down at my desk. I pull up a blank document, and the cursor blinks at me.

It all started at a party shortly after I moved in, I type. The words come slowly like even my fingers dread the idea of going back through everything that happened. *I didn't want to go to the party, but I didn't have a choice. While there, Nix and Colt forced me into performing oral sex on Nix while Colt touched me. They recorded it. The video is saved on Colt's computer.*

I typed it, and I'm still alive. The shame didn't kill me. It didn't consume me. I'm still here.

The night of my mother's wedding rehearsal dinner, I continue, *I took a painkiller before making the mistake of drinking champagne. I could kick myself for being so stupid. Nix and Colt brought me home. While I was under the influence of these two substances mixed together, Colt had sex with me. He made an audio recording of the encounter and played it for me the following day when I confronted him. The audio was stored in his phone.*

It gets easier the more I type. Even describing what's going on with James isn't so difficult anymore. Tears occasionally blur my vision, but I wipe them away, more irritated by the distraction than anything else. I have work to do here.

I don't know what I'm going to do with it or if I'll do anything at all. I only know somehow I feel better for having typed it all out. Safer, too. As far as I know, nobody has access to my machine yet—and I hope none of them will. Colt wants to keep a file on his machine? I can keep files on mine, too.

By the time I finish detailing everything that went on last night, including when James tried to break into my room, the sun has risen. My fingers are stiff from all the typing—more than I've ever done all at once before, but I feel good. Like, somehow, telling the story puts me back in control, at least a little.

That good feeling evaporates at the click of the lock. I turn in my chair, holding my breath. What is it this time? Who is it?

"Hey." Colt's carrying a plate in one hand and a bottle of juice tucked under his arm. "I thought you'd be hungry. Figured you wouldn't want to come down if you didn't have to."

"Yeah. Good call." How can he act like anything between us is even remotely normal? What has to be wrong with a person that they're able to do that? He and Nix, both.

I don't have it in me to ask, and I'm too hungry to waste time with questions, anyway.

The toasted bagel sits next to three dollops on the plate: butter, jelly, and cream cheese. A banana and a cup of yogurt round out the meal. I immediately slather the cream cheese and jelly on the bagel and take a big bite. It never occurred to me to wonder if they put anything in the food. Right now, I'm not even sure I care anymore. Whatever they do to me while I'm unconscious, they're going to do to me while I'm conscious, too. It's an illusion to think I have any control over any aspect of it. I would probably do better to get rid of that illusion now.

"You know," I mumble, my mouth full, "I have to ask myself what's in this for you. Why are you going out of your way?"

"Is making sure you don't starve to death going out of my way? It's not like I cooked you a big meal or anything." He snickers before giving me a wry smirk. "Believe me. You don't want me to try to cook for you."

"I'll keep that in mind." I peel the banana and take a big bite before the memory of having Colt's dick in my mouth threatens to sour the entire meal. No. I'm not going to let that happen. I deserve to eat.

"Are you okay?" he asks. "I mean, at least physically?"

"Are you actually asking me that question? Or did your father tell you to ask me?"

"You know what, we don't have to do this." He starts to stand, but I make a noise that stops him. I don't even know why I want to stop him. Am I this desperate for human contact? I guess I must be.

"Physically, I'm fine."

"It's easier just to give him what he wants."

"Easier for who? For me, or for you?"

"I said what I said." He looks at the floor, one knee jiggling up and down a little. "Do you have any tutoring today?"

"No, actually. My schedule was already clear."

"Okay. I guess just, you know, let me know if you have another session. Don't want a bunch of kids failing out of middle school because they couldn't get a math lesson from you." He glances up for an instant, and our eyes meet. I find myself wanting to grin, and I can't understand why.

For the first time, I get the feeling that maybe we're in this together, somehow. Like this isn't exactly his idea, either, and he would rather not go through this. Maybe it's better if I don't think too much about it. Thinking only leads to more questions, which inevitably leads to more anger and outrage. Outrage over this whole thing happening to begin with.

When I'm finished, he takes the plate. "I can bring you lunch later if you want?"

"That would be nice. Thank you." He nods, quickly turning away and disappearing from the room so suddenly it's almost like he was never here at all.

I wish I could understand him. I wish I could understand any of this.

But what good has wishing ever done me?

CHAPTER 28

I guess this is going to be a daily thing. I guess I'm supposed to expect to be summoned around the same time every evening, brought down to the basement, and ordered to strip down. Tonight, at least, there was no instruction beyond the demand that I remove my clothes. He didn't try to direct me through it this time.

And I'm still standing here, just as naked, just as cold and full of dread as before. What is it going to be this time? What has he come up with in that sick brain of his?

He doesn't keep me waiting long, settling in on one couch while Colt sits down on the one facing it. There's less space between them now, like James pushed them closer together. I guess he wants to get a good look at what's happening.

"Are you ready to get that pretty pussy filled again?" There's an edge to James's voice tonight that wasn't there before. Is it because he couldn't get into my room? I didn't have anything to do with that, but I get the feeling I'll be the one who ends up being punished for it. I can't win either way. I can only hope one of them will come to my aid the way Nix did last night. But what are the chances of that happening? I'm not fooling myself.

James turns to Colt while Nix waits off to the side, staring at my body but not yet making a move to touch me. "You know what to do." Colt lifts his hips to lower his jeans and his shorts. He isn't quite hard yet, I see.

"Look at that body," James murmurs, almost crooning the words as he turns his gaze on me. "Think of all the things you want to do to her. How you want to break her on your cock and make her sob out your name. And she wants to ride it, too. Just like the little slut she is, always hungry for more."

The man is mental, top to bottom. Making these things up in his head for his own pleasure and amusement. Colt strokes himself, staring at my boobs while he does. Either it's the sight of me or his father's encouragement—he lengthens, hardens.

"Leni, you're going to ride his cock tonight. Get on over there. Spread those legs wide, so I can see him sink into you."

It's like I'm not connected to my body anymore, dragging my feet over to where Colt waits for me with his dick sticking straight up. It's better this way. I don't want to feel connected to any of this. Colt slouches a little, making it easier for me to straddle him with my back to James. "Ease into it," James orders. "Nice and slow. I want to see every inch sink into her. Take your time."

I would rather be anywhere but here. My thighs are spread wide, and slowly Colt lines himself up with my hole before sliding inside. I'm still sore from yesterday, which I didn't realize until this very moment. I lower myself one grueling inch at a time, hissing in pain. I hate every sound James makes, his satisfied little grunts as he begins stroking himself behind us. That sound is burned into my brain now. Skin on skin.

"That's nice." He sighs once I'm as low as I can go, locked with Colt, looking anywhere but at his face. "Leni, touch him. Show him how good you feel. Reach back and grab his balls. Play with them a little." I have to put an arm around Colt's neck to keep my balance while reaching behind me. Hesitantly, I touch the place where we are joined, padding my way down to his balls. The skin there is soft and warm as I start to fondle him. His quickened breath tells me I'm doing well, so I continue the motion, massaging them a little.

"You're going to empty those balls into your pussy, aren't you?" James mutters with a nasty little laugh. "Now fuck him. Ride that cock—but go slow. Real slow."

Yes, why not drag this out? Why not make it even more unbearable? I'm not quite sure what I'm doing or how I'm supposed to move, but Colt's hands on my hips go a long way toward helping me set a pace. I let him do it, handing it over to him for now because I don't have it in me. I just don't.

"Spread her ass cheeks," James mutters. "I want to see her asshole." I close my eyes and lower my head, a tear dangling off the edge of my lashes. James's satisfied little grunt when Colt spreads my cheeks brings another tear, another. And all the while, I have to ride and pretend to enjoy it.

That isn't the worst part, not at all. The worst part is the way my body seems to wake up a little with every downward stroke. I know why, too—I can't help but grind my clit against him, and the friction is both terrible and heavenly. I don't want this. I don't want to feel good. As bad as this is, the thought of coming, of proving to James's twisted mind that I'm enjoying this, is infinitely worse.

"I'm guessing you've still never had anybody in that tight little hole, have you?" James asks. "Maybe we'll have to change that tonight." I can't help the whimper that comes out of me any more than I can help the growing disgust that spreads through me. "What do you think about that?"

"It's okay," Colt whispers. I don't want to hear it. I don't even want to think about what we're doing. I can't acknowledge him, no matter what he says.

"Nix, instead of standing there jerking off, I want you to go over there. Play with her asshole. Just stay out of the way so I can see."

"Relax," Colt whispers, moving his hips in time with me. "Just pretend it's us. Just you and me. Nobody else is here." He says it so softly, even I can barely hear him. I doubt James can over his disgusting little groans and his quickening breath.

Colt's words shouldn't make me feel better. It's not like what he did to me after the rehearsal dinner was any better than this. The thing is, it did feel better at the time. When he took my virginity, it was just us, and Colt didn't try to hurt me. He didn't humiliate or expose me. When it was just us, he was gentle, and made me feel cherished and loved.

Nix brushes a hand over my ass, and I can't help but tense up. He runs a finger around the edge of my asshole, playing with me a little, pressing but not entering right away. From the corner of my eye, I see him stroking himself with the other hand.

"Don't just play with it," James barks. "Stick it in. Fuck her ass with your finger." I grit my teeth against a whimper of discomfort and humiliation when Nix enters me, probing around with one thick finger.

"It's just us," Colt whispers. "Pretend it's just us." Leaning my head on Colt's shoulder, I close my eyes and try to do what he says. James isn't here. He's not doing this. He has nothing to do with this. It's just us. Slowly, my pain eases, the tightness in my chest, the screaming in my brain. It all eases little by little the longer I block out James's commands and focus instead on what I'm doing, what we are doing. I won't even think about Nix. Only Colt and me. It almost feels normal this way.

"Give it to her." There's no blocking him out completely, especially not now, when he's nearing the end. "Fuck her hard. Fill her up."

I place my hands on Colt's shoulders and dig my fingers in tight as he starts fucking me harder. Nix works his finger in and out in time, and god, I feel so dirty, so ashamed. That shame only worsens when the heat that already started to build, thanks to the friction against my clit, blooms into something hotter, stronger. No, I am not going to do this. This is not going to happen. I'm not going to give them the satisfaction. I grit my teeth and ride it out, reminding myself how much I hate all of them but James most of all. The filthy, twisted pig.

"Get up. Now." I can barely make sense of what James is ordering me to do, but Colt understands. He lifts me off him and practically throws me onto the couch, where I land on my stomach. A hand presses against my back—I don't know who it belongs to. I only know James is now out of his seat, crossing the small space between us, fisting himself faster, faster.

I close my eyes and bite my lip, holding back a cry of pure humiliation as the three of them come across my ass. It feels like it's never going to end; their groans, their satisfied sighs as they milk themselves all over me.

But then it ends because it has to, and all I can do is be thankful it's over.

Unlike last time, James doesn't say a word. I'm glad. I don't want to hear his voice again tonight.

Eventually, something touches my ass. Fabric. Probably my shirt or something. "Come on. Get up." It's Colt, his voice flat. When I lift my head and dare to look around, I find it's just the two of us, and my clothes are balled up in his hands. My thighs are so sore from all that work, but I fight to get on my feet, following him up the stairs to my room.

I expect him to leave me alone right away like he did before, but instead, he enters the room with me and closes the door behind him. I'm too tired, too embarrassed, and hurt to ask why. It doesn't even occur to me to argue with him when he takes me by the hand and leads me to the bathroom. It takes no time for him to strip down. I'm not even interested in looking at him or noticing his body as he steps into the shower, turning on the water before extending a hand and beckoning me.

It's just like it was before, with Nix, when I was too tired and too broken inside to care much about washing myself up. It is good to feel that water on me, though, running over my head and down my body.

He doesn't say a word. He only gently, slowly washes me with a soapy rag. I close my eyes and give myself over to him for the second time tonight, parting my legs when he nudges them apart so he can slowly run the rag over my pussy. He takes special care with my ass, too, until nobody would ever know I was violated tonight. Again.

It's only the touch of his fingers against my scar that stirs me to react. I flinch, tensing up, holding my breath. "You don't have to do that," he whispers, touching it again. I look up at him, blinking the water out of my eyes, and he's wearing something close to a smile. It's soft and almost sweet. "You're still beautiful, with or without this," he whispers, stroking my scar. "It doesn't make you who you are. It doesn't define you. Don't let it."

Tears mix with the water running down my face. Are they tears of embarrassment or gratitude? I don't know. I don't have it in me to figure it out right now.

All I know is once we're out of the shower and dried off, it feels like the most natural thing in the world to hold a hand out when he starts for the door. "Please. Don't leave. Stay with me."

He hesitates, his brow furrowing and his eyes narrowing. I pull the blankets back and crawl into bed, never doubting for a moment he'll join me.

He does, and unlike with Nix, he doesn't leave any space between us. Instead, he wraps his arms around me from behind and holds me close. For the first time in a week, I truly relax, melting against him, leaving everything else behind in favor of feeling warm. Safe.

I know it doesn't make sense to feel safe in his arms. I should be appalled by his touch, cringe away from his body, yet I lean into him for comfort. Maybe they finally did it—they broke my mind. The worst part is, I don't even care, not right now at least. Right now I'm so desperate, I'll take any kindness I can.

Even if I have no idea how long the feeling will last.

CHAPTER 29

*T*he sun is shining by the time I open my eyes again. It hits me right away. There was no middle-of-the-night drama, no close calls with James. I never thought the idea of sleeping through the night would matter quite this much. It's like this experience has changed everything I ever thought mattered.

I'm alone in bed, too. I don't register Colt's absence right away, but once I do, I look across the room, expecting him to be in the bathroom. He's not. He must have left quietly while I was out cold. I almost wish he hadn't, even if I'm glad I avoided the awkwardness of facing him this morning.

My eyes must be playing tricks on me. I blink hard and rub my fists over them, but the image in front of me doesn't change.

The door is partly open.

Right away, my heart takes off at double time. Does he realize he did it? I'm afraid to hope, afraid to think this might mean something good. Maybe he only thought he closed it but didn't all the way. Whatever the reason, I'm not going to let an opportunity slip through my fingers.

I hop out of bed as quietly as I can, then exercise just as much care in pulling jeans and a T-shirt from my dresser without making a sound. As soon as I'm dressed, I tiptoe out into the hall, listening for any voices. It's past eight o'clock, so it's not early enough that I can hope everybody's still asleep. James is probably up and around somewhere. I guess he eventually has to get back to the office, even if he is supposed to be on his honeymoon right now.

I can't help but remember the women at the rehearsal dinner. The way they all looked at him like he was some big prize. They didn't even bother to hide their interest, even with him standing arm in arm with the woman he was marrying the following day.

I wonder what they would think of him if they knew what he's really like.

I still don't hear anything coming from downstairs, so I take the chance of going down slowly, one step at a time, listening hard all the way. By the time I'm at the bottom of the staircase, I haven't heard anything to discourage me from trying to get through the front door. It doesn't come as a huge surprise when the knob won't turn—and I don't have a key for the special bolt that's been engaged.

I'm not going to give up. There has to be another way. The back door? I don't remember ever seeing a special lock on the door leading from the kitchen to the patio. When I head in that direction, I look up the stairs, expecting to find someone staring down at me. That doesn't happen, but that doesn't mean I'll take my time getting to the kitchen, starting down the hall with my heart in my throat the whole time.

The sight of my stepbrothers sitting at the island, both eating cereal, kills that idea. I should have known better. Frustration threatens to bring tears to my eyes, but I fight them back.

Colt lifts his chin in acknowledgment of my entrance. There's nothing in his posture or the look on his face to suggest anything that happened last night, or the fact that he spent hours holding me in bed. It's almost enough to make me wonder if I imagined the whole thing.

"Good morning. Here, have some breakfast." He pushes the cereal box my way, even though I haven't yet taken a seat. I don't know that I will, either.

Nix reads my hesitation right away. "He'll be out all day." There's no need to explain who he's talking about. "He said he has back-to-back meetings."

My relief is enormous, though it doesn't really change anything. He's not here during the day? He'll be back tonight. I've been granted a reprieve, that's all.

Colt eyes me like he senses my thought process. "If you want," he murmurs between spoonfuls, "you can hang around the house today. You don't have to stay upstairs. You just can't leave."

"Wow, really?" Maybe I shouldn't get snarky with him, but the way he said it is so condescending. I'm supposed to live here. This is supposed to be my house, too, but I'm being given permission to act like I live here. Does he expect my thanks?

"Whatever," Nix mutters with a shrug. "You don't have to. Just figured you might want to."

"I would rather stay in my room." I don't wait for either of them to smart off to me before I turn on my heel and leave the room. We're not friends, and we never will be. Besides, I don't want a day spent in front of the TV right now. It's a way out of here. I'm not going to waste the opportunity.

What am I going to do, though? There's got to be a way out. The house has a million windows. One of them has to be unlocked.

Rather than go up to my room like I said I would, I speed walk past the stairs and go into the family room. What a name. Like there's anything normal about this family. The windows are locked, and I would have to pull up a chair or a stepladder to reach the latches. I don't know if I have time for that or whether it would be too loud. What are the odds of them going to the gym today? If they did, though, they would probably lock me in my room to be on the safe side. So that wouldn't help.

No, whatever I do, it has to be fast. Before they get the chance to go back on their word and lock me up. I start down the hall, looking over my shoulder the whole time. I walk into the next room I find, which happens to be James's office.

I'm surprised he leaves it unlocked, but then I guess he figures nobody has the nerve to step foot in here without permission. He's that sure of himself, of how tight a grip he has over this house.

I should go straight to the windows behind the desk, but a new idea bubbles in the back of my mind. What if I can use something in here against him? I'm not sure what I'm looking for—the idea is too vague for me to have a clear idea of what to search for. There must be something. Files, pictures, a key for the front door. Something.

I go to his desk and force my way through the revulsion that threatens to choke me; it has my throat so tight. Just being in his personal space makes me want to throw up. His laptop isn't here, but that might be a good thing. I don't want to look through it. I shudder to think what I might find.

Instead, I busy myself looking through the drawers. For a man so big on security, it's a wonder he doesn't leave the drawers more tightly guarded. They open easily, but at first, all I find are letterheads and envelopes, nothing very interesting or worthwhile. I go to the next drawer, then the next, and my frustration only grows. Paper clips, a stapler. There has to be something—this desk could belong to anybody in the entire world. It's so impersonal. Doesn't he store anything worthwhile in here?

It's when I get to the deep bottom drawer that things start getting more interesting. It's full of hanging file folders, paperwork, that kind of thing. I don't have time to go through all of it, and I'm not sure I'd know what I was reading even if I did. Still no key. Maybe he keeps keys in his bedroom, but I don't dare go in there. I'd have to walk past the guys' rooms, for one thing. What I'm doing right now is already dangerous enough.

I'm about to close the drawer when something catches my eye. At the bottom of the drawer, underneath the file folders, there's a picture. Half a picture, actually, which I carefully lift before seeing the other half of the picture underneath it. It's the fact that it seems so out of place that convinces me to pick up both halves of the photo and put them together, laying them on the desk and lining up the torn edges until the full image reveals itself.

It's a woman. Smiling wide, she's dressed in a tracksuit and standing in front of a balance beam.

And I know her. Well, not really, but I recognize her. She was a coach, a gymnastics coach. I met her once at a tournament years ago—her girls were tough, well-trained, and disciplined. But instead of coming off hard and cold, the way I expected, she was warm and encouraged her team. I remember thinking it seemed like she actually cared about them. Too many coaches inspired their gymnasts by being bullies, thinking that would push them just a little bit harder, a little bit closer to winning. But no, her girls were at the top of the leaderboard, even when she seemed to take a soft, almost motherly role. I actually wished she was my coach at one point when she gave a gentle hug to a girl who fell off the beam twice during her routine.

What's her picture doing here? I don't have time to mull it over now. The guys are bound to check my room to see if I'm up there, so I need to move fast before they realize I'm gone. For some reason, though, instead of returning the photo to the drawer, I cram it into my back pocket, then turn to the windows to test them.

And when one of them moves, I have to bite back a shout of sheer elation. Instead of announcing my excitement, I ease the window up when what I really want to do is fling it open. I only have to be careful a few moments longer, then I can run.

The drop to the mulched bed below the window is an easy one, and I waste no time once my feet are on the ground. I won't make the mistake of going to the driveway this time. Sheer desperation sends me running through the woods surrounding the house. They open up onto another property. I know they do. Even if I get caught trespassing, it wouldn't matter. I just need help.

I can see another house through the trees after only running for a minute or so. There's a woman out there, weeding in a garden. I see her sun hat from here. Hope floods me, and I have to hold back tears of gratitude before I even reach the property line. How will I get them to believe me? I have no idea, but I have to try. And if they don't, I'll keep going. I'll run all the way to the police station if I have to.

I don't need to. I don't get the chance. An arm closes around my waist, and a hand slaps over my mouth before I can scream. She's there. I see her. All I have to do is scream to get her attention and beg for help. It's too late. She might as well be a million miles away.

Because Nix caught me. Nix is holding me, breathing hard in my ear. "What do you think you're doing?" he pants. "You're going to end up getting yourself killed." My heart sinks, and my tears roll over the back of his hand as he hauls me off my feet and begins carrying me back to the house. Colt is waiting for us at the edge of the tree line, arms folded, brows drawn together in a scowl. I kick out with my feet, drive my fists and elbows and anything else I can manage into Nix's body, but it makes no difference.

I'm not getting away. After this, I doubt I'll ever have another chance.

CHAPTER 30

"Here we are, trying to be nice to you, and this is what you do?" Colt slams the front door shut and locks it before Nix finally sets me back on my feet. I whirl around, furious, my breaths coming in big, heaving sobs.

"Nice?" I scream, and that feels good. Hearing my voice echoing, seeing the way their eyes widen in surprise. Like they expected me to be this meek little thing, begging for the slightest scraps of kindness. They didn't expect me to come back swinging.

"Well, yeah," Colt finally responds once he shakes off his surprise. "What did you think today was about? We told you—"

"That's not being nice. That's just basic decency, you asshole," I bark at him. Nix snorts, and I whirl on him next. "Sorry if I'm not falling on my knees and thanking you for your generosity, but nothing about treating me like a human being is generous. Why won't you just let me go?"

When he shrugs, I want to scream again. "Because we can't.

And if you would grow up and see this for what it is, you would understand that."

"Grow up? So what, that's your way of telling me to suck it up and deal with it? Because I'm not going to do that. I need to get out of here, dammit. How much farther do you think he's going to take this before he stops?"

This is the first time we've spoken about the things their father has them do to me. It's like my words have a magical effect. Immediately, the fight goes out of both of them, and they look at the floor. Like all their posturing and bullying drops away as soon as I speak frankly about their father's monstrous behavior.

"You know it doesn't work that way," Colt murmurs, his gaze still lowered.

"That is bullshit. That's what you're letting yourself believe. And I'm sorry if that's what he's making you think, but it just isn't true."

"You don't know what you're talking about," Nix growls. When he makes a move for me, I don't flinch. I stand my ground, feet planted, chin lifted. It throws him off, but only for a moment. Then he bends, throwing me over his shoulder and charging up the stairs.

"Stop it!" Though I can't exactly fight, not when he's carrying me like this. I don't need us both falling down the stairs. It's only once we reach the hallway that I pummel his back and shoulders with both fists. I might as well be punching air for all the good it does.

Colt follows us, and soon the three of us are back in my room. Nix throws me onto the bed, but I scramble off in case he decides to throw himself on top of me.

That's not what he has in mind. Instead, he thrusts a finger in my face, his own face beet red. "Now, you listen to me. You can leave as soon as this week is over. But you have to go through with this. You need to cooperate."

I shouldn't believe him. He's never done anything but lie to me. But dammit, I want to hope. I still need to hope. "You mean to say you're going to actually let me go? For real?"

"For real," Colt confirms, nodding slowly. "And the week's almost over. You don't have much longer to go through this."

"We won't stop you from leaving. But he has to get what he wants first. That's just how it is." Nix is still breathing heavy, still angry, but at least he takes his finger out of my face. I have half a mind to bite it off. He'll never stick it up anybody's asshole again.

I turn my back on both of them since the sight of their faces disgusts me. "Leave me alone. I don't want to see either of you."

But instead of leaving, somebody touches my ass. Before I can swat his hand away, Nix asks, "What is this?"

I realize the picture must have slithered out of my pocket a little when I was struggling.

"Leave it!" It's too late. He already has it, and now Colt is grabbing me, pinning my arms to my sides before reaching into my pocket to pull out the other half of the photo.

They stand next to each other, holding the two halves up and putting the picture back together the way I did when I first found it. "Where the fuck did you get this?" Nix whispers, his eyes almost bulging. Meanwhile, Colt doesn't say a word. The muscles in his jaw jump and twitch, though. The intensity coming off him is overwhelming.

"I found it downstairs." I leave it there since I'm not exactly in the mood to be punished for snooping.

I don't know why it took me so long to figure it out. Probably because I was too busy worrying about how I was going to get away. There wasn't much room for anything else in my over-heated mind, but now? "Was she your mom?" I whisper.

Neither of them says anything at first, and their silence is enough of a response. If she wasn't, they would say so right away. From what I remember, I heard their mother died in a car accident before the family came to town to start over again. I don't know how long ago that was, but it clearly wasn't long enough for the sight of her photo to keep a rush of emotion from blindsiding them.

"Yes," Colt finally whispers. I don't even think he's blinked since he started looking at it. "That's her."

I have to wonder why James would tear her picture apart. Maybe it was a moment of anger like he was venting his rage at her sudden death. But he still couldn't bring himself to let go of the photo. Not that this in any way makes up for what he's done or who he is, but it's sort of a tool in a way. It gives me an idea of the man he is, the real man inside. Not a weapon, per se, but it never hurts to know the enemy.

Nix lowers his half of the picture but doesn't let it go. "Don't ever, ever mention her again. Not for any reason. Not to us, and definitely not to Dad. Do you understand?" Nothing about the way he says it is nasty or bullying, which might be why his words have such an impact.

"And you never found this," Colt adds. "Got it?"

It must be their intensity that does it, or maybe it's the way they are obviously shaken at the sight of her. Whatever the reason, it's easy to agree. "Yeah, fine. I'll never bring it up."

With that, they leave me alone, and I drop to the bed before putting my head in my hands. That was my last chance. I know it. And since things have only escalated every day, I know it's going to be worse tonight than it was last night.

If only I had gone out the window right away instead of searching the desk. I might have gotten away.

I know he's home because I hear him down there. He's looking forward to another night of fun. He sounds upbeat, even happy. I hate it so much to know he's going to get what he wants. That's the last thing he deserves.

The click of the lock doesn't come as a surprise. By the time Nix steps into my room, I'm showered and my legs are shaved, the whole nine yards. I would hate to see what would happen if I kept James waiting, no matter how it kills me to know he'll be pleased. I'm not so stubborn that I would push his buttons on purpose.

Nix is holding a glass of wine, which he extends my way. "Trust me."

Trust him? That's a laugh. I take it to the bathroom and dump it down the sink before returning to him, glaring, daring him to say something. All I get is a disbelieving smirk and a slight shake of his head. "There's no helping some people."

"Whatever. You had the chance to help me earlier by letting me go, and you didn't. Can we just get this over with?" I don't feel half as defiant as I sound. Mouthing off and pretending this isn't tearing me up inside are my only ways of getting a little of myself back.

We start down the stairs, and there's no helping my curiosity. "What's it going to be tonight?"

"Relax and do as you're told," he replies, his voice flat. Like he's reading off a set of prepared remarks or something.

"Like I have a choice."

"Just let us do what we're going to do, and it will be over." I have to bite my lip to hold back all the many ugly, enraged thoughts running through my head. I could push him down the stairs right now, couldn't I? We're still far enough from the bottom that he might seriously hurt himself. No, with my luck, he'd end up just fine. And I would still have to go through with this, only it would be worse because he'd want to get back at me.

We go straight down to the basement, where James is already waiting in front of the TV. Some sort of sports commentary plays, not that I care, but I'd rather watch it than have to acknowledge the man smiling at me now. "Leni. I'm telling you, there's nothing better to set eyes on after a long day at the office. Knowing you're here and we're going to have all this fun together makes it possible for me to get through my day."

I don't bother hiding my contempt as I stare at him. If he's waiting for a response, he'll be waiting a long time.

His smile fades away, revealing the true man beneath the façade. I guess the game isn't as much fun if he knows he's the only one playing. "Get her ready," he grunts, turning back to the TV.

The coffee table is gone again, this time replaced by something else: a weight bench, smack dab in the center of the floor. Nix steps up behind me while I stare at the bench, wondering what it means. "Time to get undressed."

Meanwhile, Colt comes walking down the stairs behind us, his tread heavy.

I look over my shoulder, and the sight of the vinyl straps he's carrying makes my knees shake. They aren't plain straps, either. There's a cuff on either end of both of them.

When I don't start taking my clothes off, Nix decides to help me, pulling the shirt over my head almost before I know what he's doing. My thoughts are too jumbled, panic, disgust, and hatred all fighting for control of my brain.

I watch Colt arranging the straps under the bench, wrapping them around the metal legs before standing and finally looking at me.

"It's okay," Colt says in a whisper, barely audible over the TV. He unbuttons my jeans and lets them fall to the floor. "You'll be fine. Just lie there, and we'll get it over with. It'll be done before you know it."

He's such a liar. I can't bring myself to be grateful for this clumsy attempt at comforting me.

Nothing about this is fine or okay.

It wasn't enough for James to humiliate me. Now, he needs to be sure I can't move.

CHAPTER 31

*I*t's not enough to restrain me. He has to make sure I'm completely helpless.

By the time Colt is finished, and James is grunting his approval, I'm as physically and emotionally uncomfortable as I've ever been in my life. I'm kneeling on the bench. My feet hang over the edge with my ass in the air. The cuffs around my ankles ensure I can't move my legs at all. My wrists are down by the floor, the cuffs tight against the bench's legs, so there is no moving my arms, either. The side of my face is pressed against the padded surface.

I'm also blindfolded and gagged. No speaking or seeing. No moving unless I want to tip the bench over and risk hurting myself badly.

"Very nice," James decides. The way the bench is set up, the angle I'm at, my pussy and ass are directly in front of his face. "I see you shaved for me today. I appreciate that. Nothing like a nice, smooth pussy."

If I wasn't gagged, I would explain I got laser hair removal down there when I was fifteen. A lot of gymnasts do, not that he would care why my pussy is bare. I just want to get this over with.

"You can begin," he tells his sons. Immediately, I hear them lowering their zippers, ready to jump at Daddy's command. I can't stand it. How can they do this? They act like they're being forced into it, too, but that can't be true. It's not like he's holding a gun to their heads. He's a big man, but they are big, too. I'm sure they could beat him if the two of them worked together.

They don't want to. That's the only answer. And why would they? Look what they're getting out of it.

"Touch her pussy. Get her nice and wet. I want to see those lips glisten." At least I don't have to see his smug, nasty face, but I could deal without having to hear his voice. I wish somebody would put headphones on me so I could avoid that.

One of them touches me down there, stroking my lips before going deeper, parting them, dragging their fingers over my clit to tease my entrance. I'm about as dry as I've ever been, especially knowing James is sitting right there, watching every move.

"Come on. Don't tell me you don't know how to make a woman's pussy wet. Get in there. Lick it if you have to." One of them does, and I groan behind my gag. James must take it as a sound of pleasure because he groans along with me. "That's more like it. Shove your tongue up there. Fuck her with it."

Meanwhile, hands land on my back, sliding around to cup my boobs and playing with them. I feel something bump against my head, and I realize it's somebody's balls, that they're standing in front of the bench and leaning down. I certainly hope I don't end up choking to death on my own vomit with this gag in my mouth.

"That's enough of that. Nix, give it to her. Hard and deep." The first thrust pushes me forward, testing the straps. They don't give, of course, and Nix only pulls me back, closer to him, as he buries himself balls deep.

He might have gotten a little spit in there to ease the way, but that doesn't change how the sudden intrusion hurts as if I'm being split apart. My tender walls are stretched painfully, and all I can do is scream. The gag muffles my pained cry, which doesn't make Nix slow down at all.

Then he begins in earnest, slamming himself into me while pulling back on my hips. I can't hold back the pained grunts behind my gag. It feels like he's tearing me apart.

"Slap her ass. I want to see your handprints on there by the time you're finished." Now my grunts are more like cries, but again, it doesn't matter. It only makes James happy, makes him laugh almost gleefully. "That's right. I love seeing that ass shake. Colt, it's your turn."

Oh no, not both of them. I'm already so sore from the past two days.

Sure enough, the brief relief of Nix sliding away from me is soon replaced by dread as Colt takes his place. I might as well not really be here. I'm only a hole, something to plunge into, slap a little, to fill and punish. And that's what he's doing, punishing me, just the way his father wants. "Yeah, give it to her."

It isn't only my pussy that's hurting. My neck is already sore, and my shoulders ache from being driven into the bench. I try to raise my voice, to be heard and get somebody's attention. "She wants to tell you how much she loves it," James decides, and I hear him stroking himself even over the sound of a football game going on. My pain and tears are soaking into the blindfold, but I doubt he would care even if he could see them. It might even add to the experience.

"Give your brother another turn," James orders. "Fill her up. Make that ass raw. Nix, you fuck her while Colt spanks that ass until the skin cracks open. I want to see her bleed." He's spent all day planning this. It's obvious from the way he smoothly goes from one command to the next.

The two of them find a rhythm, with Colt making contact every time Nix pulls back a little. I'm openly sobbing, my body aching, my ass throbbing, and my pussy being pushed to the point of numbness. On and on it goes, with the two of them taking turns touching my body, fucking me, leaving me open and exposed to James whenever he orders it. "I want to see her pussy gape," he grunts, and when Colt pulls back, the satisfied little groan coming from the sofa makes me sick. "Oh, yeah. Spread her lips. I want to see inside her."

Dear god, he's sick. And because I can't see who's touching me, can't see their hands, he might as well be doing it. Striking me. Spreading my lips so he can see all of me. That thought alone has my panic and disgust reaching new heights. It's bad enough that Colt and Nix are doing this to me, but if James touched me like this, it would be a new level of dread.

It's a temporary reprieve, with Nix going back to it once his father tells him to. And now there's urgency. His fingers dig into me, and he grunts every time his balls slap against my clit. At least he's almost finished. "Come inside her," James tells him, his own breathing fast and shallow.

It isn't long before Nix drives himself deep and stays that way, filling me with his cum until I feel it oozing out around his dick. He pulls out with a groan and is quickly replaced by his brother. I'm so numb I hardly feel a thing. Only relief when he, too, empties himself inside me. I don't even care about what it means or how disgusting it is. I don't even care when I hear James coming, moaning, cursing, and panting for air until the sound eventually fades, then stops.

And here I am, dripping cum, aching from head to toe.

"It looks like we're in for a good second half," James announces. He's back to sounding chipper and upbeat again. "You boys should get yourself some drinks. I'm sure you're thirsty after all that exertion."

Wait a second. What is happening here? Is he bluffing? He can't possibly mean to keep me this way.

Yet the game starts up again, and I hear the three of them commenting on the quarterback and his passing rating or something like that. I have no idea. I only know I'm still restrained, still exposed, still dripping cum down the insides of my thighs, and probably onto the bench at this point. During a commercial break, I grunt, wriggling around a little. It's the best I can do to remind them of my presence.

"You better hope our guys decide to pick up their running game a little," James announces. "If not, I might just leave you this way all night. Bad luck. Women are always bad luck when it comes to football. I don't even know why they let them report from the sidelines. Caving to the woke crowd, I guess."

I have no doubt he's serious about leaving me this way. I've never cared so much about the outcome of a football game before in my life.

But the team does win, and I hear the men clapping and high-fiving each other like they had anything to do with it. I wonder if they know how pathetic they sound. Then James gets up, muttering something about having emails to catch up on. The sound of him climbing the stairs is like music, and I could weep from relief.

I'm still restrained in this awkward, now painful position. Not for much longer, though. Soon, someone's hands are on my wrists, the other pair on my ankles. Colt is gentle as he removes the blindfold, his expression unreadable while he reaches between my teeth and pulls out the gag.

I try to move but have to bite back a pained groan. I'm too stiff from being this way for hours. I flinch when Colt's hands are suddenly on me, his fingers gently rubbing away the tension from my sore muscles. "Come on, let's get you cleaned up."

He tucks his hands under my arms and slowly pulls me to my feet. I'm sore all over, all my limbs ache, not to mention my pussy feels painfully swollen. Every move hurts, and I can't help but whimper with each tiny step toward the door.

Nix doesn't bother announcing what he's about to do. He simply drapes the throw blanket over my shoulders before picking me up. A measure between a shriek and gasp falls from my lips while my arms automatically snake around his neck. I hold Nix as he carries me upstairs with Colt trailing us. As much as I hate being in Nix's arms, it's a relief to be able to rest against him. My body and my brain are too tired, too overwhelmed.

Instead of putting me in bed, Nix takes me to the bathroom, where Colt runs water in the tub. It doesn't take long to fill, and Nix is gentle as he lowers me into the scented, steamy water. It's miraculous, loosening up my sore muscles, giving me a little bit of comfort at last.

They sit on either side of the tub, both of them washing me

slowly, almost tenderly. Nix runs a soapy rag over my arms while Colt takes my legs. When the rag makes contact with my extremely sore inner thighs, he eases the pressure, barely brushing against me before gently running the rag over my pussy.

Nix gets up, returning a few moments later with a nightshirt and a couple of towels. Colt helps me stand, wrapping one of the towels around my body while Nix wrings the water from my hair with the other. They don't say a word to each other through all of this, and neither of them speaks to me. They don't need to. I don't have anything to say anyway, and I doubt I would have the strength to speak even if I did know what a person says in a situation like this.

Once I'm in bed, tucked in, Colt moves for the door—but Nix doesn't. "You coming?" Colt asks him, but Nix waves him off before turning back to me.

I'm so exhausted I can hardly keep my eyes open. "What do you want?" I whisper.

"I want to make you come."

"No, you don't have to do that. I'm too sore, anyway."

"But you deserve it." He's already pulling back the blanket that he only just tucked around me.

"You don't have to, really. I just want to sleep." I may as well be talking to myself for all the good it does. He stretches out near the foot of the bed and parts my thighs, working the nightshirt up to my hips. Now I know why he didn't bother bringing in panties. Was he already planning on this? What does it matter? My body is not really my own anymore, anyway.

The first touch of his tongue against my swollen, abused flesh makes me flinch, but all he does is stroke my legs and plant gentle kisses against my thighs, my mound. When he tries again to probe deeper, it feels better. Nicer. After a minute or two, I can't help moaning a little. This isn't like before, downstairs. He's not doing this just because somebody told him to. It's almost like he wants to do it, like he likes it. And every time I moan, it seems to please him, and he repeats whatever it was he just did to make me have that reaction. I would almost think it's sweet if it were anybody else doing it.

Before long, that doesn't matter, either. Nothing matters except the delicious heat now building, growing, and spreading from deep in my core until I'd swear I was on fire. My nerves sizzle and my back arches, my legs closing around his head until finally, it's all too much. I can't hold back. I don't want to.

Still, I bite down on my fist to stifle my pleasure. I don't want James to hear. I don't want him to know. By the time the delicious aftershocks fade away, the guilt and shame wash over me like a tidal wave. How can I come after what they did to me? How can I let Nix—someone who has caused me so much pain —make me feel good? I feel like a failure. A failure to myself and all other women out there.

A sob rips from my throat, then another, and before I know it, I'm full-on hysterically crying. My whole body is shaking, my vision so blurry I might as well be blind.

"Fuck. I didn't mean to..." Nix sounds like he is seriously shocked. Well, that makes two of us. "What's wrong?" I bury my face in my palms, but Nix grabs my wrists and pulls them away. "What the hell is wrong? Why are you crying?"

"Why? Don't you realize what a mind fuck this is? You are the one who hurt me. You used me, humiliated, and discarded me. And now you want to come in here and make me feel good because 'I deserve it'? What the fuck am I supposed to make of this?"

When I blink my tears away enough to make out his facial expression, he stares at me dumbfounded as if he seriously doesn't understand why I'm acting this way. "I did this to make you feel better."

"This is the last thing I wanted. Why in the world would you think this would make me feel better?"

Nix pushes himself up on his palms before running his hands through his short hair. "Because this is all I know, Leni. I guess I don't actually know how to make anyone feel better."

If my heart wasn't already broken, it would be now. Only Nix has the ability to make me go from feeling one thing to feeling something completely different in a split second, and this is a prime example. One instant, I'm angry, wanting nothing more than to shove him away, and the next, I want to hold and protect him from the world. It makes no sense, but I feel for him. I feel sad that he didn't grow up in a loving home.

"Thank you for trying."

"Is there anything I can do to make you feel better?"

"Promise me you won't let him touch me." It's the first thing that comes to my mind since I know the thing I really want he can't give me. "That, and that I can leave after tomorrow."

"I promise." He holds out his pinky. I stare at it for a moment, thinking he is joking, but when he keeps his hand stretched out toward me, I raise my own.

"Pinky promise?" I hook my pinky into his.

"Yes." He offers a faint smile before letting go of my finger and getting off the bed. He covers me up again, pulling the blanket up to my chin. "Good night," he murmurs before leaving the room and closing the door gently behind him.

I didn't grow up in the perfect home myself, but at least there was love and compassion in my house. The longer I'm here, the more certain I am that Nix and Colt never got that.

CHAPTER 32

"What's the matter?"

I open my eyes, which I didn't bother doing when the bedroom door opened a moment ago. Colt stands in the doorway, frowning at me. Like my being in bed inconveniences him somehow.

"I don't feel well." Please, let him leave it at that.

No. On second thought, he needs to know. For the first time in my whole life, I was glad when the cramps started this morning.

He rolls his eyes. "Come on. You know that excuse isn't going to work."

"It's not an excuse."

"What's wrong with you, then? Are you running a fever? Because you know, he's going to want proof—"

"I have my period, genius. I got it this morning. And if James wants proof, he can be my guest." Uh, maybe I shouldn't have said that. He's just gross enough to want to examine me while I'm bleeding.

At least I have the satisfaction of watching Colt fall back a step. "Oh. I guess we didn't think about that."

"Of course not. You don't have to. You're a man." I close my eyes and wince as a cramp takes hold. "You don't have to go through this once a month."

He moves closer to the bed, and I could almost laugh if I didn't feel so miserable. It's like he's afraid of me somehow. Like he's approaching an animal he's never come close to before. All I had to do was mention my period.

"Please, I can't do it," I whisper, crossing my arms over my abdomen. "I just can't, Colt."

"You know it's not going to work that way."

"Why not? I'm only human. I'm not a machine or a blow-up doll. I don't feel well. I hurt all over. Can't you try to get through to him?"

"Yeah, right." He flings the blankets away before folding his arms. "You need to eat something. You can't starve yourself to death."

"That's not what I was trying to do. But it's not like I'm in a big hurry to spend time with you guys. Don't act like you don't understand why I'd feel that way."

"You still need to eat. Come on. One more day. You just have to get through today and tonight."

"So it seriously doesn't matter that I'm begging you to help me?"

"I'm trying to help you, but you're too stubborn to see it."

"Yeah, right. You've been so helpful."

"Look, I'll try, but I'm not going to promise something I know is impossible, and denying him isn't possible."

I give up. All we're doing is talking in circles—and I am

hungry, which shouldn't come as a surprise, seeing as how I didn't have dinner last night. Not that anybody cared.

He waits while I get out of bed, then leads the way out of the room and down the stairs. I'm so tired, as I always am on the first day. Not that I would expect them to care, even if they could relate to the feeling. I go to the kitchen and sit at the table, not saying a word. Colt only clicks his tongue and mutters to himself as he passes me, then goes to the fridge and pulls out lunch meat, cheese, lettuce, and tomato. A loaf of fresh sourdough sits on the counter, and he pulls out a bread knife to slice it. That knife is so tempting. What I could do with that knife...

By the time he's finished building two sandwiches, Nix joins us. He looks like he just got out of the shower. His hair is damp, the T-shirt sticking to his back like he didn't quite finish drying off before he got dressed. "You feel like making one of those for me?" he asks his brother, jerking his chin toward the sandwiches.

"Not really." Colt slides a sandwich my way, then sits down across from me with one of his own. Nix only rolls his eyes before throwing his own lunch together, seemingly at random.

"You don't look so good," he tells me while he chews, eyeing me up.

"She's on the rag," Colt so helpfully explains.

"Oh, well, whatever. It's just one more night, and we had other plans tonight, anyway."

"Other plans?"

Colt ignores my question. "That's what I told her. Just one more night. That's all she's got to get through. He's always been clear about that. Just one more night. Amanda comes home tomorrow, and that's it."

"And it will all be in the past," Nix adds. I can't tell if they're both being dismissive or if they are this desperate to make me go along without arguing.

"That's really easy for you guys to say," I remind them. My voice shakes with anger and more than a little bit of despair. "What about me? I'm supposed to forget about this? Pretend it never happened? How is that even possible? Could you ever forget having the sort of things done to you that you've done to me?" Now I don't care about the sandwich, which I was only picking at, anyway. No matter how hungry I am, I can't seem to muster up an appetite when the time comes.

"Shit happens all the time," Nix mutters, staring down at his sandwich while he picks the crust away.

"And what about when I meet somebody? How am I supposed to tell my boyfriend about my first sexual experience? What am I supposed to say?"

"Would you shut the fuck up about it?" Nix throws his plate into the sink. "For fuck's sake, I'm sick of hearing you whine about this." He storms out of the room, and I can't pretend I'm not glad. Colt doesn't say a word, chewing slowly and staring at the wall.

When Nix comes back, this time he's not empty-handed. "Here." He slams something down on the kitchen table, something small and metal with a flared base and a rounded point at the tip.

"What is this?"

"What does it look like? It's a fucking butt plug. Don't tell me you've never seen one before."

"We're trying to help you out here," Colt murmurs. "Whether you believe it or not."

"You want me to wear a butt plug? That's the big plan for tonight?"

"The point is to loosen you up for tonight." Nix stares at me, speaking slowly and deliberately. Like he's trying to get the point across.

Finally, it sinks in. He's been obsessed with my ass all this time, hasn't he? Teasing, joking about them taking it at some point.

It looks like that's James's plan for tonight's grand finale. "You're kidding. You want me to wear this?"

"It's either that, or you go into it without getting stretched. It's up to you." Nix then adds something else: a bottle of what is clearly labeled Personal Lubricant. This just gets better and better.

"We really are trying to help you," Colt tells me. "You can either be stubborn and refuse it, or you can be smart and help yourself out a little bit. Your choice."

I can't believe this. I honestly can't.

"Don't be so nervous." Nix waves a hand, motioning for me to get up. "I'll help you. Don't worry." He smirks when I gasp in a mixture of surprise and horror. "I'm not going to hurt you."

It's either this or letting them hurt me later. When I think of it that way, there really isn't much of a choice to be made, is there? I doubt this will be very comfortable, but the discomfort of having my ass taken when I'm not ready for it would be an awful lot worse.

Still, I let out a heavy sigh as I stand, taking my time unzipping my jeans and pulling them down.

"Now, it's important that you try to relax," Nix informs me as he pushes me down until I'm bent over the table. I hear something squirting and know it's the lube. At least they thought of this much. Not that I'm about to thank them, but it's still better than hurting me.

"Okay, now. Breathe out."

I do, but a moment later, the sense of almost unbearable pressure at my back door makes me tense up.

"Relax," he reminds me, his voice low but firm. "This is a lot easier if you don't tense up." I almost want to ask how he would know, but I'm not sure I want the answer.

Finally, it's in place, and it's about the strangest feeling I've ever experienced. I'm so full and stretched. It doesn't hurt, but it doesn't feel great, either. "And you want me to wear this all day?"

"You'll be fine; just take it easy. Get some rest or whatever for your situation." Nix waves a hand over his lower abdomen while grimacing. They're like a couple of cavemen, honestly.

All I have to do is make it up the stairs when it feels like this damn plug is going to fall out of my ass at any time. But it doesn't, staying firmly in place as I crawl back into bed and curl into a ball, wishing I could go to sleep and wake up and have it be tomorrow already. That the whole nightmare in front of me would already be over, and I could move on.

I t's only a few hours before my door unlocks again. Instead of barging straight in, Colt eases the door open, peering at the bed like he's expecting me to be asleep. As it turns out, I did drift off in the middle of the book I was reading, but I got up to use the bathroom.

And the moment I got out of bed, I remembered the plug in

my ass. I actually managed to forget about it for a little bit. It was nice.

I did something else, too, and the effect is just starting to kick in. "I'm awake," I tell him, and he opens the door wider before stepping inside.

Immediately, my gaze is drawn to what he's holding in his hand. "You can't be serious," I whisper, my eyes bulging at yet another plug, this one thicker and longer than the one I'm wearing now.

"It's for your own good. Just to make sure you're ready."

"That thing looks like it's going to tear me apart," I whisper, revolted at the sight of it.

He looks down at it, tilting his head to the side. "This thing is like half the size of my cock."

And he's right. "Please, don't remind me," I mutter in absolute misery. But even the misery isn't as bad as it was before, thanks to that double dose of pills I took around twenty minutes ago. I don't know why I didn't think of it before. Nix keeps talking about wine to take the edge off, but I would much rather take my pills. At least I know nobody tampered with those.

"I can help you if you want." Clearly, he's not going to back down on this. I guess in the end, he's trying to do it for me, so I can't be mad. Instead, I roll to my side, facing away from him, then work my pants down all over my hips while he squirts lube on the new plug. This cannot be over quickly enough.

"Breathe out," he tells me, and a moment later, I feel his fingers back there. He gently but firmly pulls the plug free, and I gasp in surprise as my nerve endings fire all at once. It's not an unpleasant sensation, but there's no way I could possibly enjoy it under the circumstances. Now that the plug is out, I feel... open. It's so weird.

I flinch at the sensation of the cool lube touching my asshole. "I want to make sure this goes in easily," he murmurs in explanation. "Now, just like before. Breathe out and relax."

I close my eyes and do what he says, gripping a pillow tight. To my relief, it doesn't hurt. The pills were a great idea.

"See? Nothing to it. And now you'll be in better shape for tonight." He goes into the bathroom and washes his hands, but to my surprise, he comes back to the bed rather than leaving me alone. Honestly, I'm not sure which I'd rather have him do right now. It isn't exactly that I want to be alone all the time, but if the alternative is talking to him?

He doesn't stop at sitting with me, either. No, he stretches out across the bed, lying beside me. "Do you want me to do it now?"

"Huh?"

"Fuck your ass?"

"Why in the world would I want you to do it now?"

"I'd be gentle. It would be just the two of us. It's your first time, so I thought it might help."

I'm still on my side, facing him. He is on his back, staring at the ceiling, lost in thought. From this angle, I get a perfect shot of his profile. Strong jaw, soft lips, a smooth-shaved face, and eyes that hide so many dark thoughts.

I take a few deep breaths, taking in the fresh scent of his shampoo and aftershave while trying my best to figure him out. What could possibly be going on in his head?

And then it clicks.

It's your first time, so I thought it might help. He's referring to my first time with anal today, but what about my actual first time?

"The night of the rehearsal dinner. Did you have sex with me because you thought it would be easier on me?"

"Yes," he flat-out admits. "We knew you were a virgin, and we figured it would be better for you this way."

"We?"

"Nix and I."

I take a minute to let that sink in. My whole perception shifts, and I remember what happened that night in a different way. I don't know what to think. I didn't want it to happen like it did, but thinking about how my first time would have been downstairs with James watching has bile rising in my throat.

Colt turns his head toward me. Our eyes lock.

"Was I wrong?"

"No, but it doesn't make it less bad. None of this should happen."

"It was the best-case scenario I could think of at the time."

Part of me wants to ask him why Nix wasn't there, but an even bigger part doesn't, so I remain quiet.

"How are you feeling? Are you still crampy?"

"Yes," I admit. "But it's not too terrible today. I've had worse days."

"What does it feel like?"

"Are you seriously asking me that question? Or are you just screwing with me?"

"I want to know. I always hear girls talking about cramps, but I don't know what it feels like."

"It's kind of like having a stomachache you can't get rid of," I explain, even if that doesn't quite describe it. "I mean, it's a muscle, you know that, right? A uterus?" He grimaces a little at the word but nods anyway. "So it cramps up. It tightens. And sometimes, it feels like there's something kicking me half to death from the inside out."

"That sounds like hell."

"It's even better that you're supposed to walk around like everything is normal and you feel fine. And that's only one symptom. You don't want to hear about some of the other ones."

"That really sucks."

It's definitely a surprise when he reaches out and places a hand on my stomach. "Do you need anything else? You didn't really eat very much lunch."

"I usually feel nauseous on my first day. Another lovely symptom. Besides..." My throat tightens up, and my tongue is heavy and clumsy. How am I supposed to have an appetite when I know what's going to happen later?

"You know, I wanted to apologize for something." He won't look at me, just at my stomach, which he rubs in slow, gentle circles. It's almost sweet. "When I let Deborah write on you after the wedding. That was wrong. I shouldn't have let that happen. We should have never brought her home. Shit, we shouldn't have invited her to the wedding."

Am I hallucinating? Or did he seriously just say that? "For real? *That's* what you're apologizing for?"

"It was a shitty thing... and unnecessary. I'm sorry."

"After everything you've done to me, you're apologizing for that? That's probably the least of what I've had to deal with." I can't help but laugh—quietly, gently since I'm still in that warm, fuzzy place the pills have taken me. I'm only dimly aware of how hilarious and sad it is at the same time, hearing him apologize for something so trivial in the grand scheme of things. Back before James came home, and things took this sickening twist? Yes, I would have appreciated an apology.

Now, I haven't even given it a moment's thought. It's amazing how quickly perspectives can shift when all hell breaks loose and everything falls apart the way my life has the past several days.

CHAPTER 33

*H*e expects me to wear this? I'm not even sure if I can figure out how to put it on. This so-called dress Nix dropped off in my room is so flimsy, it might as well not exist. "Trust me," he muttered when all I could do was stare in a mixture of surprise and revulsion. "Just wear it and don't make a big deal over having to. It'll all be over after tonight."

Somehow, that doesn't make me feel much better as I stand in front of my mirror, having worked out how things are supposed to go. This isn't a dress. More like a fetish outfit—if that's what they're called. Tight and black and sheer and barely long enough to cover my pussy. My nipples are tight points pushing the see-through fabric, and every time I move, the hem hitches up over my ass. I pull it down a little, but that's no use. It will only creep up over my cheeks again.

The butt plug is still firmly in place, and I've started to adjust to it a little. Not that I have any plans to make this a regular thing, but at least I'm not in pain. I can almost imagine how the sensation would be pleasurable if it wasn't for the circum-stances, and once again, I have to mourn for something I've lost. I will never be able to wear one of these again without so many ugly memories bubbling to the surface. The man has taken so much from me, things I didn't even know existed until now. How much more is he going to take before this is all over?

I shouldn't let myself think like that, but I'm so tired, so sore and used. Heartsick. On top of that, there's my whole hormonal situation. I'm already miserable, so this isn't exactly helping.

Hanging out in my room isn't doing anything to get this over with. I have to survive; that's all I need to do. I have to get it over with. After tonight, it's finished. I've gotten through everything else they've done to me. I can do this, too.

So even though I want more than anything to curl up in bed with a heating pad and a book, I step out into the hall, prepared to meet my fate.

Colt is waiting for me, leaning with his back against the wall across from my door. He can't help but look me up and down. At least he keeps it brief and doesn't make any comments. All he says is, "It's going to be a little different tonight."

"No kidding. I still have this thing up my ass."

"That's not what I mean."

The way he says it makes the hair on the back of my neck stand up. "What's happening?"

"Come on. You'll see." It doesn't take long for me to figure out at least part of what he means since, instead of leading me downstairs, as usual, he heads down the hall.

My heart clenches when I realize what's happening. Where we're going. "No," I whisper, grabbing him by the arm like that will do anything to slow him down. It doesn't, of course. "In there?"

"Like I said. Tonight will be different." Then he opens the door to the bedroom James shares with my mother. Nix is already waiting, as is his father, standing at the foot of the bed.

In here. In my mother's bed. It's enough to make my blood run cold.

James flashes a broad smile that widens with every step I take. "Good evening, Leni. Let's see you do a little spin in that outfit. As soon as I saw it, I knew it was made for you."

And here I am, trying to ignore the fact I've never felt less attractive in my whole life. The fact that I'm crampy and bloated isn't helping things, either. Still, I know better than to hesitate, so I do a little spin with my arms held out to the sides.

"Very nice," he declares. Already I can hear the change in his voice. How it's gotten sort of breathy and raspy. All the blood's leaving his brain and traveling south. He even runs a hand over his crotch, rubbing himself a little while he stares at me.

He then takes a step back from the bed and waves an arm like he's directing me that way. "I thought tonight we would keep things a bit more intimate," he explains. There's a throb of eagerness in his voice, like a little boy who can't wait to start having fun. "Besides, we want you to be comfortable. I understand last night might have been a little rough on you, and I would like to make up for that."

Yeah, right. Like I believe a word he's saying. Especially when he uses that fake, sickeningly sweet tone, like all he cares about is doing right by me. He must think I'm really stupid. Either that or he gets off on being an absolute bastard. I wouldn't doubt it, all things considered.

Not that I'm in any hurry to get on the bed, but I hesitate more than I normally would, biting my lip and glancing at James before looking away. "Do you know... I mean, did they tell you..."

He clears his throat. "Yes, I've been informed of your condition." And oh, does he sound grossed out. For once, I'm the one grossing him out. What a change. "But don't worry. We'll keep that in mind. Nobody will touch your pussy tonight." The way he announces it, it's like he's also reminding his sons. Like he's being the generous, doting parent. Am I supposed to thank him?

With that, his expression hardens, and I know we're about to begin. "Now get on the bed. On all fours."

So this is it. I just have to get through it, that's all. And once it's over, it's over. That's all that keeps me going as I climb onto the king-size bed where my mother sleeps, where I'm sure she's had sex with this man and will again. And all the while, he'll know he made his sons take her daughter's ass in this same bed. I wonder if he'll think about it while they're fucking.

What is wrong with me? Why am I even entertaining these thoughts? I guess it's because they're easier to think about than the reality of what's happening to me and what's about to happen.

"Colt, you can go first. Remember what we talked about. Take her hard. Make it count." James lowers his zipper as he speaks, taking himself in one hand and beginning to stroke.

Colt makes the briefest eye contact with me before taking off his clothes. I don't know if the lube was his idea or his father's—I'm guessing his or Nix's, definitely not James's. James would never put any thought into my comfort or protection.

He squirts a little onto his palm and uses it to stroke himself, to make himself hard, while he climbs onto the bed and positions himself behind me. I'm shaking, already fighting off panic-induced nausea that would be bad enough if I wasn't already feeling so ill, thanks to my period. I should have taken another pill, but I didn't want to run the risk of taking too many in too short a timeframe.

It isn't like before, earlier this afternoon. Instead of talking me through it, reminding me to relax and breathe, Colt merely takes the base of the plug and yanks it out. I gasp, stiffening, and James merely laughs as he slowly walks around the bed. "You think that was something? Wait until you take two cocks up that ass tonight. Go ahead, Colt. Make her feel it. I want her to gasp again."

It's like he hates me. Like he genuinely hates me and wants me to suffer. Why else would he sound so gleeful when he gives instructions like that? Why would he be so damn determined to humiliate me, hurt me, break me?

I barely have time to form those questions in my head before Colt enters my gaping ass. Yes, he is much bigger than that plug, and I can't imagine the pain that would have come from him forcing himself inside before I was ready. I'm hardly ready now, even with the lube he so generously applied.

"That's right," James calls out over my pitiful whimpers. "Tear that ass up."

He doesn't exactly do that, but he isn't exactly gentle, either. He takes me by the hips and pulls me close, lining us up better before pulling back, then plunging in again. It's the strangest feeling. My body keeps telling me I have to go to the bathroom, but that's not the case. I don't know what to think or feel besides humiliation and outrage.

Just get through it. Just hold on, get through it, and it's over.

"How's that feel, son?" James asks Colt as our bodies bang together, and I have to grit my teeth against a pained cry every time he drives himself home. "Is that ass as tight as I think it is?"

"Yeah," Colt grunts. No matter what he's thinking about this, his body is another story. His body is loving it, his dick plunging in and out so hard his breathing is getting faster. "Really tight."

"Nothing like a virgin ass," James says with a sigh like it makes him happy to think about it. "Let your brother get in there and enjoy it before you stretch it out too much."

At least it gives me a moment to catch my breath. I touch my forehead to the mattress and tell myself to ignore the cramps threatening to make me even more miserable than I already am.

Nix is already hard, prepared, and he wastes no time working his way inside me. His satisfied little grunt makes James laugh and stroke himself faster. "Now fuck her. Fuck her good and hard. Fuck her until she passes out."

My head tells me he can't mean that, but deep inside, I know he does. I need to stop thinking of him as a normal human being. Nothing about him is normal. He wants me to hurt.

And I am hurting. My ass is raw, and my stomach is in knots. I didn't realize until now how gentle Colt was trying to be. Now that I'm under Nix's control, and he slams into me for all he's worth, I really wish Colt would come back. I can't hold back the tears of pain, and soon the pain comes out in the form of wracking sobs. The last thing I want is for them to see me break down, but this is too much. It's all too much.

"Not quite enough," James announces. He's breathing hard like he just sprinted, coming to a stop at my side, so he can see Nix pumping in and out. "She needs to scream. Make her scream."

"Please!" I wail, my pride forgotten in the face of the pain while Nix only pounds me harder and faster. "Please!"

"Please, what?" James taunts. "Please, fuck your ass harder? Nix, I think she wants you to do it harder. Give the slut what she's begging for."

"No!" I sob. My hands are twisted in the blankets, tears dripping from my face and soaking in. "No, please stop!"

"Who the hell said you get to decide that?" As I continue sobbing, he shouts, "Harder! Show her what happens when she tries to call the shots."

Nix is panting now, his body getting slick with perspiration. I feel it on my ass and the backs of my thighs every time we slam together.

"Tell him to fuck your ass," James grunts, standing close to me. "Do it. Say please, fuck my ass."

"Please..." Just one more night. One more night, and it's over.

"Please, what?"

I don't want to, but I have to. I have to do it, or else they could seriously hurt me. It's that fear that makes me do it. "Please, fuck my ass!" I shout. I barely recognize my own voice. I sound like some broken animal howling while James laughs.

"I don't think I heard you. Say it again. Louder this time."

A roar bursts out of me, and all the pain, humiliation, and shame come with it. I'll do anything, say anything to make it stop. "Please, fuck my ass! Fuck my ass! Fuck my ass!" I scream it until my throat is raw and maybe bleeding. Until I lose my breath and my voice breaks.

But that's nothing compared to the other scream that fills the room.

The scream coming from the doorway.

I open my eyes and look up to find my mother's horror-filled face.

CHAPTER 34

*I*t's like all hell has broken loose, everything happening at once. Mom is frozen in the doorway, screaming while James immediately puts himself back in his pants, babbling the entire time.

Mom is hardly listening, too busy reacting to what she walked in on. "What the fuck is this? What are you doing? Leni, what is this? James!"

"I can explain. I didn't mean for this to happen!" James insists while the guys offer their own excuses behind him, frantically pulling their clothes on.

She knows. She's seen it with her own eyes. She can't tell me it didn't happen because she's seen it. I've never felt this ashamed in my life. My heart is breaking, and I haven't stopped crying yet, but at least she knows and can't pretend otherwise.

"She's been doing this from the beginning!" James thrusts his arm toward me when all I'm trying to do is cover myself up with the blankets as best I can. "She's been seducing me from the minute you brought her here! I'm so ashamed."

My insides go cold. After all the things he's done so far, how did I not see this coming? "That's not true!" I scream over him. "Mom, that isn't true at all!"

"She tried to get to Colt, but he turned her down, and she's been using me to get back at him. From the very beginning, she did everything she could to turn me on and get me to look at her and not you, sweetheart."

"Mom, he's lying!" I'm still sobbing, but now it's for a different reason. "Mom, they hurt me. They made me do this!"

"Please." James shoots me a filthy, cold look. "Everybody in town knows you've been obsessed with this family, with my sons, for years. It's disgusting. I'm only sorry I was weak enough not to call you on your pathetic little blackmail scheme."

"What blackmail scheme?" I look at the guys, but they're turned away from me.

"You've conveniently forgotten the recording you made the night of the rehearsal dinner?" He even has the nerve to glare at me. He's that devoid of a conscience. "When you seduced Colt, recorded it, then threatened to take it to the police and say you were under the influence, and he raped you?"

I can't breathe. There isn't any air in the room. My mouth moves, but nothing comes out. He would stoop this low?

And not only him. Colt speaks as he pulls a shirt over his head. "He's telling the truth."

"What?"

He won't look at me, the coward. "She said we had to do things to her, or else she'd go to the police."

"Look at the tattoo on her ass," Nix continues. "Alistair. She had our last name tattooed on her ass. That's how obsessed she is."

"None of this is true! Mom, they drugged me while you were gone. That's when I got that—"

"Shut the hell up with your lies," James warns. "I'm only glad your mother came back when she did. I'm sorry she had to see what a filthy degenerate she raised, but at least she'll see what you've been doing to us all this time. You can't stand to see us happy. You need to have your way, no matter who it hurts."

She won't look at me. Why won't she look at me? I have to get through to her somehow. "Mom. You know that's not what I'm like. I swear, I didn't want any of this."

"You certainly sounded like you wanted it when I walked in."

That's it. That's the gut punch. I've lost. I never stood a chance.

She folds her arms over herself, and I can see she's shaking. I guess she would be. She just walked in on her husband and stepsons using her daughter. While her daughter cried out and begged for more. Jesus, could this be any worse?

"I swear, I didn't want any of this to happen. Please, believe me."

"You know what? I'm through with you. I don't want to hear another word out of your lying whore mouth. Get the fuck out of my house. Pack your things and go. I don't care where you end up. I don't care if I never see you again. In fact," she adds, viciously ripping the comforter away from me, so I'm fully exposed again. "It would be better for you if I never do. Because if I set my eyes on you again, I will kill you. Do you understand? I will finally be rid of you, one way or another."

I don't know what to think. How to feel. All I know is I need to get out of here.

I run out of the bedroom without looking at any of them,

fleeing for my own room and slamming the door. I tear the flimsy garment away from me and throw it on the floor, stepping on it on my way to the dresser, where I quickly pull on a hoodie and a pair of leggings. After that, I grab my backpack and jam in as much as I can. It's the best I can do in a hurry, and I am definitely in a hurry.

My brain never stops turning the entire time. I hear them down the hall, still arguing, with James defending himself while his sons back him up. I would say I can't believe it, but that's not true. I wouldn't put anything past them. It's like they rehearsed the whole damn thing. Like they had their excuse already and waiting just in case we ever got found out. And, of course, she didn't believe me. Why would she? She never has. From the beginning, she's been sure I would ruin this relationship for her.

And the thing is, even now, after she's rejected me and basically kicked me out of her life, I still want to warn her about who he is, how he is. I seriously doubt I'm the only person who brings this out in him. Eventually, those dark needs of his will have to be fulfilled. Either he does it with her or somebody else —either way, this isn't going to be the last time a situation like this happens. Even though she's hurt me more times than I can count, I really hope she's not the one he decides to hurt.

Once I'm sure I have everything that matters, I put on my shoes and listen at the door to see what's happening now. I don't want to run out into the hall and come face-to-face with her. I don't even want to know what James has told her since I left the room, but I imagine it's much worse. God, how can he live with himself? And how can his sons live with themselves, for that matter? Lying the way they did. They know damn well how I ended up with this stupid tattoo, but they're willing to pretend it was my idea, that I'm obsessed.

The hallway is empty, thank god. I take off running, dashing down the stairs with my backpack slung over one shoulder. At least I get to leave. I don't know where I'm going, but I have a little bit of money in the bank. I can figure things out once I'm away from here.

But the sight of my two worst enemies standing in the driveway makes me stop short and backpedal a little. Nix is standing at the open driver's door to the truck while Colt steps forward, closer to me. "Come on."

"Go to hell," I fire back. "Like I would go anywhere with the two of you—you fucking liars. You sick fucking liars."

"Get in the truck," Colt growls. "Or I'm going to put you in it."

"You know where you can put your truck? Right up your ass. See how you feel." I begin to walk around him in a wide arc, but of course, it does me no good. He picks me up and unceremoniously dumps me in the back of the truck before slamming the door. By the time I sit up and reach for the handle, Nix has already engaged the locks.

"This is kidnapping, you assholes. What, do you want to add that to your list of crimes? It wasn't enough to rape me. Now you have to fucking kidnap me? I bet this is your father's way of keeping me quiet forever, isn't it? Are you supposed to take me somewhere, leave me there to rot?"

"Are you finished?" Nix mutters as we drive away from the house. I don't bother looking back. I'll never see it again, anyway. Not once they're finished with me. Considering everything that's happened, I don't think the idea of them murdering me at their father's command is that far outside the realm of possibility.

It's not a very long ride, but it's a silent one. I don't say another word until it's clear they're not taking me out to the woods or anything like that. No, in fact, we're rolling through a cute little college campus with pubs and shops sprinkled around the outside. People are all over the place, wandering in and out of restaurants and cafés, hanging out at tables on the sidewalk.

This is where I'm supposed to be starting school. Not for another few days, but this is the place. "Why are you bringing me here?" I finally have to ask.

"Why do you think? A deal is a deal." Nix pulls to a stop in front of a long, three-story building on the edge of campus.

Colt turns in his seat and holds out a key. "Your room number 312. This is the key to your door."

I feel like I've walked into a movie halfway through, and I'm the only one who isn't caught up on the plot. "I don't get it."

"You're here. You're at school. And you're all set—everything is paid up, and there's money in your account, so you can go to the cafeteria, the bookstore, or whatever. It's all there."

"Like I said, we had a deal," Nix reminds me. "And we confirmed everything is set up for you. Go ahead. Take the key and get out of here."

Can this be true? I want it to be, but it all seems so sudden. Like being thrown from one insane situation into another with hardly any time to gather my thoughts in between.

"You're sure about this?" I whisper, staring at the key in my palm. "This isn't a trick?"

"You'd better hurry," Nix grunts, staring straight ahead. "We've got to get back home. We'll be missed."

"It's for real," Colt tells me in a quieter voice. "Go on. Go, like, be a college student."

Even though I should be happy, all I can do is hate them. They've even taken this from me. I should be joyful, full of hope, and looking forward to the next phase in my life. Instead, I'm afraid to get out of the truck because I just know I'll end up finding out this was all a trick.

Still, I have nowhere else to go, do I? I guess I'll find out whether they've been fucking with me all this time if I try to use this key and it doesn't work. Maybe I didn't really believe they would follow through with their part of our agreement. I mean, it's not like they've ever given me a reason to believe they're sincere.

I climb down from the truck without saying a word and slam the door for good measure before starting up the pathway toward the entrance to the building. People walk in and out, some carrying boxes, and the energy is happy and upbeat. Even though class doesn't start for another few days, today was the first day we were allowed to move in. To think, all these people were finishing last-minute stuff before moving in while I spent the day dreading having my ass fucked.

I take the elevator to the third floor and walk down to room 312. I'm still holding the key in my palm, my fingers closed tight around it. Is this for real? If I try this key and it doesn't work, that might be what breaks me. I might finally fall to pieces here in this hallway with a bunch of strangers wandering back and forth.

But it does fit, and it turns in the lock, and the door opens to reveal a room that's actually a hell of a lot nicer than I ever would have expected. There are two beds, one on the left-hand wall and one on the right, two dressers, and two nightstands. There's plenty of space, lots of room in the closets, and the windows overlook the campus.

There are also two desks; on one sits a new laptop and a new phone. I can't believe I forgot my old laptop. Luckily, everything is saved on my cloud.

Since the other side of the room contains no items—the closet's empty, and nothing is in the dresser—I'm assuming it's supposed to be mine.

Is it really over? Did they really let me go and make sure I'm set up comfortably here? There are even clothes in the dresser and hanging from the rod in the closet. All of it is new, with the tags still attached. Like whoever bought it went by the sizes of the clothes in my room. But which one of them would be that thoughtful?

It's almost too much to be believed, but the evidence kind of speaks for itself. I'm still waiting for somebody to jump out and yell *Gotcha* and laugh themselves sick while I fall to pieces, but that's not happening. The bed even has clean sheets on it, the whole nine yards.

I think this is it. I want this to be it.

But instead of releasing the breath I'm holding and letting myself relax, all I can do is sit down on the bed and stare at the new computer and wonder if this is all part of their fucked-up game.

CHAPTER 35

*C*lasses start tomorrow. All around me, both inside and outside the building, there seems to be nonstop laughing and talking, music playing, and doors opening and closing. Life, in other words. Everybody is looking forward to starting the semester. I hear people talking about parties as they walk past my room, things they're looking forward to.

While I hide out in here, wondering if I'll ever be able to actually enjoy this.

I mean, I haven't even slept a solid night since I got here. I can't escape the nightmares. I keep expecting to open my eyes and find James standing over me, demanding I humiliate myself for him again.

I wish I knew what to do. This will always hang over my head unless I find a way to get closure. The problem is, I have no idea what that looks like. They can't get away with this. I can't let them get away with it. No punishment would be too severe after everything they've put me through.

What do I do, then? Go to the police? And who would believe me? Not even my own mother believed me. The one person who was supposed to protect me and love me. How could I possibly convince a stranger? Plus, I'm sure they've already thought about that. James probably has a plan for just such a situation.

Nobody would believe me. Not against somebody like James. Somebody with money, a career, and a reputation. And what would end up happening? Word would get out somehow because it always does. *Has-been gymnast accuses powerful lawyer of sexual assault*—like that's not exactly the kind of story that makes headlines. Every aspect of my personal life would end up being torn to pieces. My only shot at living a somewhat normal life would be to change my name and move to the other side of the world.

I guess that's out. I'm going to have to find a way to live with it. I'll have to, or else I'll have no hope of a future. Not if I stay stuck in what they did to me. I need to find a way to move on.

Obviously, that time is not now since the clicking of the lock on my dorm room door makes me jump a mile, heart in my throat, and ready to defend myself from an attack.

"Piper?" She's the last person I would ever expect to see, even if it's strangely fitting that she would show up. Yet another example of a disappointment in my life. This is becoming a greatest hits playlist of all the most fucked-up aspects of my existence.

She manages a shy little smile. "Yeah, hi."

"What are you doing here?" Even the fact that she's carrying a mesh bag full of clothes over one shoulder and wheeling a suitcase with the other hand doesn't clue me in right away. I'm too busy being surprised by the sight of her.

"We are... roommates." She drops her bag of clothes on the other unmade bed. "This is my room, too."

I launch myself out of my chair so fast that she backs into the bed and ends up flopping down on it. "Did they put you up to this?" I demand, leaning down until I'm in her face. "Are you here to spy on me? Is that part of their plan? I knew it. I knew there was something more to all of this!"

She only stares at me with wide eyes, leaning back a little. "I don't know what you're talking about. Who do you mean? Why would anybody be planning against you?"

"Oh, give me a fucking break. Don't act like you don't know."

"But I don't, I swear. This is my room, room 312. It's the room I was assigned, along with you. I don't know what you mean by a plan." She hesitates, biting her lip. "But if you want to talk about it, I don't have any place else to be. What's going on?"

I don't know what to think about this. I back away, never taking my eyes off her. I don't trust her, for one thing. And I don't know if I can believe her.

"Leni, you can trust me. I know I made mistakes. And I know I'm probably the last person you think you can trust now. All I can say is I'm sorry, and I wish I had never done it. I really miss you, and I'm so sorry I hurt you. If you need a friend right now, I'm here. I want to listen if you want to talk."

It just so happens that the one thing I need more than just about anything in the world is somebody to listen. Still... "I don't know. You really hurt me. That's not the kind of thing I can just forget."

"I understand. And I'm so, so sorry. I hate myself for hurting you. And I know trust isn't something you can just magically get back. I've done a lot of thinking about this, especially since those couple of days we were together at the gym. All I wanted was to be able to talk to you the way we used to. It's like you were so close, but you may as well have been a million miles away. And that hurt so much. That, more than anything, reminded me of what I lost because I made the wrong choice. I will do anything I can to make it up to you. I just want us to start again. I'm willing to earn your trust back if that's what it takes."

She doesn't know it, but she's saying exactly the kind of thing I need to hear right now. All of a sudden, my legs are too weak to hold me up, so I plop down beside her on the bed. "I don't know if I should tell you or not."

"You don't have to tell me anything you're not comfortable talking about, but I'm here for you. So whenever you feel comfortable, just let me know. The least I can do is listen. And I'll tell you something else," she adds in a softer voice. "I noticed when we were at the gym together that you didn't look very good. I'm not trying to insult you, I swear. You looked kind of pale and extra tired, run down. I was already worried about you, but I knew you wouldn't want to hear me talk about it. Nobody wants to be told they're not looking good, but especially not when it's somebody who hurt them."

"I have really missed having you to talk to," I admit in a whisper. "I have really needed you the past few weeks."

"Leni, please tell me. What's happening?"

I can't believe I'm about to do this, but I have to. I'll die if I don't get it out. It will eat a hole through me just like if I swallowed acid. This isn't the kind of thing I can carry around for the rest of my life. "You have to promise this stays between us. At least until I figure out what I want to do about it. Swear it."

"I swear. I won't say a word to anybody."

I'll test her a little bit first. Just to see how she reacts. "You know, now that I think about it, you didn't go back to the house after Mom's wedding. It was just Deborah."

"Yeah." Her teeth sink into her lip. "They were being weird. They all had way too much to drink, and nobody wants to be the sober person around a bunch of drunks. But I don't know, Deborah kept talking about you, too. And she kept saying things like how she was going to take both of them on that night. I didn't want to be any part of it. Really, I haven't talked to her since that night. I don't know why I ever... forget it." Her cheeks are red now, and her lips pursed tight.

I believe her because that's exactly what Deborah would say —she probably did screw them both that night, come to think of it. "Did either of the guys ever tell you why they hate me like they do?"

"Honestly, they never really got into specifics. But they did say that you were kind of obsessed with them."

"Like how I had to go to that party? Where I ended up in the pool?"

"Yeah, honestly. They sort of made it sound like you forced your way into it."

"Do you seriously think I would force my way into that party? Nobody even wanted me there. You know me better than that."

"I do. I sort of thought they were full of shit."

"And that so-called job at the gym. I bet they made it seem like I was just tagging along with them, following them around."

Her head bobs up and down. "Does that make any sense, either?"

"No, I thought it was really weird."

"What if I told you they've been setting me up all this time? They wanted to make it look like I was obsessed with them. Do you want to see what else they did? Honestly, this might be the most disgustingly brilliant part about the whole thing." I stand up and lower my pants just enough for her to see the tattoo. "Now you tell me. Would I ever, ever get anything like this on my own?"

"What? No way!" She leans in, eyes going wide, her nose wrinkling. "You're saying they gave you this? How?"

"They drugged me. Put it in my food and told me it was because they were having a party and didn't want me getting in the way. But I got this, too. To make it look like I was totally obsessed with them."

"I don't get it, though. Why? Why go to all that trouble?"

This is it. This is where she either believes me or calls me a liar, and I know this was all a waste of time. I have to tell myself I can trust her. I need to.

"Remember, you don't tell anybody about this."

She gulps but nods, looking me straight in the eye.

So I tell her. I tell her all of it, even the parts I'm too ashamed to admit. All about James, all the awful things he made me do. From the hand around my throat in the hallway to that last night when he turned everything around on me.

And by the time I'm finished, we're both crying. "I haven't left this room except to get something to eat since I got here. You are the first person I've spoken to since that night. I can't sleep. I don't know what I'm going to do. I keep thinking they're going to come back for me. I can't believe it's all over, even though I want it to be, so much. I want to go to the police, but I'm so fucking scared that no one will believe me."

She doesn't say anything for a long time, blowing her nose and wiping her eyes. Eventually, curiosity made it impossible for me not to blurt it out. "Do you believe me?"

"Yes, yes, of course, I do." She throws her arms around me, and I stiffen in surprise at first. "I'm sorry. But I just feel like I have to hug you. I can't believe you went through all of this alone. I am so, so sorry. You are the last person in the world to ever deserve something like what happened to you."

I hardly hear most of what she says. The only thing that matters is she believes me. Finally, at last, somebody believes me.

But it isn't long before the truth comes rushing back. I can't avoid it. "You're the only one who believes me."

She pulls away, wiping her eyes again. "I know. They've done a really good job of making it look like you're super obsessed. That tattoo is just, like, diabolical."

"I know. And it's not even the worst thing they've done."

"But they can't get away with it."

"I know. I don't want them to."

"Do you have any proof at all? Anything?"

"I wish I did. James was really smart about making sure I didn't have any, but he has things on me." Even whispering his name makes me shudder in disgust. "At least I don't have to see him anymore."

"But god, we have to do something. Not that I'm trying to push you or anything like that," she insists, "but it just doesn't seem right for him to get away with this."

"I know. I don't want him to. He doesn't deserve to."

"Whatever you need, I'm here. I'll help with whatever I can. You're the best friend I ever had, and it's my fault I forgot about that—but I'm going to make it right."

I believe she means it. And for the first time in weeks, I have a little bit of hope to cling to.

CHAPTER 36

"I didn't even know they offered fencing as a class."

Piper nods, all glowy and smiley after her first fencing lesson. "It counts as phys ed credits. Who knew? And I think it'll be fun. You know I've never been athletic like you."

"So what, you just wave those pointy swords around?" I slash my arm through the air, attracting the attention of a few people walking our way. All they do is go back to their conversation. It's strange, being able to walk around all free and whatnot, saying and doing pretty much whatever I want without anybody using it to taunt me. That doesn't mean I won't pay attention to the people around me when I do something like that, and they notice—maybe once enough time passes. Once I get used to nobody caring very much about what I do and just letting me live my life, I won't be so quick to look around and make sure nobody is making fun.

"I think it's a little more than that." She giggles. "And they put something on the end of the foil, by the way. So we don't end up stabbing each other to death."

"Ooh, a foil. You already know all the technical terminology."

"Yeah, I'm a real expert after one class."

"Well, it's good to know you won't end up impaled. And it seems like it's going to be fun?"

"It really does. How about you? How was your lit class?"

"You know me. Any excuse to read a book is just fine. We're covering *Beloved* first. I have to read five chapters before the next class."

It's almost too bizarre how normal this feels. Walking across campus with my best friend, chatting about our classes now that we've been through almost the first full week of school. Finally, I've got somebody to talk to, and Piper seems so relieved that I want to be friends that it feels like we've done nothing but catch up and laugh since she showed up at our room.

I can almost believe I will live a normal life now. I can almost believe it's possible to forget and move on. After walking around campus these past few days, I know that nobody can look at me and tell what I've been through. I don't have any reason to be paranoid or ashamed. I might have a small tattoo on my ass—which nobody can even see—but there's no tattoo across my forehead saying what I've been through. I need to remember that.

"Heads-up!" We barely have time to react before a football sails not very far over our heads. A tall, athletic guy comes running past at top speed and grabs it at the last second, bobbling it a little on his fingertips before pulling it in close. Piper does a slow, joking sort of clap, and he touches a finger to the brim of his ball cap before running away.

It's only when she continues and realizes I'm not with her

that she stops and turns around. "You okay?" she asks with a light laugh.

I don't know. I should be, but I'm not. I can't move, and my heart is racing. She approaches slowly, glancing around like she wants to make sure nobody is watching us.

"I can't breathe," I whisper before struggling to suck in a lung full of air.

"You're safe. That guy, he's nobody. Just a guy playing football with his friends. Nobody is going to hurt you. Okay? Remember that. Tell yourself that. You're safe here. Nobody is going to hurt you anymore."

Nobody is going to hurt me. I close my eyes and force my way through a few shallow breaths before the tension in my chest loosens and my pulse settles back to a more normal speed. The world was starting to dwindle to a pinpoint there for a second, and all the color had started to drain out of my surroundings, but now it's back, just the way it was before.

And now I feel like the biggest idiot. "I'm sorry."

"You don't have to apologize to me, not ever. I guess it's only natural."

"It's just that it will probably take me a while to get used to people randomly running at me from out of nowhere."

"I get it. Like I said, you don't have to apologize or explain yourself. I'm here. We can get through this."

I'm so grateful I could cry, but I've done so much of that. It's amazing there's any moisture left in my body.

That's going to change with time, too. I have to believe it will. Piper's right. I'm safe here—not that I'm going to run around being reckless or anything, but I don't have to worry about whether everybody around me is going to hurt me somehow. I hate knowing how James managed to work his way so deep into my head, him and his sons. It isn't fair.

But they aren't here. The guys are at MIT by now, living it up. I haven't heard another word from them since they dropped me off, and my mother hasn't bothered to reach out to me, either. What a surprise.

That's for the best, too. Even though it burns me up inside, knowing she believes all those ugly lies about me, that's just something I'm going to have to accept. If it means I no longer have to deal with her, so be it. I'll make that sacrifice. I know the truth, anyway. I know I'm not the person James made me out to be. That needs to be enough. Maybe it's for the best that I've learned to live without her approval. I'd probably be in much worse shape if that wasn't the case.

"They still haven't reached out, have they?" Piper asks as we enter our building.

I shake my head. "You would know if they had. I would have told you."

"I mean, that's good, though. They're moving on and letting you move on."

"I know. And I know I should be grateful."

"But..."

We climb the stairs side by side, and suddenly, my heart is much heavier than it was before. "But I can't help thinking it's unfair as hell for them to just go on with their lives like none of this ever happened. I can't even walk across campus without getting freaked out because somebody ran too close to me. But I'm sure they're living it up, already going to parties and having fun."

"I wish they would fry for it. I really do."

"I know. But still..." We reach the third floor, and I lean against our door while Piper unlocks it. "Is it wrong that I just kind of want to let the whole thing go away? Is that selfish, do you think?"

"I've seen what this has done to you. And I've heard you while you're having nightmares."

I can't help but cringe. "I didn't know it was that bad."

"It's not terrible. But you're obviously going through a lot. I can see why you'd want them to suffer, but I can also see why you would want to let it all go away. That's totally normal."

"So I'm not selfish?"

"No. You're not selfish. You're doing what you have to do to take care of yourself. That's not selfish at all." She drops her backpack on the floor next to her bed before throwing her arms over her head and stretching. "I need a shower. I really worked up a sweat earlier."

"Please, don't let me stop you." I wave a hand around in front of my nose like she smells, and we're both laughing as she disappears into our shared bathroom.

I'm still mulling things over as I kick off my shoes and pull out *Beloved*. I heard a couple of people groan when the professor assigned the first five chapters before our next class, like reading five entire chapters is so tough, but all I could do was smile. I know it's nerdy, but I can't help it. It's an excuse to curl up with a good book, and I've never been able to resist that.

I'm barely a few pages in when my phone vibrates. I jump at the sensation in my pocket. I forgot the thing was even there; I only carry it around more out of habit than anything else. I still don't quite trust it, seeing as how Colt and Nix left it for me.

What if they're tracking it somehow? I hate how paranoid they've made me.

I should ignore it. I really should. After all, only a few people know my number, and I don't want to speak to any of them. The sooner I completely cut them out of my life and my memory, the better.

But my curiosity is too much to resist. I won't absorb any of this material, not if I try for the rest of the day unless I at least see who texted and what they have to say. My heart is heavy with dread as I reach into my pocket to pull out the device. The text is from an unknown number.

Unknown: How is school? - Colt

The phone shakes until the words blur. Finally, I have to put it down and clench my hands together, taking deep breaths to work my way through the flash of panic that's gripped me. It's okay. I'm okay. I'm safe here. He's miles and miles away, where he can't hurt me. None of them can.

What I ought to do is block his number. I need to ignore this message. It's the only way to cut him out of my life, right? If I engage with him, that only opens the door to more of the same bullshit. I have to be smarter than that, or else there won't be anybody to blame but myself for the misery that will surely follow.

Then again...

I bite my lip, staring down at the phone like I'm waiting for it to snap at me. If I can get him talking, I might be able to eventually get some proof. Maybe not right now since it would look too obvious, but eventually. If I convince him I can move on and we can talk like two normal people, he might be more likely to open up. He might spill something he didn't mean to, something I can use against him—but mostly against his father.

And so, though I don't want to, I type a message in reply.

Me: It's pretty good. I was just about to dig into some reading for my lit class. How's it going there?

Immediately, an ellipsis pops up like he's replying. I can almost see him sitting with his feet up on his desk or windowsill, or maybe he's out with new friends. Perhaps he misses having somebody to torment.

Colt: Pretty good. It's going to take a little bit of getting used to, new people and all that. But the coursework seems like it should be a breeze.

I roll my eyes.

Me: At MIT? Those are some pretty big words.

Colt: Yeah, but how do you think I got in? I know what I'm doing.

Whatever he says. I'm sure his father's money had a little something to do with the two of them getting in, as well, but I don't want to think about James, much less mention him.

Colt: Any hot girls there?

He would ask that question. I can't help but bristle at the way he managed to change the subject so quickly.

Me: I don't know. I don't really pay attention to girls, in case you forgot.

Colt: Come on. Even a straight girl knows when another girl is hot.

Me: I've sort of been a little too busy getting settled in. And having nightmares, but he doesn't need to know about those. Nor does he deserve to.

Colt: I didn't think there'd be so many here. I figured

they'd all be nerds. But there are a couple of smoke shows in my classes. I fucked one of them the first night we got here.

Something about that sets my teeth on edge. I really wish it didn't. I also really wish I understood why. What do I care who he fucks? If anything, I feel bad for the girl. Somebody should warn her about him and his brother. Somebody should definitely warn her against letting him take her home for a visit over the holidays, for sure. Then again, what am I saying? He's not the relationship type, is he? I'm sure he wouldn't even recognize the girl if he walked past her this very minute.

Whoever she is. Why do I even care?

I don't know what to say, and I know he's waiting for an answer. What, do I congratulate him? Extend my sympathies toward the poor girl, whoever she is? All he's going to do is keep taking me farther down this road, and I have no desire to go in that direction with him. Not ever again.

So instead of playing along, I do the only other thing I can if I want to save face and get rid of the burning lump of betrayal his message lodged in my throat. I turn the phone off and toss it onto my desk before returning to my reading.

Though something tells me it's going to take a long time to plow through these chapters now that I have so much on my mind.

CHAPTER 37

*J*ames Alistair wife
I hit enter, and immediately the Google screen populates with search engine results. Unfortunately, all I find are little bits from the wedding announcement my mother made a point of sending out to the local papers. Everything I'm finding has to do with her, but she's not the one I'm interested in.

I can't forget about that picture. I can't forget the way Nix and Colt reacted to it the day I found it in James's desk. I need to find something I can use against this man, and she's what I keep coming back to. There's something very wrong, but I can't figure out what it is. I hoped a little digging around on the internet would help, but I keep hitting dead end after dead end.

I stare at the ceiling, pursing my lips. I wish I could remember her first name, but there were so many coaches over the years. It's all a blur. I only remember her face and how kind she seemed. I'm having a hard time wrapping my head around that part. How somebody so kind, so warm and maternal, birthed two monsters like her sons.

Even thinking that to myself makes me frown and shake my head. I doubt they were born that way. James must have somehow found a way to twist them up.

Instead of putting James's name in there, I type *Alistair gymnastics death*. I mean, there's got to be something about her team mourning her, her accomplishments with them, something. The woman could not have disappeared off the face of the earth.

Still, I don't get anything worthwhile. Nothing that mentions her. Was her name even Alistair, or did she keep her maiden name? This time, I type in *gymnastics coach dead*.

Nothing. I mean, there are lots of articles and blog posts about various gymnastics coaches who died, but when I pull up images related to the links, none of them are her.

"Hey. Class let out early. You wanna go get some dinner?" Piper hasn't fully entered the room, only poking her head in from the hallway.

I turn to her, tapping my nails against the desk with one hand. "Question. Did Colt or Nix ever tell you anything about their mom?"

She comes in and closes the door, then leans against it. "It's funny, but now that you mention it, no. I really don't think so." I can tell she's thinking about it, too, frowning, staring toward the windows. After a few moments, she shakes her head with a shrug.

"That's really weird, isn't it? She was supposed to have died, right?"

"I think that's what I heard back when they first came to town, yeah."

"I heard it was a car accident."

She nods. "Yeah. Now that you mention it, I remember hearing the same thing."

"So why can't I find anything about her online? No obituary. No anything. It's like she never existed."

"That's really weird. What do you think it means?"

"You're going to think I'm crazy."

"I doubt it."

"I think James did something bad and covered it up. I really think that." It would explain why he freaked out when I mentioned her at dinner that one night. Why the guys are so guarded when it comes to her, telling me I could never mention her. If he did something to his wife, he wouldn't want me bringing her up, even in casual conversation, would he? I'm sure he would rather pretend she doesn't exist, just gloss over the whole thing. As if such a thing could be forgotten.

And if that's true? No wonder his sons are the way they are. They never had a chance.

"Come on," Piper urges. "Let's get something to eat. You need to let this go for a little while. Be around people."

I lift my eyebrows. "That's an interesting choice of words."

"Why?"

"Because I was invited to a party. One of the girls in my lit class lives off campus and is having a little casual thing. She must have repeated that part like a million times. They'll order some sandwiches and some pizza, and we're just going to hang out. I was thinking of going, and it would be really cool if you'd come, too."

"You're the one who was invited."

"So what? I don't think they'll check a guest list at the door. It sounds pretty chill, but I would feel a lot better if you were there with me. No pressure," I add at the last second. "I'm not trying to guilt you or anything, I promise."

She scoffs, rolling her eyes. "I didn't think you were. Yeah, if you don't think it would be weird for me to go, I'd love to. Let me get changed and stuff."

I need to do the same thing. This is the first party I've been to in... I can't even remember how long. I don't count the party the guys forced me to. That was more of a shit show than a party, one I'd rather forget about forever.

Back when I was popular, and people actually wanted to talk to me, I didn't have time for parties because I was too busy training. Then I lost all my friends and all my social standing.

I have to remind myself nobody knows who I am here. I can start fresh. That's an empowering feeling, and my confidence climbs as I get ready and put on a little makeup. Piper puts on music and even dances around, which lifts my spirits even more. It's times like this I understand how much I missed her, even when I didn't realize it.

By the time we're walking across campus, I feel like I can actually handle this party. "I do hope it's as quiet and low-key as it was described," I fret to Piper because I can't help it. I don't need to end up in a drunken frat party with a bunch of guys who will only remind me of the two I want to forget but can't seem to.

When we enter a large, comfortable apartment, my hopes climb. I recognize a handful of people from class strewn around, hanging out on sofas and around the kitchen table. There are other clusters here and there, voices overlapping and almost drowning out the soft, upbeat music playing through the TV. Pizza boxes are on the kitchen counter and a tray of sandwiches beside them, plus what looked like endless bottles of alcohol and mixers. "There's beer in the fridge, too," one of the guys tells us. "I'm Trevor, by the way."

"Leni," I tell him, shaking his hand. "And this is Piper."

"Leni, Piper, make yourselves at home. What brings you here?"

"Oh, I'm in lit class with you," I tell him with a laugh. "But I usually sit in the back of the room, so you probably never noticed me."

He snaps his fingers, chuckling. "Of course. Sorry, I've had a few, so my beer goggles have me a little fuzzy. I guess Maya invited you."

"Yeah, is she around here somewhere?"

"She's out on the balcony. Everybody is supposed to just make themselves at home, so I figured I'd help out with that a little bit." He pulls a beer from the fridge before looking at Piper and me, his brows lifted in a silent question.

"Sure, I'll have one," she murmurs.

"I'm good, but thanks."

While his back is turned to us, she elbows me, wiggling her eyebrows up and down. Sure, he's cute, but there are a lot of cute guys. I think I can be forgiven for not wanting to jump right in and flirt with somebody so soon after everything I've been through.

Over the next hour or so, another dozen people come in until the place is pleasantly full. The music is louder now, and I'm glad we ate some pizza when we first got here because it's pretty much gone. Somebody offers to go out for more and starts getting money together from interested people who didn't get a chance to eat, but Piper and I both shake our heads.

"If all college parties are this laid back, I can see going to more of them," Piper admits while the two of us stand back, watching a game of beer pong taking place out on the balcony. It's a little tricky because sometimes the ball bounces off into the parking lot, but whoever brought the supplies has a bag of what looks like hundreds.

"Wanna play?" somebody calls out to us, holding up a red cup before draining it and crunching it in their fist.

"No, thanks." I laugh, shaking my head, and Piper does the same.

"You don't like playing beer pong? It's actually pretty fun, you know." I look up to find Trevor standing beside me, and he grins. "If you don't mind drinking out of a cup that has a dirty ball floating in it."

"Which is exactly why I'm not interested."

"But it's alcohol. Alcohol cleans things, right?"

"He sort of has a point," Piper tells me with a giggle.

"See? She knows what I'm talking about. Loosen up a little. You would actually enjoy it."

It happens so fast. An arm slides around my waist from behind. "How about you mind your own business and don't talk to my girl?"

So many things happen at once. Piper gasps. Trevor backs up a step. And I freeze solid because I know that voice. I've heard it every night in my dreams.

I shove his arm away from me and spin on my heel to glare up at Colt, who has the nerve to sneer down at me like I belong to him. He's here. Why is he here? "What the hell do you think you're doing?" I demand. I don't care who hears or if anybody gets the wrong idea. I'm too shocked, too flustered, and too damn angry. When will enough be enough? Why can't he leave me alone?

"What do you think? I couldn't reach you on your phone, so I had to come and see if you're okay."

"I'm fine, obviously. Now get the hell out of here!"

Trevor clears his throat behind me. "Do you need help with this asshole?"

Colt goes from sneering at me to glaring at him over the top of my head. "Back the fuck up, pal. You don't know what's happening here."

"Don't I? Because it seems pretty fucking clear she wants you to go away."

"I don't remember asking you for a recap, prick." With that, Colt closes a hand around my wrist and pulls me off the balcony and back into the apartment. I throw a panicked look over my shoulder and find Piper weaving her way through the crowd behind us, right on my heels. Trevor's back there somewhere, and I want to apologize to him, even if I'm not the one who's being rude and obnoxious.

Only once we're out of the apartment do I yank my arm free. "You've got a lot of nerve," I growl, my teeth gritted. I'm practically vibrating with rage. "Who do you think you are? And why are you even here? You fucking psycho. You're supposed to be at school. Are you seriously telling me you came all this way because I turned my phone off? And how did you even know where I was going to be?"

"Man, you've got a lot of questions. You're giving me a fucking headache." He jogs down the stairs, and for one moment, I'm tempted to let him go. It's obvious he thinks I'm going to follow him, and the last thing I want is to give him what he wants.

At the same time, he knows where my dorm is. He could go there anytime he wants. And now I want to be sure he's not going to hang out in front of my building or something creepy like that, demanding I talk to him if I want him to leave.

How does he always manage to put me in this position?

I hate myself for it, but I run after him, and Piper follows me. He wastes no time, walking with his hands jammed in his pockets, a man on a mission. Why me, dammit? Why does it always have to be me?

Rather than scream at him the entire way back to the dorm, I manage to hold back my anger until we're inside the building. "Now. What are you doing here? Are you insane?"

"Yeah, something like that," he retorts with a snicker, going straight to the stairs and climbing them two at a time. "Obviously, I'm smarter than you since you were practically letting that prick hang all over you."

"He wasn't doing anything like that. We were just talking. You know, like normal people do. I understand how you wouldn't be able to relate to that, but it does happen."

"Hang on a second. What are you doing?" Piper barely manages to get the question out before Colt opens our door like he lives here.

And nausea threatens to knock me on my ass when I find Nix sitting at my desk, doing something on my laptop.

"Get off of that!" I rush across the room and reach for the computer, but he holds it too far away.

"You should have let it go," he says as I reach for the machine. "But no, you had to go digging, didn't you?"

Dammit, I should have known better. They never give me anything without there being strings attached. "So what? You gave me this laptop so you could monitor what I do online? Do you have any idea how fucking sick that is? What are both of you doing here? Get out—now! I never want to see either of you again!"

"Just hold on, take a breath." Colt gets between us. "You still don't know how dangerous it is to fuck around with things you don't understand, Leni. So yeah, that's why we're here. Making sure you didn't dig up anything you're not supposed to know about."

"You guys need to go," Piper tells them in a quiet but firm voice. "Now."

I hear her, but there's something else in my head. Something louder. "What happened to your mother?" I demand, my gaze bouncing back and forth between the two of them. "Obviously, it's a big enough deal that I'm not even allowed to Google her without you coming all this way. How did she die? Tell me the truth. We're not in the house now. Nobody is stopping you."

Nix rolls his eyes. "Our father didn't kill her if that's what you're thinking."

"That's exactly what I was thinking, now that you mention it."

"Because she's not dead." When my head snaps up at Colt's admission, he lifts a shoulder. "She's still alive. And I'll tell you everything, I really will. It's safer for you to know than for you to get caught digging around. But you have to listen to us."

"I don't need to know that badly." I fold my arms, shaking my head. "Absolutely not. I am not leaving this room with the two of you. You need to leave now. You do not belong here, and you were not invited." But dammit, they've got a key. I should have known! Maybe we can get the lock changed.

"I'm not letting her leave with you, either." Piper steps up next to me and puts an arm around my shoulders. That's just what I need right now because I might seem big and tough on the outside but on the inside? I'm crumbling. I need her support more than I've ever needed it before. If she wasn't here, I shudder to think of the lengths they might go to get me out of this room.

They exchange a look, and finally, Nix shrugs. "Whatever. Some people can't be helped."

"That's what you're calling it? Go to hell. And if you don't think I'm getting the lock changed, you're sadly fucking mistaken." I follow them to the door and slam it behind them, then motion for Piper to bring me the desk chair. I can't believe I'm doing this again, but it looks like I'm not out of the woods with these two yet. I wedge it under the knob to make sure they can't come back.

It seems like history keeps repeating itself. Is there ever going to come a time when I'm out of this constant loop with the two of them? Because I don't know if I can spend the rest of my life looking over my shoulder, wondering if they're following me. Watching. Waiting to strike.

CHAPTER 38

*a*t least I managed to smooth things over with Trevor after class. We part ways outside the lecture hall, and I wave as he jogs off on his way to his next class. It took a while to convince him I'm not in an abusive relationship with Colt, even though I sort of am. Just not the kind he's thinking of. Once I explained Colt is my stepbrother and extremely overprotective, he loosened up a little. He seems like a nice person and somebody I can see being friends with. What a shame we started off on the wrong foot.

I'm out of class for the rest of the day, and Piper has a three-hour lecture on Thursday afternoons, so I'll have the room to myself for a while. I'm sort of glad, as much as I've been loving spending time with her. I'm still kind of shaken up by what happened the other night, and I know she is, too. I can't stop feeling like I have to apologize even though she tells me every time that I don't need to, that it wasn't my fault. *It's not like you invited them*, she's told me, and of course, she's right. But now her privacy was violated just like mine was, and I can't help but feel a little guilty about it. If it wasn't for me, nobody would have barged into her dorm room while she wasn't even there.

It happens so fast. One second, I'm considering grabbing lunch and taking it back to my room, and the next, somebody much bigger and stronger than me is strong-arming me into a classroom. An empty one, but still. I barely have time to register what's happening before I'm alone with Colt. Again.

And this time, I don't bother holding back. I shove him with both hands as hard as I can. "What the hell is wrong with you?" I hiss. "I'm going to get campus security on your ass, you know that, right? You don't belong here. You don't go here, and I don't want you here! So just leave."

"It's not that easy."

"What are you talking about? Not that easy. What do you think you're doing?"

"I'm protecting you."

"Protecting me from what? Do you even know what you're talking about? Who gave you this savior complex? Because I'll tell you, they were wrong. I don't need you. I don't want you here. So leave."

"It's not going to happen. I can't leave you unprotected."

"What do you think you're protecting me from? Your father? Because you weren't able to protect me from him before, so why now?"

He flinches at my outburst, and I know that statement hit home.

"What do you think?" he whispers, his eyes darting over my face. "Seriously. Think about it. Why do you think I can't leave you alone? Why do you think I can't stop watching you?"

There goes my bravado, quickly replaced by trembling fear.

"Are you telling me... I have to watch out for him? You think he'd come here?"

"I don't know, and that's the problem. I'll never know for sure. But how am I supposed to go to MIT and pretend everything is normal when he's so close? He could find you easily, and then what?"

Is that what this has been about all along? I don't want to believe him because he's tricked me so many times before, but when I give it serious thought, I can't help but remember times when he wasn't hurting me. When he was trying to help me, like with the butt plug. I'm sure that was his idea—I doubt Nix would have cared either way. He wanted to make sure I didn't get hurt. And when James forced us to fuck in front of him, Colt whispered to me and tried to make it easier. And he held me. He was kind and gentle.

"Fine, so let's say you tried to protect me from your dad. What about all the other times? You treated me like shit back in school. I never did anything to you, and you know that damn well. But you hurt me. Humiliated me. And then, before your father ever started with me, you made my life miserable after I moved in."

"Did it never occur to you that we did it to keep you away? That we dragged you into that fucking party to make sure you weren't alone with him? Or the lock on your door—you never figured out we were locking him out, not locking you in?"

"You locked me in during the day plenty of times."

"It was all to protect you. That job at the law firm? What the hell do you think would have happened there if we had let that happen?"

I hate that he's making a good point. Now that I look back,

knowing what I know, I can see it from his point of view. Still, I shove him again. "Fine. But you sure as hell never had a difficult time performing when he forced you." I make big, sarcastic air quotes around the word. "If you were against it, why were you always ready to go?"

That one, he doesn't have such a quick little answer to. He looks at the floor, in fact, his jaw twitching. "I don't know. I guess I'm fucked in the head. I'm not hiding that. I got off on seeing you naked, on having you at my mercy, but I'm nothing like him."

"Oh no?" I taunt.

"No." His head snaps up, and he glares at me. "I can admit I get off on controlling you. I already told you that I think you're beautiful, so of course, I get hard when I see you naked. Yes, I like fucking you in messed-up ways. That's part of who I am. But I also feel remorse and have a conscience. I want to take care of you and make you feel good. I don't want you to be scared or trapped in a house. I want you to be happy and have friends."

He reaches out to touch my cheek. I want to pull away, but something stops me. I don't know what. "I don't want to hurt you anymore. That's one thing I know for sure. All that is over. Nothing matters more than keeping you safe."

"Did you ask Piper to move in here?"

"No, I didn't ask her, but I set it up. I didn't want you to be here with a stranger." I should have seen this before. Even now, when I thought I was free, he's still controlling my life.

I need to get my head on straight. And that's not possible while I'm in his presence and he's touching me. When he's this close to me. "I can't do this."

He sighs heavily as I open the door, flinging it wide and

marching out into the hall. Why does he keep doing this to me? And why do I make it so easy for him?

I should know better than to think he'll let me go just because I want him to. He walks beside me the entire way back to the dorm, not saying a word. Anybody who sees us together would probably think we're just two normal everyday people. And it does occur to me that I could scream for help. If I really wanted to be rid of him and make him pay at least in part for what he's done to me, I would.

And I do, don't I? I want to get rid of him. I want him to pay. So why can't I bring myself to scream?

When we reach my building, he makes no move to leave. "Bye," I mutter, glaring at him. "Thanks for walking me back to my room. You can go now."

"Do we really need to play this game?" When all I can do is gape at him, he shakes his head and opens the front door, strolling into the lobby like he lives here. As soon as I get a chance, I'm going to write a strongly worded email to the school and ask them about upping their security because this is ridiculous.

Rather than make a scene, though, I follow him inside, then up the stairs to the third floor. He's waiting for me at the door by the time I reach it. I hate how sure he is of himself. How sure he is that he's going to get his way.

But he did try to protect me. And if he's telling the truth, which I think he is, he didn't go to MIT because he wanted to stay here and make sure I was safe from his father. I can't help it. It warms my heart and makes me soften up toward him.

And that's why I let him follow me into my room rather than ask security to kick him off campus. Why I let him pull me onto the bed until we're sitting together. I'm too tired to fight on top of everything else.

"You have no idea how long I've been wanting to do this," he whispers, wrapping his arms around me and holding me close. His heart is pounding under my ear.

Why? Why do I matter so much to him? No matter how I tell myself to be careful, I can't help wanting to believe him. I want to believe this is true, that he means it, that I matter to him. Because I'm finally starting to figure out that somewhere along the way, he started mattering to me.

When I lift my head, prepared to tell him this can't happen, he covers my mouth with his before I can speak. His kiss is exactly the opposite of what I would expect from him. He's tender and sweet as his mouth moves slowly over mine. He kisses me like he's got nothing he'd rather do—like he has all the time in the world. Before I know it, he's pulling me down, and I'm following him until we're lying together on the bed.

"Let me stay here with you," he whispers between kisses, one hand moving slowly up and down my back.

"You can't do that. You know we'd end up getting caught." And I doubt Piper would be a big fan of the idea.

"Fine. Then stay with me. I have an apartment just down the street."

"You what?"

"I couldn't stay in that house anymore," he explains, pulling back enough to look me in the eye but still caressing me as he speaks. "And I sure as hell couldn't go to MIT. So I got an apartment down the street from campus. How else do you think I've managed to be here? You could stay there with me."

"Colt... I couldn't do that. I could never do that." I shrug away from his touch, backing myself up to the wall to put as much space between us as possible. It still isn't much, but I can think more clearly when I'm not in his arms. "I could never trust you. After everything you've done? No way."

"You already trust me."

"Bullshit."

"Did you or did you not ask me to stay with you that night? You know what I'm talking about. You like it when I hold you. You like it when I'm with you. I make you feel safe. And I meant it when I said I'm never going to hurt you again. All of that is over."

"I don't know…"

"I know something else, too." He reaches out, this time placing a hand on my hip. "You like it when I make you come."

"Don't do that."

"Don't do what? Touch you? You can't pretend not to like it when I touch you." And he keeps doing it, too, his hand sliding over my hip and around to my ass. I wish it didn't feel so good. I wish I was strong enough to make him stop.

I wish I *wanted* him to stop. That's at the heart of the problem. I can tell him to stop all I want, that this is wrong, that I don't want him touching or kissing me, but it's all a lie. He has a way of lighting me up inside, of making me feel things. Of making me want when I was so sure I wouldn't want anyone, for any reason, for a very long time.

It turns out I want him. That's the issue. I only want him touching me like this. Holding me, caressing me, refusing to stop because somehow he knows what I need better than I do.

Like how he drapes my leg over his thigh before running a hand over it. "I don't think I could ever get tired of this," he whispers. "The feel of you. The way you come apart in my hands, under me."

"You have to know this brings up all kinds of bad shit for me, right?"

"You can forget all of that now. Let's replace it with good memories." He pulls me closer and holds me tight, so tight there's no chance of getting away. Not that I want to. I can't resist the warmth and comfort of his embrace. "And this is how you do it. By taking back what you want. What makes you feel good."

His touch is featherlight as he grazes my ass again, this time allowing his hand to drift between my thighs. "What makes you feel good? What do you want?"

What do I want? I want him to stop talking. More than that, I want to do what he described. I want to take this back for me. I want to do this because I want to. Not because somebody else told me to or because they're directing me. *I want.*

When he leans in, pressing his lips to mine, I don't resist. No, I kiss him back as hard as I can, hard enough that our teeth clash as our tongues touch, then tangle together in our joined mouths. We tangle the rest of ourselves, too, arms and legs, and this time, I know it's not a dream.

He wants me. And I want him. I want this.

One kiss at a time, one touch, he undoes every last reservation left in the back of my mind. And this is how it's supposed to be. Not forced. It's more like we're following what instinct is telling us to do. Like when he pulls my tank top out from my waistband. When his hands brush against my bare skin. I don't even mind when he touches my scar on the way up my back so he can unhook my bra. Even that doesn't bother me because he's already shown me how little it matters. He told me I'm beautiful not because of it and not in spite of it. That it doesn't define me.

I have that in mind as I unbutton his jeans, running the zipper over his already hard dick. When my palm brushes against it, he groans, his eyes closing, his throat working. It's so much better this way, and I do it again and again, just for the sheer joy of watching his reaction and knowing I'm the reason for it.

"Fuck, I want you so bad," he groans, opening his eyes to stare deep into mine. The look in them leaves me breathless. The intensity, the heat, the desire. Desire for me.

And then he kisses me again, again, rolling me on my back before burying his face in my neck, running his lips over my skin until I run my fingers through his hair, moaning helplessly. "So sweet," he whispers, and something like joy flares to life in my heart. Every touch, every brush of his lips over me, brightens that joy like fuel on an already blazing fire.

And now nothing could stop me from being with him, from taking him inside me. I need to get rid of my clothes. I need to be as close to him as I can. "Get this off me," I whisper, frantic, sitting up partway to pull off my tank top and bra. Immediately, he lowers his head to take one of my nipples in his mouth, sucking almost playfully, teasing me before releasing it with a popping sound. He does the same on the other side, then switches back and forth until I'm ready to scream. I'm so wet, my clit aching until it hurts.

"Touch me. Down there." I fumble with my jeans, and he helps me unbutton and lower them over my raised hips and down my thighs. When he cups my pussy, rubbing his palm against the soaked fabric, I have to bite down on his shoulder to hold back what would be a scream otherwise. I can't forget there are people on either side of the room, and it's the middle of the day.

Something about that is sort of hot—like we're doing something wrong. And all that thought does is get me hotter, wetter, and before I know it, I'm humping his hand, my body so desperate for what it needs that it's acting on its own.

"That's right," he rasps, his breath quickening. "Take it. Take what you want." I can only groan in agreement and frustration combined. I just want to come. That's all I want. I want to feel good.

"Come for me," he whispers in my ear. "Come for me like I know you can. Let yourself go."

"So close..." I breathe, rising higher and higher, the tension building until I want to scream again. "So close!"

"Give it to me. Give me your orgasm, Leni." And then he presses his fingers down hard, tight against my clit, and I see stars. The whole world explodes in a shimmering cloud of light. All I can do is cling to him or else risk shattering into a million pieces.

But he holds me together, helping me through it, and when I come back to my senses, he's kissing me again, my forehead and cheeks and throat. "The most beautiful thing I've ever seen," he grunts, driving himself against my hip. He's so hard; his precum soaks through his shorts, dampening my palm when I touch him again. "Oh fuck, I need to be inside you. I need it."

I don't say a word, only working my thong down and tossing it aside before welcoming him between my spread thighs. I need this, too. "I want you inside me," I whisper, my voice shaky with nerves.

He lowers himself on top of me, stretching out, and I strain upward to catch his mouth before he slides in, filling me up all at once. Our mingled groans are lost between us, and he begins to move, taking me with slow, deep strokes.

I close my eyes and focus on the feeling. The growing heat, the friction between our bodies. The way his heart races against my chest, against my lips when I run them over his throat. It's pounding the way mine is.

"Yes," I whisper, holding him tight with my legs and pulling him deeper. I need him to know I want this. That he was right, that this is how it needs to be. "Yes, more."

And he gives it to me, driving himself deeper, harder. Maybe I never finished coming in the first place, or perhaps it's happening all over again. All I know is I feel it building almost on top of the last one, stronger this time. Every time our bodies meet and he rubs against me, he pushes me a little closer to the edge.

"Getting tighter," he pants close to my ear before lifting his head. "So tight."

"Getting close..."

"You're going to come for me again?"

I whimper my response, unable to speak.

"I want you to come on my cock. I want to feel every ripple of those muscles. I want you to milk me dry. Will you do that?"

"Yes. Come with me," I plead.

"I'm... going to." Yes, he's moving faster, losing his rhythm. And I love that, too, feeling him lose control, knowing I'm the reason. "Fuck, I'm going to..."

"Yes." I jerk my hips, meeting his rapid thrusts, losing control the way he is. "Yes, Colt! I'm—" It hits all at once and cuts off anything else I was going to say, but there's no need to announce it when he feels it happening from the inside. He crashes against me one last time before grunting out his release. The warm rush of his cum filling me is a deep, satisfying sensation. So much better than it ever was before. How have I lived without this?

How can I go back to life without it?

"Leni." He collapses on top of me, and I hold him, listening to his ragged breaths and his soft grunts as he comes down from the high he drove us both to. "Are you okay?"

That he would even ask me—breathless, muffled against my neck—brings tears to my eyes. But these aren't tears of pain or sadness. More like gratitude. I smile through them even though he can't see them. "I'm fine. Better than fine."

CHAPTER 39

I'm sure the last thing Piper expected when she got back from her lecture was to find Colt in the middle of putting a shirt on. "What are you doing?" she shrieks. "Get out of here! Oh my god!"

Colt and I look up in unison. I lost track of time, and we scrambled out of bed to try and get him out of here before Piper returned from class. We didn't make it.

And now she's standing in the doorway to our room, looking horrified. "I'm getting security."

"No, wait. It's not like that."

"What, did he tell you to say that?" I don't think she could give him a filthier look than she is right now. "I ought to cut your balls off for what you've done. How could you? What was it this time? How did you convince her?"

Colt doesn't say a word. I don't know if he's shocked or amused by her reaction. I reach her, take her by the arm, and pull her into the room, then close the door so we have at least a modicum of privacy. "It isn't like that this time. I know it sounds crazy, but it's complicated. I promise, though. He didn't force me into it."

Then I shoot him a look over my shoulder. "This time."

Understanding dawns in his eyes, and he waves a hand between us. "You told her?"

"I told her everything, yeah. I had to talk to somebody. I was going crazy."

"Don't even pretend it's not true." The look Piper's giving him could melt steel. If I didn't truly believe she meant it when she said she wanted us to be friends again, I would believe it now. She's ready to kill for me.

He lets out a long breath before finally shrugging. "I'm not going to pretend. It's all true—I'm sure she didn't exaggerate anything. I'm not proud of it, believe me."

"That doesn't make me feel any better." Piper turns to me, her eyes going wide. "I don't get it. Why would you?"

Even if Colt wasn't here, I wouldn't know what to say. "It's complicated. I don't understand it myself."

"It is complicated," Colt adds.

"I don't even want to look at you." She throws her backpack on her bed and plops down, arms folded. "Even if your dad made you do it, you could have told Leni why."

When I turn to Colt, lifting an eyebrow, I find him staring at the floor with his thumbs hooked through the belt loops on his jeans.

"She does have a point," I tell him. Amazing how her being here makes it easier for me to say all the things that have been on my mind. He has a way of mixing me up, but Piper's presence gives me back a little bit of myself.

"It's not that easy, and it wasn't like I knew everything ahead of time. We knew my dad was obsessed with you and that he wanted us to befriend you. We figured if we did the opposite, you wouldn't want to be around us... including my dad."

"Oh..." That does make sense, but it doesn't explain many other things. "That was before. What about the past few weeks?"

"Again, we didn't think he would ever take it this far. He did this whole thing in stages, always telling us to do one more thing and then he would be done. Well, that one more thing always turned into more, and by that time, we were already so entangled he would have blamed all of it on us anyway."

"I know he's your dad, and I know you feel like you have to be loyal to your father or whatever, but I can't let him get away with what he did. And if you care about me the way you say you do, you'll have to prove it by helping me make him pay for what he did."

He's slow to sit on my bed, and suddenly, he looks drained. "I can't do that."

"Why the hell not?" I blurt out. All the pain, frustration, loneliness, and confusion are in that question, ringing out in the room.

"Because I just can't." His voice is so small, almost reminding me of a little boy's. "And I can't tell you more than that. I wish I could. I wish I could help you. I want him to pay, too. For all of it, for everything. But it's just not possible. You aren't the only person involved here."

I'm not the only person involved.

I don't know why it took me so long to figure it out.

The way they reacted when I mentioned her. The torn-up picture and the way they stared at it. All the secrecy.

"Is this about your mother?" I whisper, knowing it's true but also sort of hoping it isn't. "She's supposed to be dead, but you told me she's not. Is he... using her against you somehow?"

He lifts his head slightly, his eyes barely meeting mine before darting away. But he nods, and Piper gasps softly.

"We can't go into this. I don't even know... just forget we ever talked about it." He practically jumps up from the bed and crosses the room in three long strides. "I'm gonna go. Please, whatever you do, don't tell anybody we had this conversation."

"Wait a minute." I'm cut off by my phone buzzing away on my desk. I wish I wouldn't have turned it back on. I'm tempted to ignore it since it can't be anybody important, anyway—I almost never get calls.

But I glance over anyway because isn't that what you do when your phone rings? Even if you have no intention of answering, curiosity makes you look. And that's what I do.

I only programmed her number into my phone just in case I had an emergency and thought she might give a damn for once. "It's my mom." Nobody could be more surprised than I am as I answer the call, holding up a finger in a silent plea for Colt to stick around.

"Mom?" At first, I can't figure out what I'm hearing. "Mom?" I call out over the sound coming through the phone. "Are you okay? What's wrong?"

"Oh, Leni!" It finally hits me that she's sobbing.

Loud, gusty sobs. "Sweetie. I didn't know. I swear I didn't know! I'm so sorry!" Whatever she says after that is lost to another burst of sobs, louder than before.

By now, Colt is standing beside me, and I can tell from the look on Piper's face that she can hear everything, too. It would be impossible not to, the way Mom is screaming.

"Mom, slow down. Please, I don't understand what's happening. Are you okay? Did he hurt you?" I mean, I have to ask that question. It's what I've secretly been dreading all along. As much as she's hurt me, I don't want him hurting her.

"Am I okay? No, I'm not okay! Oh, Leni, this is all my fault! How did I not see it? And all the things I said to you, oh, my god! I could die! Can you ever forgive me?"

Now I'm crying because, for the first time in as long as I can remember, there is true, genuine regret in her voice. I believe every word of it, even if I don't understand. "What happened? Please, slow down so I can understand. Did he say something?"

"I found what you wrote! I was going through your room, and your old laptop was sitting there, and I opened it up because... I don't know why I did it," she confesses. "But it was right there, all of it. Everything you wrote down. How did I not know? I will never forgive myself, I swear. My poor girl. My poor baby."

"You didn't know," I whisper through my tears, sinking onto the bed. It's all too much. I can't cope.

"But there's more than that," she continues, the words pouring out. "I went to his computer. I don't know what made me do it, but I told myself I had to find some kind of proof so we could nail the bastard. So I looked through his computer and, oh my god, you would not believe what I found."

Fear freezes me stiff. He never took video, did he? What if he had cameras hidden somewhere in the house? "What did you find?"

"So many files. He didn't hide them very well. Right there on his computer, saved to their own network like he was looking at them while he was at the office. I can't even begin to imagine.

Oh, Leni, can you ever forgive me? We've got to find out what to do about this. I swear, whatever you need, you've got it. Please, forgive me."

"One thing at a time." I can barely think. I'm so over-whelmed. She believes me. Maybe we can finally be a team the way we're supposed to. All this time, I figured she wouldn't care even if she knew the truth, but now I know. And so does she.

"Okay, here's what I need you to do. Come here. Come to my dorm, and we'll talk about it. But I think it would be smart for you to get out of the house." Colt's head bobs up and down, his eyes as hard as his expression. "Can you do that? Can you come here?"

"Yes, I will. Oh, honey, I'm so—"

"What the hell do you think you're doing?" I reach out and grab Colt's arm, my nails digging in at the sound of his father's voice. That voice. I still hear it in my nightmares, but that's nothing compared to hearing it for real.

And he is very, very angry.

"Mom, get out of there!" I don't even know if she hears me because James is shouting, the voice getting louder like he's coming closer.

"Put that fucking phone down!" That's the last thing I hear before the line goes dead.

"Mom? Mom!" But she—or most likely, he—already ended the call.

"Come on. We have to go." Colt practically has to pull me off the bed, but once I get moving, the shock wears off, and he's the one who ends up having to follow me outside when I run past him, flying down the stairs and dashing through the lobby. Mom. What is he doing to her?

The tires squeal as we peel out of the parking lot and almost fishtail onto the road. Horns blare, and people shout at us, but none of it matters. Mom. What is he doing to her?

"She said she found files on his computer?" Colt asks as he tears down the road. I have no idea how he can focus on driving so fast while speaking.

"Yeah. I guess he saved them to their own network so he could access them from wherever he was. She didn't say exactly what she found," I whisper, and just the thought of it makes my insides freeze up. I don't know what I'll do if I find out he took video of everything. What if it got out somehow? What if he posted it online and shared it with his friends? What if, what if? The questions will never stop. Will I ever know for sure?

There I was, thinking I would never step foot in that house again. Just turning into the neighborhood is enough to make me tremble in fear and dread. "Should we maybe call the police?"

"You know it wouldn't matter," Colt grunts. "He'll find a way to pretend nothing was happening and it was all a big misunderstanding."

"But it might stop him from whatever he's doing now."

We're already turning into the driveway. "You should wait out here, just in case."

The words are barely out of Colt's mouth when it happens.

When the windows of the house blow out.

When a fireball shoots into the air.

At first, I don't know what is happening. It looks like a scene from a movie, so unreal, so intangible.

Then the truck shakes. The aftershock from the explosion rocks the vehicle. My heart clenches in my chest.

My ears are ringing, and everything's blurry. I try to speak, try to scream, but I can't hear myself. Colt grabs my arms, and I can't figure out why at first. Why can't I hear? His lips are moving, but I can't hear anything he's saying.

The ringing subsides after a few moments and so does the strange, foggy feeling in my head. Once it's gone, there's only one thing on my mind. "Mom!" I'm already unbuckling my belt with one hand while throwing the door open with the other.

"Leni, wait!" But I can't wait. How am I supposed to wait? The fucking house exploded and is now on fire, and my mother is in there. She's in there somewhere.

"Mom! Mom!" I scream as I run across the lawn to where the house is in flames. Glass and wood and siding and shingles are everywhere, and I run through them with Colt behind me, shouting my name. "Mom!"

"Leni, wait!" Colt grabs me around the waist and pulls me back before I can reach the front door. "You can't go in there!"

"But Mom!" I strain and stretch, trying to fight my way out of his arms. She was trying. She knew she was wrong. Why didn't I tell her I forgave her? I ignored what she needed, my forgiveness. I could've given it to her. I have to tell her.

Colt pulls me backward and away from the house. My lungs burn, my throat is raw from screaming, and my muscles ache from fighting Colt.

A moment later, the left side of the house collapses in on itself. The deafening sound of glass breaking and wood splintering fills the area. The smell of burning rubble invades my senses, and all I can do is collapse just as the house did.

"No!" I croak, dropping to the ground. Colt's arms are still around me, and I think that's the only reason I'm not falling apart. Because of him, my heart is still in my chest instead of spreading out on the driveway in a thousand little pieces.

He holds me for a long time, well past the point when flashing lights dance over the ruins as fire trucks come speeding our way.

CHAPTER 40

$\mathcal{I}$t's late by the time we reach Colt's apartment, hours after the explosion and everything that happened after. I'm pretty sure if he didn't help me out of the truck and into the building, I might have sat in the passenger seat and stared through the windshield until morning. I don't feel anything. Why don't I feel anything?

Once we're inside, Colt leads me to the sofa and has me sit before pulling out his phone and placing yet another call. "Hey, it's me. For fuck's sake, call me back, text me, something. Let me know where you are." I don't need to ask who he called. Nix is MIA and has been since Colt first called him after the police arrived and pulled us away from the house.

I don't think I've ever been asked the same questions so many times in a row. Yes, I received a phone call from my mother that inspired my stepbrother and me to go to the house. No, I didn't see anybody who shouldn't have been around—no strange cars, no people. No, we didn't hear anything coming from the house before the explosion.

No, I can't imagine who would do this.

Then again, the detectives we spoke to made it a point to remind us there's no way of knowing just yet exactly what happened. Why did the house explode like it did? "It could be a faulty gas line. Unfortunately, these things do happen. Did your mother say anything about a strange smell in the house?"

The question shouldn't have made me laugh, but it did, laughter I couldn't hold back no matter how embarrassing it was. The two detectives exchanged a look I knew was one of concern but not surprise. They've probably seen enough people in shock to dismiss things like that.

No, there wasn't a strange smell in the house. It was something much worse.

Did he do it? Why would he have done it? No, I can't believe he would deliberately blow up his own house to cover up what he'd done. Not while he was still inside. Granted, we don't know for sure whether he was, but facts are facts. There's no reaching James on his phone, he wasn't at the office, and his car was in the driveway. It's now ruined, of course, buried under a mountain of rubble.

"We still don't know for sure." Colt crouches in front of me, taking my hands and rubbing them briskly like he's trying to rub life into me. "They could have gone somewhere. He could have set something up and taken her away to cover it up, you know? I wouldn't put that past him. We still have to hope."

It's like I've never seen him before. Who is this person? Kind and helpful and sweet. "You don't really believe that, do you?" I whisper. It's the first thing I've said since we parted ways with the detectives, who promised they'd pay a visit as soon as they knew anything.

"I would believe just about anything right now because I would put nothing past him. I'm so sorry. You have no idea how much I've wanted to tell you everything all this time. I just couldn't."

I can't even process that right now. Too much is going on, too many layers to pull back.

At the heart of it is the certainty I know I can't make him understand. Deep inside, I know she's gone. No way would he let her live, not after she found the truth. He must have decided it would be easier to kill both of them. After all, she had already called me. So he knew I was aware of what she'd found. No way was he going to be able to keep his secret much longer.

If only we had gotten there sooner. Then again, we could have been caught in the explosion if we had.

"I'm so tired," I whisper. That doesn't even begin to describe it. The total exhaustion, the weakness in my muscles. "I should go back to my place."

"No, you should stay here. The police said they will come by as soon as they know more."

"Is that the only reason you want me to stay?"

"No. I want you to stay because I want you here. I don't want you to be alone, and I don't want to either. Please stay. You can lie down in my bed."

I nod. The truth is, I would rather stay here as well. He doesn't say another word, helping me up, showing me to the bedroom. My clothes reek of smoke, and I pull them off and toss them in a heap on the floor before crawling into bed and curling up on my side. I hear Colt calling Nix again and leaving another message as I close my eyes, grateful sleep is already pulling me under. I can't stand being awake anymore.

"**Y**ou need to eat something."

"I'm not hungry. I already told you." I've already told him multiple times, but he is relentless. I curl up, burying my face in Colt's fluffy pillow. It smells like him.

"This isn't about being hungry. This is about you taking care of yourself. You have to put something in you." Turning my head enough to see him, I catch Colt looking out the window, frowning. "It's almost dark, and you haven't left the room all day. You at least need to eat."

"I said, I am not hungry. I don't think I could eat a bite of anything." I roll onto my other side, away from him, but that doesn't spare me the sound of his heavy sigh. I can't bring myself to care very much right now that I'm making life difficult for him. My mother is dead, and I'm too busy trying to make sense of everything to care either way about food. It seems so trivial when I know she's out there somewhere in that wreck of what used to be a house, buried under all that tile and marble, granite and hardwood. All the luxuries she ever wanted. They're now her tomb. I squeeze my eyes shut and tuck my chin against my chest, fighting back another wave of emotion that levels me flat no matter how I try.

She died knowing she let me down. We never even got the chance to work things out.

"It isn't like I don't know how you feel." He sits on the bed, the mattress shifting under his weight. "I still can't get ahold of Nix, either."

I roll over, now sorry for glossing over what I know he's going through. His back is to me, and I place a hand against it. "It could be a coincidence. I'm sure that's what it is."

I'm lying. It's been twenty-four hours since the explosion—more than that, actually. Nix hasn't so much as picked up his phone to send a quick text and let his brother know he's okay. I can't imagine why he would have been at the house, but anything is possible.

We both jump a little when the doorbell rings. Immediately, Colt hurries from the room, and I follow him with my heart in my throat. Who is it going to be? What will they have to tell us?

It's the detectives from last night, people whose names I don't quite remember. There are still a lot of things that are a blur. "Mr. Alistair, we wanted to come and speak with you personally about developments in the case."

The woman—I think her name is Jones, maybe—looks over his shoulder to find me standing in the doorway leading from the bedroom. "Miss Peters, I'm glad you're here as well. Why don't we all sit down?"

And now I know it's bad news. Not that I expected anything else. I'm not a little girl anymore. I know certain things aren't possible, like surviving an explosion and the destruction that followed it. I sit on the sofa, my hands clasped between my knees, and Colt sits beside me. To these two, we are a step-brother and stepsister family. I have to remember we're not supposed to be more than that.

The man—Patterson? Maybe?—leads off. "It's an ugly thing, what I'm about to tell you," he warns. "After searching Mr. Alistair's computer at his law firm, we have a pretty clear image of his state of mind."

"What does that mean?" Colt asks.

"It means we found thousands of images and videos recorded over the course of several years." His eyes drift my way. "Of you, Miss Peters."

"Me?"

"You were a gymnast, were you not?" I nod, mute with surprise. "It seems Mr. Alistair had what can only be described as an obsession. He took videos of you during competitions and oftentimes zoomed in on specific body parts." He clears his throat, his face darkening a little as he looks at his partner.

"The dates on the files stretch back four years to when you were fourteen years old," she explains in a gentle voice. "I'm sure this must come as quite a shock, especially seeing as how he was your stepfather for a short time."

"Mr. Alistair," Patterson continues, looking at Colt. "Did you know about any of this? Did you ever have any idea of your father's feelings toward your stepsister?"

He doesn't hesitate. "Yes. I did. My brother and I both did. He moved us here so he could be closer to Leni. I knew about it even before we moved. It was the reason he..." His face crumples a little like there's something he has to say, but he doesn't know how to say it. "It was the reason he tried to kill our mother."

I can't wrap my head around it. I hear what he's saying, but it makes no sense. Like he's speaking another language.

"Would you care to elaborate on that?" Jones asks, and now I see she's taking notes.

"I guess he first saw Leni during a competition. My mom, she was a coach. Leni was one of the gymnasts on another team. And I don't know. He was obsessed with her. He started taking random business trips, just out of nowhere, last minute. We found out later he was actually traveling to the places where Leni was competing."

All I can do is dig my nails into my palms as I absorb this. All that time.

"That was what first clued my mom into what was going on," Colt mumbles. "He was supposed to be at a conference or something, then she found out there was no such conference going on, so she started digging into his travel arrangements and stuff. And then, I guess she found some of his pictures, something. And when she confronted him with it... we thought he killed her, my brother and me. He told us she was in a coma after he took her to the hospital."

My mouth is hanging open, and I can't seem to close it for long before it falls open again. That's what he was holding over their heads?

"He wouldn't tell us where she was, but he did send us a picture once when he visited her. She had tubes coming out of her and one of those braces around her neck. She was on a ventilator. And he told us if we didn't do what he wanted, and if we ever told anybody about the things he did, he would end her care. And we would never know where she was, or when she died, or any of it."

He hangs his head and whispers, "And if she died, it would be our fault."

"We are going through your father's financial records, as well," Patterson tells us. "And it does look like he had some payments through a shell corporation going to a hospital out of state. In fact, we were going to ask you about that. If you knew why your father would be sending money to a hospital under seemingly anonymous circumstances. We'll dig deeper into that and let you know what we find."

"You think you can find my mom?" There's the tiniest bit of a tremble in his voice, and it goes straight to my heart. All this time, James was using her to manipulate them. He knew how much they loved her, and he used it against them to get what he wanted.

I hope wherever he is now, he's suffering. Alive or dead, I don't care. I want him to hurt.

Jones clears her throat and stands in front of the two of us. "The fire marshal's report will say the explosion and the subsequent fire were set purposely. It was arson. The jets on the stove were all turned on, all the way up, along with the oven. That sort of thing doesn't happen accidentally."

"And you know it was my mom in there?" I whisper.

"Yes, one of the bodies identified is that of Mrs. Amanda Alistair. Again, I'm very sorry." Her brow wrinkles. "And I'm sorry to give you more bad news, but the firefighters recovered three bodies."

"Three." Colt sinks back on the sofa and covers his face with his hands.

"Yes, besides your father, it would appear that your brother, Nix, was also inside the house. We're very sorry to have to break this to you."

"You're wrong." Colt jumps up, shaking his head and waving his hands. "You're wrong. Somebody made a mistake. Nix wasn't there. He couldn't have been. This is all a mistake. It was somebody else."

"Do you have any idea who else might have been in the house? An employee, maybe? Domestic help?"

There was no such person, at least nobody I ever saw.

"No, but there has to be another explanation. It wasn't him. It's not him."

The two of them exchange a look that's easy enough to read. "Again, we're very sorry," Jones murmurs. "And as my partner said, we will call you as soon as we find anything about the first Mrs. Alistair. Please, take care of yourselves. Take care of each other. And let us know if you can think of anything else that might be worthwhile in the investigation."

I'm the one who has to show them to the door because Colt is in no condition. Pacing, shaking his head, snarling.

When we're alone, I turn to him. "Colt, there's really nobody else it could have been, is there? I'm sorry, I hate to believe it, too."

"You don't know. All these fucking years. And this is how it ends? Having to do what he wanted all this time because otherwise, he would have let our mother die. Do you think he wouldn't have? Do you think that was an idle threat?"

"I don't think it was an idle threat."

"So what? He dies in a fucking explosion along with that sick bastard? How does that make sense? How is that fair?" He leans against the nearest wall and slides down until he's on the floor, folding his arms over his knees and touching his forehead to them. I feel so helpless—useless. I don't know the right thing to say or if there is any right thing at a time like this.

All I can do is sit down with him. Be close to him and let him know he isn't alone.

Because, after all, we have to take care of each other. We're all we have.

CHAPTER 41

J lower my head and look down at the two graves covered in flowers, notes, and even a few stuffed animals. The dirt around it is freshly turned, the headstone meticulously carved and beautifully inscribed.

Amanda L. Peters.

Beloved mother.

I refused to have them put Alistair on her gravestone. The marriage was annulled anyway since James was still legally married to someone else. My gaze moves to the grave next to hers.

Nixon C. Alistair

A life taken too soon.

His grave holds even more flowers than my mother's. Half of our high school is here to say goodbye to one of their favorite alumni. We thought about holding two separate funerals but decided we didn't want to go through all of this twice.

As the pastor reads a passage from the Bible that vaguely fits my mother's life as a mother, I glance up into the sniffling crowd. A lot of people who came I only know from the wedding, but most of the attendees I don't know at all. Piper is the only person here who actually came for me, to support me in any way she could.

My grandma couldn't make the trip down here. They had a rocky relationship, but her own daughter's death hit her so hard that she ended up in the hospital.

We had James cremated. The funeral home told us they would send us the ashes in the mail. I hope it gets fucking lost. I didn't think I could ever hate someone as much as I hated James. Not only did he do unspeakable things to me, but he also terrorized his own children, put their mother in a coma, and now because of him, my mom and Nix are dead.

Losing a parent—your only parent—is as confusing as it is heartbreaking. My brain has still not fully processed that my mom is gone. There have been moments when the pain has been so overwhelming that I couldn't breathe. Then other times, I simply forget she is gone. Those are the worst. I would reach for my phone, ready to text her, just to be reminded that I won't ever be able to text her again. We had drifted apart after my accident, but she was still my mom, and there was a time we were actually close. I miss those times more than anything. A part of me always hoped we could find our way back to that relationship. Now we'll never get a chance to try.

A sob rips from my throat without permission. I don't want to cry in front of everyone, but my treacherous tears keep coming. I'm surrounded by people, but I feel so fucking alone. The thought has no time to take hold when I feel a warm hand wrap around mine, interlacing our fingers like they belong together.

Blinking the tears away, I look down at Colt's hand holding mine. Colt stole my first kiss, my virginity, and many other things. We have been together in every way possible, yet this feels more intimate than anything else we have shared.

The rest of the funeral goes by in a blur. Most people come up to Colt and give him condolences; some ignore me completely, and others turn to me briefly with fake well wishes. I don't really care about any of it. I think the only thing keeping me sane is Colt's hand, which stays securely wrapped around mine through it all. Even when people hug him, he never lets go of me.

By the time we get back to the apartment, I'm beyond exhausted. All I want to do is curl up in bed and sleep for the next week. The only thing keeping me from doing so is Colt. All day, he has been my rock, my lifeline, the glue that held me together.

Now it's my turn to be there for him. His nervous energy is enough to fill the room. "It doesn't feel right without him."

"I know. But you have to remember he could be, you know... watching from another place." I wince at the way he looks at me, like that's the dumbest thing he's ever heard, and maybe I shouldn't talk anymore. "It's possible."

"But it's not the way it is. He's alive."

"If he was, why would he stay away all this time? He could at least have gotten word to you that he's alive, Colt. I want him to be alive, I really do." When he scoffs, all I can do is put my arms around him. "I do. I want it for you."

He hugs me back, stroking my hair. "He's trying to give us space to be together."

That's a new one. "What do you mean?"

"It's exactly the kind of thing he would do. He'd want to stay away to give us space because he knew."

"Knew what?"

"He knew I loved you first."

I can't have heard that correctly. "What did you say?" I lift my head from his chest and look up at him in confusion. "You what?"

"I loved you. I still love you," he whispers, taking my face in his hands. "I have for a bit. But I couldn't exactly come out and admit that, so I went too far in the other direction. Like I was covering, I don't know."

"You're telling me that you loved me all that time? Even when you were so cruel and mean?"

"I did. Very much." A faint smile starts to stir. "I still do. I understand if you can't love me. I don't deserve it, not after everything I put you through."

He loves me. Something about that feels right. The first truly right thing to happen in the past few months. On the other hand, could he really be this good of an actor?

"I want to believe you. Maybe a part of me already does..."

"But?"

"But... it felt real. If you really did care about me, how could you hurt me so badly? How could you watch me suffer?"

I can see the turmoil in the depth of his blue eyes. He is thinking about what to tell me. I just hope it's the truth.

"Because hating you came so easy to me."

He might as well slap me in the face. His words sting more

than I like to admit. I'm about to ask him where the hell he is going with this when he continues on his own.

"I knew it wasn't your fault that my father was obsessed with you. Nothing he did was your fault. Yet if it wasn't for you, none of this would have happened. At least not in my mind. If you hadn't been there competing that day, my dad would have never seen you. He wouldn't have risked his marriage, and he wouldn't have hurt my mom."

"Colt..."

"I know, I know." He throws up his hands. "I know I shouldn't have blamed you. *I know that.* I'm just explaining to you how it was easy to do."

"It came so easy to you then. How do I know we won't go back to that? How can I trust that you won't wake up one morning and decide to hate me again?

"Because I let that shit go. You have to believe me. I let it go, and now if I simply think about it, I feel so fucking guilty. I'm sorry. I hope you can give me time to prove it."

"I didn't feel the same about you," I admit. "I wasn't pretending to hate you. I really did."

"I can't blame you."

"But you were right about me trusting you before. When your dad made us do those things, I felt the safest with you. I was glad it was you touching me and not him. However, that doesn't mean I love you."

"Do you hate me?"

"I don't hate you anymore. I haven't for a while. Now, all I want is for us to have a life. Maybe together. You think we can figure that out?"

For the first time in a long time, he looks genuinely happy.

"Yeah. I think we can if we put our heads together. It might take a while, but we can figure it out."

I stretch up on tiptoes to kiss him, smiling when I pull back.

"We've got all the time in the world."

CHAPTER 42

*I*f someone had told me a few weeks ago that I would be dating Colt Alistair, I would have bet millions of dollars against it. Yet here I am, having dinner at a restaurant because neither one of us felt like cooking or eating frozen dinners again. I guess this is considered a date. Even if it came out of necessity, we're still two people eating a meal in a public place. We also sleep in one bed every night and have sex almost every day. So yeah, dating seems like the right term, even if we have never actually called it that.

"Are we dating?" I ask point blank.

Colt stops chewing, though his cheeks are still filled with his last bite. His elbows are resting on the table. He lowers the burger he is holding with both of his hands and looks at me over the bun. His eyebrows rise, then he quickly chews and swallows his food.

"Yeah... I mean, I guess. We live, sleep, eat, and take showers together. What else would you call it?"

"Roommates? Friends with benefits?"

"I told you how I feel about you."

"You also told me about banging some girl at MIT."

A grin spreads across his face, and I don't miss the sparkle in his eyes as I mention other girls.

"You know I didn't go to MIT."

"The girl could have been from around here. I didn't know if that part was a lie."

"I didn't have sex with anyone else. Not that time or any other time. And just so we're clear, if another guy so much as looks at you too long, I'll fuck you in front of him, then cut his eyes out and shove them down his throat," he tells me casually before taking another bite of his burger.

I glance around us to make sure no one heard his over-the-top threat. Luckily, we're sitting in a quiet corner, and the restaurant isn't too busy right now.

"So why did you say that?"

"I wanted to see if you were jealous. Clearly, you are."

I chew on the inside of my lip. Yeah, I guess I am jealous. "I don't want you seeing other girls."

"I know, and I won't. You can trust me."

"Did it ever bother you that I had sex with Nix?" This is a sore subject, so I'm treading lightly, but I also really want to know.

"No, not Nix. That was different. There was never any jealousy between us. I'm not sure why. Maybe because I always shared everything with him. Or maybe because I trust him so completely." He drops what's left of his burger onto his plate. "Let's get out of here. I've lost my appetite."

"What? No! I'm sorry, I shouldn't have brought it up."

"It's not that. I don't mind talking about Nix."

"Then what—"

"Hey, Colt."

UGH.

Deborah's voice makes me cringe worse than nails on a chalkboard.

She walks right up to our table but doesn't greet or acknowledge me in any other way, which I guess is a step up from belittling and bullying me. Alongside her is a guy I've never seen before. He seems to be our age, maybe a little older, judging by all the tattoos on his arms and hands.

Unlike Deborah, his eyes are on me, zeroing in on me in a weird and creepy way.

"Funny meeting you here." She waits for Colt to respond, but he is more interested in the leftover fries than her. "So, did you hear Bradley went on a weekend trip and never came back?" Another moment of awkward silence. If she was anyone else I would feel bad for her.

"Do you mind if we sit with you?" Deborah asks Colt as if I'm not even here at all.

Colt ignores Deborah like she does me and directs all of his attention to the guy next to her. "You know what's funny, Jeremy? I was just telling Leni if someone looks at her too long, I'll fuck her in front of him, then cut his eyes out and shove them up his ass."

"Down his throat, actually. That's what you said earlier," I correct him with a grin.

"You heard her. Down your throat."

Jeremy turns ghostly pale, takes a few steps back, and casts his eyes to the floor.

Deborah giggles nervously. "Well, can I sit with you?"

Now Colt does look at her. "Deborah, I don't understand how you are this stupid and not realize when people don't like you. No, you can't sit with us. Not now, not ever. You are nothing but a stuck-up bitch, latching on to every guy who gives you a sliver of attention. So do us all a favor and get lost before I throw up the burger and ruin this date."

I've never liked Deborah, but I can't help feeling sorry for her. She turns her head away like she is about to start crying and doesn't want anyone to see. "Let's go, Jeremy." She takes him by the hand and pulls him out of the restaurant.

I should be happy that Colt stood up for me, that he sent them off while also making it clear we're dating. I should be giddy that Deborah got some of her own medicine, but instead, I'm reminded of how Colt can be.

The past few weeks have been so nice. He has been kind to me, even loving, and so attentive. I almost forgot this side of Colt. Just like his dad, he has two versions of himself, and though I'm glad I'm on his "good side" now, knowing that he could change his mind about me any day has my stomach in knots.

Dread pools in my stomach. My mind is so hazy with fear I barely notice the server coming to clear our plates and bring us the check. Colt throws a few twenty-dollar bills on the table.

"You okay?"

"Yeah. I'm fine."

He slides out of his seat and comes to stand beside me. "Let's go home. You look a little pale—"

"What if you change your mind again?" Still sitting in my spot, I look up at him, waiting on his answer.

"What?" He looks confused. "What are you talking about?" He sits back down, but this time, he takes the seat next to me.

"Seeing you talk to them like that reminded me of how you used to talk to me."

"I told you, I let that hate go. It'll never be like that again between us."

"But how can I be sure? How can I admit to loving you if I always have that fear?"

His concerned frown turns into a triumphant smile. "You love me?"

Shit.

"That's not the point." I try to play it off, but of course, Colt has no intention of letting it go.

"Well, it should be because that's all that matters. I love you, and you love me. Why should we let the past get in the way of us being together now?"

"Because I'm scared that our past will be our future. I can't go through that again, not after everything that's happened. If you turned your back on me now, I don't think I would survive it." That's it. I'm putting everything on the table. My darkest fear, my deepest thoughts. We had to go through hell to get here, but now we've made it. We came out on the other side together.

"It won't be. I just know it, and if I have to, I'll spend the next twenty years proving it to you. I love you, Leni. I want to be with you, and I won't ever do anything to hurt you again. I swear."

"I love you too." The words have barely left my mouth when Colt's lips are on mine. He buries his hand in my hair, pulling me closer into the searing kiss.

He holds my heart in his hand, and now it's up to him to keep it safe.

EPILOGUE
ONE MONTH LATER.

"Are you ready for this?" I take Colt's hand and find it damp with sweat. It's not difficult to imagine why he's feeling this way. It's been years since he last saw his mother in person, and she's still comatose. There's a good chance she always will be, thanks to how badly James beat her all those years ago.

But she's alive and here in a hospital only a few minutes from his apartment. It took a lot of work, a lot of phone calls, and arrangements, but he managed to get her moved from the hospital in Florida, where James had stashed her.

He takes a deep, shaky breath. "She won't even know I'm here. It doesn't really matter."

"It matters a lot. And you never know. They say people in comas can hear what goes on around them." I mean, I've heard it before. I don't know if it applies in this situation, but I can't let him keep feeling this way without at least trying to help.

"Let's do this." He blows out a long sigh before leading me into the hospital room, holding a bouquet of her favorite flowers in the other hand. Lilies. It was important to him that she had her favorite flowers.

I feel like I shouldn't breathe too loudly once we're inside the room. It's like entering some sacred space, breaking into this poor woman's peace. She's in her bed, of course, with a tube in her throat and various monitors beeping all around her.

She's the woman from the picture, only she isn't. Older, for one thing. Her face is relaxed—that big, winning smile is gone. But it's her, and now I see the resemblance between her and her sons.

"Mom." Colt's fingers tighten around mine as we move closer to the bed. "It's me. It's Colt. I'm here. I don't know if you can hear me, but I'm here."

He leaves the flowers on the table next to the bed before sitting in a chair at her side. He rubs his hands together, obviously nervous. "I'm sorry it took so long for me to find you. We wanted to for a really long time. Me and Nix." His voice catches on the name. "But I found you. And now I'll be able to see you all the time. You get to hear me talking about nothing important. Aren't you lucky?"

I can't help but smile, even with tears in my eyes. I've been standing back, away from them, but he waves me closer. "Mom. You remember Leni Peters? I remember you saying she had the best floor routine you ever saw." I stare at him in surprise—he never told me that.

"She's safe," he whispers, taking her hand in both of his. "We both are. He's gone now. I don't know if you can hear me, but he's gone. He's never going to hurt anybody again. Only..."

He hangs his head for a moment, and I can feel his sorrow. "Only the cops think it was Nix who did it. I don't believe them.

It's been a whole month, and I haven't heard anything from him. They're trying to say he set an explosion in the kitchen at the house. That was what killed him. They're saying Nix was there, in the kitchen; that was where they found him. But I don't believe it."

It hurts to hear him say that. Even after a month, he refuses to believe Nix set the explosion. Even though the third body— Nix's body—was found in the kitchen. It was never identified as Nix. That's the problem. There was too much damage.

So long as there's no positive identification, he has hope. I almost wish he didn't. He can't move on if there's no closure.

He talks to her for a long time while I sit and listen. And think. About what she lost. What we all lost. I lost the opportunity to settle things with my mother. I never had the chance to tell her I understood how she could be blinded by a man like James. He basically love-bombed her from the minute he figured out she was my mom. I'm still not even sure how she ended up hiring her or what brought them together. She never did tell me, and she never will.

Neither will he.

I don't know if it makes me a bad person or what, but I can't bring myself to care much about James dying. I'm glad he's not here anymore; that's about it. I do wish Nix could've waited until Mom was out and safe, but... something tells me she might not have made it out, anyway. She could've ended up like this poor woman before me. In a hospital bed, unable to move or speak.

"I'll be back to see you next week. I promise." Colt lifts his mother's hand to his lips and presses a kiss against the back of it. "I'm so glad you're here. I'm glad you're with me now." My heart swells almost painfully when he says it. All this time, he wasn't even allowed to mention her. It was like she never existed.

I hold his hand the whole way to the garage, only letting go once it comes time to get in the truck. "How do you feel?" I ask once we're inside.

He doesn't answer right away. "Better. I feel better. She looks good—I thought she would look a lot worse than that. But she looks like... Mom."

"I'm really glad you got the chance to see her again. It's like a miracle."

"It would be a miracle if she woke up." He tightens his grip on the wheel before sighing. "I know that's not going to happen."

He can face the truth about that, but he can't face the truth about Nix. I guess because he's seen his mom in person, for himself. Nix? That will always be a mystery, and he can't let himself give up hope. I understand his feelings. I would probably feel the same way in his place.

It's clear we're both thinking about it throughout the ride back to the apartment. I moved in with him shortly after that terrible day. Piper got another roommate once I confirmed with the school's administration that I'd be taking the rest of the semester off. We only had a couple of weeks as roommates, but it gave us back our friendship. I'll never stop being grateful for that, especially since I don't know how I'd be able to hold it together without her.

Not that living with Colt is terrible or anything like that. But it isn't always easy to live together with all this shit between us. His undying hope that sometimes seems a lot more like delusion. All the terrible memories. There are moments when I look at him, and I might as well be back in that basement.

But I can't leave him. I don't want to, either. I don't want to be without him, even if it means having to remember. It isn't as if I'd be able to forget, anyway.

"I wish Nix could visit her." He opens the refrigerator door and pulls out a bottle of water, which he opens and hands to me like it's second nature before taking one for himself. "I think he'd feel a lot better if he did. I know I do. Like it's a way of reminding myself why we had to do all that shit and keep his secrets." He rarely, if ever, speaks of James. I'm certainly fine with that.

"You kept her alive. You did everything you could for her. I'm sure she would've done anything she could for you, too."

He wraps his arms around me. "Thank you. I hope you know how much I love you."

I lean into him, enjoying his warmth. "I love you too."

The End... for now.

Thank you for reading Lock me Inside. Please keep reading for a bonus chapter told from Colt's perspective. Trust me. You DO NOT want to skip it.

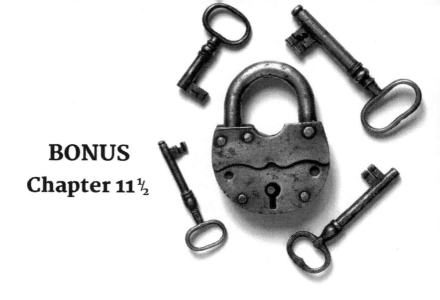

BONUS
Chapter 11½

Told from Colt's perspective

"What a way to make an exit." I chuckle as I follow her out of the restaurant. I didn't want to be there either, so I'm actually glad Leni is playing sick.

"Look. I'm really not feeling well. Can you please just leave me alone?" Leni pushed past the hostess. Using her shoulder, she presses open the heavy door leading to the street. Stepping outside, she sucks in an audible breath. Her shoulders lift before dropping back down with an exhale.

Just as I'm about to call her out for acting, I realize her body is swaying from side to side. Her legs start to shake, and she looks like she is about to hit the ground.

Nix appears at my side. We reach for her at the same time, keeping her upright by holding onto her arms on either side. Her head lolls to the side, her body about to give out.

"What the fuck did you take?" Nix snaps.

"Hydrocodone... it's just for pain." Her voice is nothing more than a sleepy whisper.

"That's some strong shit. How much champagne did you drink?"

"Um, two... I think."

"Great. Can you go and get the car? I don't feel like carrying her," I tell Nix. Even though I wouldn't mind carrying her, I do, however, want a moment alone with her. Nix curses under his breath and disappears down the alley toward the parking lot.

Wrapping my arms around her, I pull her closer, holding up most of her weight now. Her silky red hair dances in the wind. Parts of it reflect the colorful neon sign from above the restaurant, making her skin glow.

Closing her eyes, she actually leans against me. Her head ends up on my chest, her arms hanging useless by her side. If I wasn't already sure she was really out of it, I am certain now. Clearheaded Leni would never lean on me like this. She would never be this trusting.

"Don't drool on my shirt," I whisper when she cuddles up to me even more. I don't really care if she messes up my shirt. She looks up at me like she's about to say something, but her lips stay sealed while her eyes slowly close. Her facial features relax, and her legs give out completely.

A moment later, Nix pulls up, parking a few feet away from us. Noticing she is out completely now, he gets out and opens the back door. I carry her to the car and place her limp body on the back seat. She instantly relaxes. Curling up on her side, she tucks her hands under her head like a pillow.

"You'd better get in with her or buckle her up or something."

Nix isn't wrong, especially considering he is driving. My brother takes the speed limit more as a suggestion than a requirement.

I close the door at her feet carefully and walk around to the other side. There, I slide my hands under her head and lift her up slowly, just enough for me to sit down and let her head rest on my knee.

Her breathing remains even, her body motionless beside the subtle rising and falling of her chest. Her red hair fans over my leg, and I use the moment to catch a few strands between my fingers.

Even though the sun has already set, there is plenty of light in the city illuminating the inside of the car. Enough to see the freckles painted over the bridge of her nose and the frown line between her brows. I run the pad of my thumb over the creases, trying to flatten them out. She looks so much better smiling.

I can't get too close, I can't let my guard down, and I definitely can't make her smile.

"You're getting attached," Nix tells me as if I didn't know. "Remember where this is going. The more attached you get, the worse it will be."

"I know." *I fucking know.*

I spent the rest of the drive memorizing her face, running my fingers over her smooth skin and through her silky hair, knowing she would never let me do this if she was awake.

Too soon, Nix pulls into our driveway. The car stops in front of the door, and he cuts the engine. I wait for him to walk around and open the door before I carefully lift her into my arms and get out of the car.

Leni is still out cold, her head leaning against my chest as I carry her up stairs. It's not until we're inside her room that she shows first signs of waking up.

"Mmhhhh..." She moves her shoulder like she is trying to escape my hold, but then she turns her face toward me and buries it into my shirt with another moan.

"Get her zipper," I whisper as low as I can. Leni's cheek is pressed against my chest, and I don't want to wake her.

Nix moves closer, unzipping her dress while I hold her. Just as he finishes, Leni tilts her head up and opens her forest-green eyes for a moment. Her gaze is unfocused, but still, there is recognition. I'm expecting her to start fighting, kicking, and screaming.

Instead, she simply looks at me as if she is happy to see me. A faint smile appears on her lip. I keep searching her eyes for an ounce of hate, fear, or resentment, but there is none.

I'm well aware that the only reason for this is the mixture of pain meds and alcohol, yet I can't help but enjoy it. She's never looked at me this way before, and I doubt she ever will again.

The way she looks at me is so foreign, it takes me a moment to even recognize the feeling. It's trust. Right now, she places a kind of trust in me that couldn't be more misplaced.

Her eyes flutter shut, and the moment is gone. Forever lost in the dreadful chaos that is our life.

"Are you going to put her down?" Nix questions when I don't move.

"Yeah, I was just enjoying the moment. The absence of loathing in her eyes is kind of refreshing."

"You know it's better this way."

Yes, I fucking know it. Now more than ever.

Gently, I move Leni around so Nix can pull the dress off her before I place her on her mattress. The dress must have had one of those built-in bras because I'm a little surprised when I find her chest bare underneath.

Fuck, she's perfect. Spread out in her bed in nothing but panties, I get to take her in, feast on the view like she is a fine piece of art. For a while, I wondered what it was about her that had my dad so fucking obsessed with her. I understand now.

She's flawless.

Her red hair falls into a fiery halo around her angelic face. Her slender neck is begging to have my fingers wrap around it, the smooth skin of her collarbone and shoulder needs to be kissed, and don't even get me started on those tits.

I groan, readjusting my slacks to make room for my rock-hard cock.

"You know..." Nix trails off.

"What?" Turning my head, I stare at him over my shoulder. He rubs his chin like he is deep in thought.

"You know she's a virgin."

"Of course I know."

"What if she wasn't?"

"Huh?"

"We could help her lose her virginity... tonight. She is not going to fight you. She might not even remember any of this tomorrow."

My first thought is no, absolutely not. But the more I think about it, the better the idea sounds. I'm sure this is not how should want her first time to go over, but this would still be a hundred times better than what my father had planned for her.

"I'll do it," I blurt out before Nix can get the wrong idea. I know he wouldn't mind popping her cherry either.

"I figured. But I'm staying." Nix flops down on the chair in the corner.

"No video."

"The old man is going to be furious if he doesn't get a recording of this."

"I know." I'm willing to take the risk. "He can punish me later. Maybe we get lucky, and he gets so angry he has a heart attack." That would be too good to be true.

Quickly, I slip out of my shoes, unbutton my slacks, and let them slide down my legs. I discard the rest of my clothes in a hurry, eager to crawl onto the bed with her. Once I'm naked, I do just that.

Kneeling on the bed, I dip my fingers into her panties and slide them down her long toned legs. Using my knees, I wedge myself between her thighs before blanketing her body with mine.

She squirms beneath me, a nervous energy builds, and her eyebrows draw together in a frown.

"Relax…" I whisper before placing a soft kiss on her lips.

"Colt?" Her voice is so small, so fragile and innocent. "Colt, please."

"Please, what?"

She doesn't answer for a few moments. Her eyes are still closed, and I'm certain she went back to sleep when she finally answers softly. "Please… don't hurt me."

"I wasn't planning on it. At least not tonight." If it was up to me, I would never cause her any pain.

"What are you doing?" she murmurs when my lips brush against her cheek, then I move down her jaw and brush against my throat.

"Just relax. Let me take care of you."

She shivers in response, her body moving against mine, causing a delicious friction.

"You're so beautiful," I whisper, placing another kiss against her collarbone. "So perfect."

Moving down to her breasts, I take one in my hand while gently sucking on the other.

"Oh god," she moans, and I can't help but chuckle against her skin. I roll my tongue against her nipple, and she bucks her hips.

"Let's see if you taste as good as you look." I trail open-mouthed kisses down her flat stomach to her hot mound. "Such a pretty pussy."

Then my tongue is on her clit. I flatten out my tongue against the small bundle of nerves, making her squirm again.

"Yes... Colt..." She buries her finger into my hair, raking her sharp nails over my scalp.

"You taste so sweet. Like honey."

I work her clit until her thighs shiver and her back arches. When I know she is about to come, I suck harshly, pushing her over the edge. She moans my name as she comes apart on my tongue.

Her body relaxes back into the mattress, and I slowly make my way back up over her stomach, her breasts, and her throat. "I love making you come." I kiss her cheek, then cover her mouth with mine, wondering if she can taste herself.

Lining myself up with her entrance, I rub the head of my cock against her, gathering the moisture there.

"Let me inside you," I whisper between kisses. Groaning helplessly, she moves against me, only pouring gasoline into the already pit of control fire inside me. "I want to be inside you."

"Yes," she whispers, spreading her legs wider to make room for me.

"Do you want me to fuck you?"

"Yes, Colt..."

My chest swells with pride. She might hate me, but a part of her must like me as well.

Carefully, I push myself inside her. She's wet enough to ease the way, but she's still impossibly tight.

She raises her hands, placing her palms against my chest. "It hurts," she whimpers, making me stop. It takes an enormous effort not to shove into her the way I want.

"Shhh, you're doing good," I soothe, peppering featherlight kisses over her face. "Just relax, and I promise it won't hurt after this."

After a few seconds, I move another inch. Slowly, I move in and out of her, creating a delicious friction that makes us both moan while I breathe heavily against her neck.

"See. The pain is already over. Now you can enjoy the rest."

We both can.

Her pussy has my dick in a chokehold, but I manage to move, thrusting into her all the way until my balls touch her skin.

"Leni..." I groan, barely recognizing my own voice.

"Yes, Colt. Yes."

I move faster, and she moans as encouragement. The heat is building again, the tension, and her pussy starts to tighten again with every deep, driving thrust.

"Come for me," I grunts. "Come for me again."

"I think... I think I'm... oh god...!" And then she explodes. Her whole body stiffens, and her nails dig into the skin on my back, making me hiss out in pain. Her release sets off my own. Stars dance over my vision, and an unbelievable orgasm rolls toward me. I want to come inside her so badly, but I don't have a fucking condom.

My balls tighten and the tingle in the base of my spine grows. Right before I blow, I pull out. Wrapping my hand around my cock, I pump frantically until I shoot my load across her stomach.

Slouching over her, I catch my ragged breath before moving off the bed slowly.

"Wow," Leni whispers, making Nix laugh.

Fuck, I forgot he was even here. Turning around to face home, I find him standing in the doorway to the bathroom. He takes a step closer, holding out a wet washcloth to me. I grab it, giving him a nod of thanks.

The small towel is warm, which doesn't seem to help when I clean her up. Leni's eyes fly open on contact. She stiffens when she sees me, taking in the situation carefully. When I do nothing besides clean her up, she relaxes back into the mattress.

"Now you go to sleep," I say softly before draping a blanket over her. Leaning over her, I brush a strand of hair from her face. She stares at me in confusion, as if she has no idea what just happened.

"Why can't you be this nice to me in real life?" she whispers, fighting sleep.

"Don't worry about that, love bug. Just sleep." I place one last kiss on her forehead, tucking up the blanket to her chin.

When I straighten up, she is out once again. Her eyes closed, her lips slightly parted, and her breathing even.

"You think she'll remember this tomorrow!" Nix appears at my side.

"I fucking hope so."

I hope she remembers this. I hope when she looks back in a few years, this is all she remembers of me.

***

For the rest of this chapter, a second bonus chapter told from Nix's point of view, and much more bonus material, join our Patreon now!

Authors Note

My therapist recently asked me a question that threw me into a loop of more questions and deep thoughts.
She asked: How do you grieve?
At first, my answer came quite easy.
I grieve alone.

I'm not the kind of person who feels better when given a hug, I don't reach out to friends or family to be consoled, and I don't share my feeling even with the people closest to me. My husband knows that if I'm going through something, I want to be left alone. I pull away. I cry by myself and go through the motions until I get myself together and rejoin society.

Then my therapist asked: Have you ever tried sharing your pain with someone else?
I was baffled. Because the answer was very simply no. I have never tried, never wanted, or even thought about sharing my pain with anyone.
This is how I grieve. This is how I deal with loss, pain, fear, and everything in between. I don't know how to do it any other way. I don't share my feelings, and I don't think I ever will be that kind of person.

It took me another few days to realize that I was lying to myself. Because the truth is, I do share my feelings, I do share my pain, my fears, and my grief.

I share it all in every single book I write.

My stories might be fiction, and my characters and their problems are made up, but nothing is more real than the emotion I put into my books.
Writing is my outlet, my way of dealing with all the things I normally keep bottled up inside.

Writing is such a crucial part of my life, and now, you are part of it too.

About the Author

C. Hallman is a *USA Today* Bestselling author and one part of the international bestselling author duo Beck & Hallman.

For a list of all of our books, updates and freebies visit our website.
www.bleedingheartromance.com

For all links, SCAN code below.

Made in the USA
Columbia, SC
27 February 2023

13026930R00209